全新英语读写一体化教程
阅读 与 写作

教师用书
（修订版）

主编 梁晓晖

编者 杨岸青 金 铭

审订 陈颖卓

F. A. Kretschmer, Ph. D.

北京航空航天大学出版社

图书在版编目(CIP)数据

全新英语读写一体化教程.阅读与写作.—修订版./梁晓晖编著.
北京:北京航空航天大学出版社,2008.6
教师用书
ISBN 978 - 7 - 81124 - 344 - 4

Ⅰ.全… Ⅱ.梁… Ⅲ.①英语—阅读教学—高等学校—
教学参考资料②英语—写作—高等学校—教学参考资料
Ⅳ.H31

中国版本图书馆 CIP 数据核字(2008)第 059714 号

全新英语读写一体化教程·阅读与写作(修订版)(教师用书)

主编 梁晓晖
编者 杨岸青 金 铭
责任编辑 江小珍

*

北京航空航天大学出版社出版发行

北京市海淀区学院路 37 号(100083) 发行部电话:(010)82317024 传真:(010)82328026
http://www.buaapress.com.cn E-mail:bhpress@263.net

涿州市新华印刷有限公司印装 各地书店经销

*

开本:787mm×960mm 1/16 印张:15.75 字数:353 千字
2008 年 6 月第 1 版 2008 年 6 月第 1 次印刷 印数:2 000 册
ISBN 978 - 7 - 81124 - 344 - 4 定价:28.80 元

Contents

上

（下）

给教师的话[*]

——写在《全新英语读写一体化教程·阅读与写作》(修订版)丛书即将出版之际

一、给教师的话

感谢《全新英语读写一体化教程·阅读与写作》丛书出版四年来老师们的大力支持。通过这四年的教学与科研,我们更加深切地意识到我们的学生对用科学的方法进行英语读写训练的渴求。

去年我在英国做访问学者期间,对那里的英语语言文学专业学生的阅读能力颇有感触。他们的本科生平均每学期有三门课,研究生每学期有两门课。除了大班讲座以外的所有课程,老师只负责介绍基本知识点,启发学生按照正确的方向提出问题,并对学生的观点加以评述;而一半以上的时间学生可以发表自己的观点,或者评论同学的观点。学生发言的思路全部来自课外阅读指定的参考书。每门课的教师都会列出书单。低年级本科生平均每月至少阅读一本大部头评论书籍,中篇著作两至三本,另外还有很多评论性文章。高年级同学每周至少阅读一本中长篇小说,两篇以上评论性文章和若干评论书籍的章节。研究生需要每两周阅读一本长篇小说和一本理论书籍。这是基本阅读量。为了准备期中、期末、毕业论文,学生还会尽可能多地阅读理论书籍。这样才能使他们在写论文时思路灵敏,文章写得有理有据。当然,他们阅读的是母语。但我们的中文系学生阅读母语时也很少有人能够达到这样高的阅读速度,更不用说要一本本地阅读英文书籍了。

值此教材再版之际,把几年来使用这套教材的心得与大家共同分享。

既然提倡学生要变通地阅读,这套教材也可以变通地使用。比如:上册 Unit 5,Text A 中的第二至第五段是同样内容的不同句式安排。可以要求学生在看完第二段后根据教师的提示自己试写出第三至第五段,然后与课文对照。Unit 6,Text A 中有一些中文式英语语句,可以找出来让学生修改。Unit 7,Text A,可以让学生通读原文,找出文章结构,画出生词,从头到尾猜测所有的生词词义。在教师的引导下,学生是可以猜出大多数单词的大致含义的。下册的 Unit 2,Text B 选自刘润青的《语言与文化》,这本书简明实用,又是中英文对照,可以鼓励学生阅读英语书籍。另外我们有一些 Reading Skills 里的难句摘自《傲慢与偏见》,如果学生已经阅读了一定数量的英文简写本小说,就可以开始阅读一些故事情节的原著了。

二、授课大纲

下面附上我其中一次公开课的授课大纲,材料选自《全新英语读写一体化教程·阅读与写

---

[*] 另附一份授课大纲和一份教学计划。

作》上册的 Unit 6,Text C。因为是给听课教师们的公开示范课,所教阅读方法没有按照教材的顺序安排,仅供参考。(中文部分是给教师的建议,英文部分是课堂的授课内容。)

I

In this lecture today, I am going to introduce to you one of the most important reading skills: **to grasp the main idea of an article through detecting the author's opinion.**

A very important academic skill for university students is **to capture the main idea while reading. And finding the author's point of view is one efficient way to achieve this purpose**, especially **in those complex articles.** If you fail to identify the author's opinion, all details seem to be jumbled together and the reading process could become a torture to you. Even **in easier articles**, without sorting out the author's view among different opinions, you may also misunderstand the whole message altogether. Today, I'll illustrate my point by Text C of Unit 6 in the 1st vol..

II

Before analyzing the article, I want to know whether it is difficult or tolerably easy to you. When you previewed the text, how did you feel its degree of difficulty?

Where is your difficulty with the article? Is it in the new words, or in the long sentences? Or what else?

No new words? But you do not know what the author is talking about.

Why?

The most disturbing problem arises when you don't understand the general meaning of an article without any question in language points. Now I'll show you the method to tackle this article.

1 **Let's start with a basic question: the article is informational or fictional?**

2 **Please draw the diagram we learned the last time to show the structure of an informational article and to identify the thesis statement.**

请三位同学到黑板上画出信息类文章结构图。确定 thesis statement 的规律性位置。

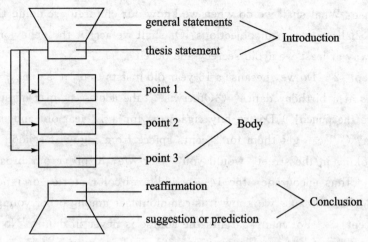

The thesis statement usually appears at the end of the beginning paragraphs.

让学生阅读第一、二段,找出本文的 **thesis statement**。"There isn't any."

启发学生:但第一、二段的信息是从 **general** 到 **specific**,所以 **thesis statement** 只能在"the end of the first paragraph."

启发学生:从第一段的三个问题中可归纳出几种观点?"Two",即对孩子的不当行为要么(1)公然反对(**oppose openly**),要么(2)默认(**accept reluctantly**)。可把这两个观点写在黑板上。

③ **作者的观点会是什么**。提问几个同学,整合他们的想法。"反对"?"默认"?还有第三种可能性吗?还有一种可能性,即综合的观点:synthesis——家长可以采用(1)、(2)相结合的观点。那么文章中是(1),还是(2),还是第三种综合的观点呢?

④ 阅读末段,找 conclusion,以及作者的观点。大家已经学过在首尾段多注意转折连词"**but**"后的信息。在这篇文章末段 but 后有两个观点:(1)while still keeping in mind the inexperience and immaturity of youngsters which make them need a strong foundation from which to move forward;和(2)it is quite possible to encourage individual thinking,二者结合即为作者的综合性的观点。而且末段的最后一句说得很清楚:We must give them both "roots and wings",这更验证了作者所持的是综合的观点。结合首尾段总结 **thesis statement**:**The adult should give their children both guidance (roots) and freedom(wings).**

这是一种综合的观点:synthesis! 这也正是全文的主要意思,main idea。

⑤ 让学生对所有中间段落进行归类,看大致属于支持(1)还是(2)。全文大意和细节就都清楚了。每段的倾向见下面标示:

Text C Coexisting with Teen-Agers

Eda J. Leshan

1 In any discussion among parents of adolescents, sooner or later one question is almost

certain to arise: What shall we do when we know our children are doing things we don't approve of? Shall we voice our objections? Or shall we accept the behavior on the theory that in this way at least we avoid secrecy and deceit?

观点(2) **Accept:** 2   Do we, because a 16-year-old insists that "it's done," serve cocktails to youngsters at a birthday dance? ("Otherwise," the adolescent may insist, "somebody's liable to spike the punch!") Do we buy cigarettes for a 12-year-old and sit by while he smokes them? (" I can get them for 2 cents apiece from a guy at school. You wouldn't want me smoking in the street, would you?") Do we, to prove our broad-mindedness, laugh at—and thus encourage—the 14-year-old's off-color stories or ignore his locker-room language just because we know it is commonplace among other youngsters his age?

观点(2) **Accept:** 3   For many parents the course is never in doubt. No child of theirs will do thus and so! Others, however, may have been confused by warnings against "indoctrinating" their children with their own thinking. Or attempting to "mold them in their own image." These are the ones who suffer doubts when questions like the above arise.

观点(2) **Accept:** 4   Methods of control that worked in earlier years are useless now. (The 12-year-old who wants to try smoking will not be "distracted" for long by a lollipop!) By this time too, youngsters have learned to hide what they are doing. Or they may not even resort to subterfuge but will announce, "If I can't do this in front of you, I'll just do it behind your back!"

Facts: 5   The adult wish to get a clear picture of the youngster's social scene today has prompted an increasing number of surveys among parents and students of various schools on such matters as clothing considered appropriate for school and parties, use of makeup, smoking, dating behavior. (One recent survey included a question on whether or not lights should be left on during parties.)

观点(1) **Oppose:** 6   Interestingly enough, the results of A recent questionnaire given to 2,000 parents and students in a big city junior high school indicated that the students were just as uncertain about standards and limits as their parents. While the youngsters demonstrated a wish for many signs of increasing freedom (such as being permitted to earn money and have full responsibility for handing allowances), they also showed a strong desire for parental controls in matters where they seemed aware that their own impulses might get the best of them.

观点(1) **Oppose:** 7   These youngsters said they thought parties should be planned, should have adult supervision; felt their parents should know where they were and with whom. Two-thirds of the students thought they ought to be home by midnight on weekends and holidays, and seemed to want help in scheduling homework and keeping to a reasonable bedtime during the week.

观点(1) **Oppose**:8 The results of such a questionnaire suggest that, useful as such surveys may be in giving parents a picture of the social scene today, youngsters in the complicated business of growing up need more than the statistical analysis of a questionnaire to guide them. It is important for children of all ages to have direct guidance and a clear understanding of what their parents expect of them, even though they cannot live up to parental standards all the time.

观点(1) **Oppose**:9 Often mothers and fathers can help youngsters understand what behavior is appropriate and acceptable merely by their own steady example of maturity and good judgment. At other times they may have to point out in no uncertain terms the hazards of certain conduct, and suggest more acceptable ways of doing something.

观点(1) **Oppose**:10 But growing up is slow. Even with the best of adult guidance, youngsters will experiment with new forms of behavior in ways that parents may not like. There will be times when their self-control will fail, when they will feel they must challenge parental authority, when they must satisfy special needs whether their conduct has parental approval or not. Adult sanction for inappropriate behavior, however, may just add to adolescent confusion.

观点(1) **Oppose**＋观点(2) **Accept** 的综合：11 It is certainly true that young people must learn to think for themselves. In a time of rapid social change they will inevitably face situations requiring new judgments that we cannot make for them. But it is quite possible to encourage individual thinking, while still keeping in mind the inexperience and immaturity of youngsters which make them need a strong foundation from which to move forward. We must give them both "roots and wings."

6 推演：In many English articles, since the author holds **a comprehensive or synthetic view**, **that is**, neither (1) nor (2), but a combination of both (1) and (2), it is difficult for us to grasp the author's view and to detect the main idea of the article. In that case we may adopt the 4-step approach：

Step 1：**to determine the type of writing**

Step 2：**to use your knowledge of structure as a tool**

Step 3：**to identify the thesis statement and the author's opinion**

Step 4：**to put the details in an organized way**

III

I would like to conclude today's lecture by saying that, in an informational article, the main idea and the author's point of view is far more important than the details. If you find any strange word or any involved sentence in a newspaper, in a journal or an examination paper, don't be nervous, for you can always appeal to this 4-step approach to **grasp the main idea of an article through detecting the author's opinion.**

It has to be practiced over and over again before you can use them with ease. My hope is that you will improve steadily and finish the course with well-developed reading skills.

三、教学计划

最后是一份 Unit 7, Text A 的教学计划,希望能对老师们有一些借鉴作用。

Teaching Plan

Text A, Unit 7
Reading and Writing Course

Unit 7　Human and Animal

◇ 教学目的

1. 揭示阅读内部规律:一篇有一定量生词的文章,学生不必词词查字典,也不应逐字逐句匀速阅读。学生可利用文章结构知识以及句段之间的衔接手段判断各部分之间的关系,在阅读中保持思路清晰;再利用上下文或自身所掌握的背景知识以及基本的字、词知识推测生词词义,做到融会贯通。

2. 以语言功能为统领,从语篇中帮助学生掌握词、句、篇中的知识,引导学生建立语义场,从词汇关系入手用科学的方法记单词;针对句子结构在语篇中功能的学习,改变学生孤立学习语法条目以及写作时中式英语的状况;着重培养学生对谋篇机制及文章结构的认识,这样既可以大大提高学生的阅读速度和理解能力,又能够解决学生在写作时句与句之间意思交错、跳跃、逻辑关系不清的问题。

3. 利用阅读与写作的互动关系。第一,通过写作调动学生对阅读的兴趣:在写作实践中学生在词语表达、文章组织上的困惑激发了他们的阅读兴趣,并增强了他们在阅读过程中吸收知识的敏感度。第二,通过阅读提高写作:帮助学生积极阅读,善于思考,充分汲取文章精华,并运用在自身的写作实践中。

4. 对阅读中涉及的文化现象善于观察,勤于总结。

◇ 教学时间安排

1. 第 1—2 课时
   (1)议论文结构
   (2)Text A

2. 第 3—4 课时

(1)记叙文结构

(2)Text B

3. 第 5—6 课时

(1)利用记叙文结构预测 Text C

(2)针对 Text C 中的问题展开课堂讨论,为写作做准备

4. 第 7—8 课时

(1)讲评作文

(2)总结本单元,介绍下单元

◇ 教学重点

1. Reading Skills

- The knowledge of **article structure** as a help to grasp the relations of different parts in the article (an argumentative article as represented by Text A and a narrative as represented by Texts B and C).

- The knowledge of **article structure** as a help to guess the meanings of new words (practice in Text A).

- The knowledge of **article structure** as a help to predict the unread part of the article (practice in Text C).

2. Writing Skills

- The words that form **situational sets** and **semantic sets** with *dog*.

- The sentences that describe *dog*.

- The sentences that compare *dog* with other things and therefore show **comparison of equality** and **comparison of superiority**.

- The way to write a **well-organized argumentation**.

3. Cultural Background

- Westerners' general attitude toward a *dog*.

◇ 具体内容与方法安排

Text A   Canine Crisis

(一)课前预习(课前布置)

1. Write down all the words and expressions that you know are about the specie of the dog and people's comment on a dog.

2. Write briefly your attitude toward raising a dog.

(二)课上训练

1. 检查学生预习情况

Since *dog* is a general word related to this unit, to develop a word associative field centered on this word will be illuminating both to the reading and the writing of a similar subject.

(1) Write DOG on the chalkboard and then ask the students to associate it with any words connected with it.

(2) Have the students make up a few general categories into which these words can be grouped, like situational sets, semantic sets and those with positive or negative connotations.

(3) Choose the words they think can form a comment on raising a dog.

(4) Conclude the Westerners' general attitude toward a dog.

2. 议论文、说明文的文章结构知识

A general structure can be found in an argumentative or expository article, as shown by the following diagram:

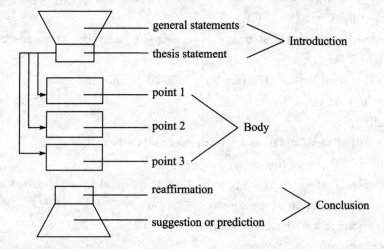

3. 略读打乱次序的课文内容并排序

Hand out the leaflets of Text A with paragraphs not in order. Let students skim it in one minute and put them in order with the help of article structure knowledge.

The last sentence of the second paragraph serves as the thesis statement of the whole article. It contains two controlling ideas "a dog is *expensive* and *annoying*" that will be used in the topic sentences of the body paragraphs: "Providing for the dog's needs is ... *expensive*", "A dog is ... a *nuisance*." The thesis statement discloses both the content and the sequence of the body paragraphs. The relationships of different paragraphs can be shown by the following chart of the article structure:

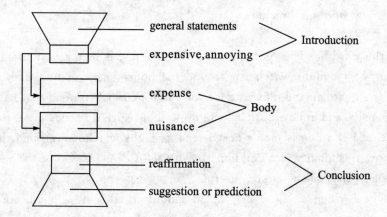

general statements — Introduction
expensive,annoying

expense — Body
nuisance

reaffirmation — Conclusion
suggestion or prediction

4. 快速阅读并记录下生词

Read the text quickly from the beginning to the end within 5 minutes. Find out how the argument (the thesis statement) is supported throughout the article and underline all the new words.

While the two body paragraphs support the thesis statement, the details of each body paragraph also support their respective topic sentence. Here is the first body paragraph with the important key words underlined:

Providing for the dog's needs is so expensive that the animal should be an income tax deduction. There's the medical bill for shots to keep the mongrel healthy. Unless it's kept in the house, a female must be given "preventive maintenance," a ten-to twenty-dollar investment. Otherwise, before you know it, you'll have more canine deductions in your family. And dogs have to eat. Don't think you can buy a case of Ken-L-Ration and be done with it. A dog can be as particular about food as a French connoisseur. To feed even a Chihuahua, you'll spend three to five bucks a week. If you own a big mutt, you need a dog-house. They're expensive. A carpenter will build a deluxe model for about seventy-five dollars. For about thirty dollars' worth of materials, a weekend's work, and a smashed thumb, you can build a leaky, 5'×4'×4' plywood box yourself. And these are only the major costs. Only those who can afford mink can really afford a dog.

5. 细读并试猜生词词义

Read the text closely within 10 minutes and guess the meanings of new words. The knowledge of article structure, word relations and word formation can together help the detective job.

Here are the first three paragraphs with students' new words underlined and clues of guessing these new words in brackets.

For ages the word has been going around that the dog is man's best friend. I agree. A dog can be <u>handy</u> as a night watchman around the house, as a <u>pointer</u> and <u>retriever</u> on a hunting trip, as a guardian and playmate for the children. But I <u>contend</u> that having a dog for a pet is so expensive and annoying that I can do without such a friend.

(<u>handy</u>: clue 1-If a dog is man's best friend as night watchman around the house, the adjective to show this quality of a dog must mean useful.

clue 2-formation: handy, hand is sth. useful.

<u>pointer</u>: clue 1-When a dog is helpful on a hunting trip, it will indicate to its owner where the game is.

clue 2-formation: pointer, person, here animal, who shows us where sth. is.

<u>retriever</u>: clue-formation: person, here animal, who retrieves the game for us.

<u>contend</u>: clue- The conjunction "but" introduces sth. opposite to the previous opinion. While the part before "but" is about the good points of having a dog and the part after it the bad points, this verb *contend* may mean "to say from a different angle" or, in an argumentation like this text, "to argue".)

Providing for the dog's needs is so expensive that the animal should be an income tax deduction. There's the medical bill for shots to keep the <u>mongrel</u> healthy. Unless it's kept in the house, a female must be given "<u>preventive maintenance</u>," a ten-to twenty-dollar investment. Otherwise, before you know it, you'll have more canine deductions in your family. And dogs have to eat. Don't think you can buy <u>a case of Ken-L-Ration</u> and be done with it. A dog can be as particular about food as a French <u>connoisseur</u>. To feed even a <u>Chihuahua</u>, you'll spend three to five bucks a week. If you own a big <u>mutt</u>, you need a dog-house. They're expensive. A carpenter will build a <u>deluxe</u> model for about seventy-five dollars. For about thirty dollars' worth of materials, a weekend's work, and a smashed thumb, you can build a <u>leaky</u>, 5'×4'×4' <u>plywood</u> box yourself. And these are only the major costs. Only those who can afford <u>mink</u> can really afford a dog.

(Main idea: This whole paragraph displays the high expense of raising a dog, so words here are mostly in the fields of 1) those about dog, 2) those about the expenses for a dog's food, house and other items.

<u>Mongrel</u>, <u>mutt</u> are types of dogs, and they form semantic sets with a dog.

<u>Connoisseur</u>: In a sentence that shows comparison of equality, this word refers to a person with good judgment on food, an ability equally enjoyed by a dog.

A case of Ken-L-Ration：dog food.

Plywood：material for building a dog house.

The above two expressions form a situational set with "dog's expense".)

A dog is such a nuisance that no one in his right mind would want to own one. Consider the dog owner blessed with a dog that fetches-slippers, rubber toys, newspapers. Have you eased your bare feet into slippers fetched by a slobbering basset hound, seen a living room demolished by a toy-retrieving boxer, tried to read a newspaper chewed to wet confetti by an obedient Boston bull? And dogs make noise. Some mutts howl all night. But you aren't the only one to endure sleepless nights; your neighbors let you know they didn't sleep either. Cops are frequent visitors to dog owners' homes. They inquire about holes reported dug in neighbors' flower beds, prize cats maimed and bleeding, and pet chickens and ducks sent to their eternal reward. Suspect: your pooch! You deny everything, of course. Rex, you assure the officers, was asleep by the hearth. But you secretly suspect him, because you don't really know where Rex was all week. And you remember wondering why feathers were floating in his water bowl yesterday. Dogs are pests. Neither a fire-breathing mother-in-law nor a nagging spouse will prove more annoying to man than a dog.

（Main idea：how annoying a dog can be.

Nuisance：things that annoy you.

Pests：things that annoy you.

Both the two words form elegant variations to "annoying".

Fire-breathing, nagging：Although a sentence in a form of comparison, it shows an idea of superlative. The two words convey the troublesome qualities of two family members, but still not so annoying as a dog.)

6. 完成课后练习

7. 总结

（1）Apart from the word-by-word approach, you have more effective ways of reading.

（2）The knowledge of article structure is important in reading comprehension.

（3）The article is made a whole by related words.

（4）It is useful to look for sentence functions beneath a sentence structure.

（三）课后作业

1. 分析其他教材中议论文、说明文的文章结构。

2. 模仿 Text A 的结构写一篇150字的作文，阐述 Text C 中的男孩没有射死狗的原因。

A Few Words to Teachers

From what aspects can teachers help their students improve their reading ability?

The primary duty for teachers even before students begin to read is to enhance their students' reading readiness; that is to say, on the one hand, determining the students' preparation in prior knowledge, and, on the other, encouraging their impulse to read. A well-designed pre-reading activity is the spur to students' thinking. I have included at the beginning of each unit various Pre-reading Focuses. You may create other or additional activities that best serve your purposes.

I would like to stress that there are no simple routines for teachers to observe. In fact, routine is a sure way to kill interest. But a few general ideas may be helpful:

1. The teacher may always use the title, heading, and the first paragraph to make predictions about the probable content of the selection, and to form questions about the text. In order to test their own predictions or to find the answers to their own questions, students will definitely read the text more eagerly.

2. The teacher may ask the students to skim the text in a very short period of time (say, one minute). Then, they may write a brief outline (or call it out to a student at the blackboard) of what they feel the text is about. Finally, they may read the text again, more carefully, and compare what they have written with what the text says. It is important to note that this also involves *projecting* or *forecasting* meaning. Some students may be better at it than others, but, as this is a reading skill training, the teacher had better not stress that there are *incorrect* answers.

3. For nonfiction texts, the teacher may give students an incomplete outline and then ask students to read the text to fill in the outline.

The teacher must constantly be aware that although students cannot understand reading material without a certain linguistic competence—without a certain amount of vocabulary, syntactical awareness and semantic knowledge of the language—linguistic competence alone cannot ensure students' comprehension. Do not insist, therefore, that the meaning of each and every word must be understood in order to say something about the passage. A knowledge of the ways writers organize and construct paragraphs and whole articles will assist them in understanding meaning at least as much as, if not more than, the knowledge of individual words. That is why a reading course, combined with a writing course, may be a more effective approach. In class, writing activities may also be handled by asking a student to write on the blackboard the answers as supplied by the rest of the class members.

Last but not least, teachers must aid students to build their skill in drawing inferences from the material. This will assist students in forming their own critical views of a text.

It is upon these considerations that the exercises and teaching directions (ways of approaching the text: not "orders") are designed, and upon them you as a teacher may build your own teaching plan.

In the textbook, I use the following terms in specific ways:

Read quickly: to read the whole text at the quickest speed the students can in about three minutes (or more) without using a dictionary and skipping those words they do not know.

Skim: to read for the general idea or the whole picture of the material.

Scan: to look for exact answers for specific questions.

These terms will be more fully discussed as the course progresses.

Teachers may instruct the students to read the explanations in the reading skill section of every unit. Then the teacher may call upon them at random to explain the parts in their own words and assign them a grade for their explanation. The teacher should also ask for the definitions of technical terms: situational sets, semantic sets, associative field, and so on, and should return to these definitions from time to time in subsequent class meetings to ensure that the students remember them. This suggestion is made in order to encourage active learning (where the students are responsible for their learning), rather than passive learning (where the teacher is responsible for everything).

When a pre-reading question is asked, the teacher may tell the students to close their books to answer it. This would guarantee that the students are not continuing their slow reading beyond the time limit, and encourage them to try to speed up their reading by skipping what they do not understand and by focusing on what they do understand.

Section One   Human Relationships

Unit 1   An Open Heart

Suggestions for Teaching

1. In order to assist students in making quick judgments about the meanings of unknown words with the help of context clues, you may give them some classifications for the types of context clues. Below are some of the clues, with their signal words or structures, which may aid students in their thinking:

(1) Explanation Clues

In job *evaluation*, all of the requirements of each job are defined in a detailed description.

A *contributory* cause is one that helps to produce an effect but cannot do so by itself.

Signal structures:

—placing words side by side or next to each other to explain (apposition)

—explaining the meaning (attribution)

Signal words:

—be, mean, can be taken as

—similarly, that is, in other words

(2) Example Clues

It seems that such *maladies* as colds, fevers and sore throats will always be a part of life.

Signal words:

—such as, for example, for instance, ... belong to...

(3) Comparison-contrast Clues

John likes to spend his money. On the other hand, his girlfriend is very *frugal*.

Signal words:

—but, instead, however, or, rather than, on the other hand, unlike

3

（4）**Experience Clues**

Anne disliked Terry so much that everything Terry did *infuriated* her.

Signal structure：

—continuation of the thought with the result continuation

（5）**Summary Clues**

Ted refused to do homework. He lacked respect for his teachers. He was disobedient. He cut school. Finally, the principal had to take *disciplinary* action.

（6）**Co-occurrence Clues**

A large computer can add or subtract nine thousand times a second, *multiply* a thousand times a second, or divide five hundred times a second.

（7）**Mood or Setting Clues**

The speed, with which he moved across the room, quickly reached the door, and dashed down the steps, showed his great *agility*.

2. In the early stages of language learning, words are usually learned in lists of paired words. The lists contain a word from the target language and a synonym in that target language or a translation in the mother tongue. But the more words are analyzed or are enriched by imagistic and other associations, the more likely it is that they will be retained. Therefore, when the students become more proficient, help them learn to rely more on their own inferential skills by decoding words in context and retaining words through semantic relations. **Synonymy** (the quality of having the same meaning) and **antonymy** (the quality of having an opposite meaning) are the two basic semantic relations between words. These two relations alone can serve to group a number of words and expressions in certain texts.

Finding a theme for a group of words in the discourse can also build up a type of relation for these words and, therefore, ease the mastery of them. If the theme is connected with the thesis of the whole article, the grasp of these words can be even easier.

3. In a narrative, the general structure may go in the following pattern: the category *setting* includes those elements indicating time, place or other circumstances of the episode. In a given setting the *character*(s) is/are introduced, whose personality(ies) is/are greatly influenced by and may be inferred through the setting. The character will form *conflicts* with the environment, one certain situation or other characters. Readers will follow the character to pursue his/her goal. Many events may happen before the goal is reached, and

readers will feel tension when the character tries to overcome the difficulties. Near the end of the story, one important event will happen which becomes the turning point or the *climax* of the story; at the same time the conflicts are coming to their *resolution*. Stories are usually sequenced: one thing happens before the next, and the introduction of the time for each episode will form a *time line*. The relationship of these categories may be shown clearly by the following chart:

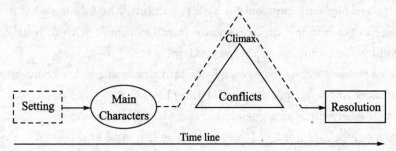

It is advisable that the teacher point out to the students for each text the above basic elements and give them outside assignments to read in order to draw up their own chart. The knowledge of the narrative's structure will activate student's reading readiness for the story reading and promote their ability to make guesses about the unclear parts of the content.

In **Text A**, the story happens in an economically depressive setting. The main character Ben is depicted as a joyful and warm-hearted man despite the gloomy situation— the setting. But his kindness seems to have been made use of by a pitiable woman customer. Will Ben remain a warm-hearted man or become a sour person? This is the biggest problem for the character. After a period of psychological struggle, Ben conquers his small self and solves the problem for himself by accepting the narrator's advice. At the end of the story, the woman customer returns the money and this episode forms the climax of the story. The resolution is that Ben refuses to take the money in spite of his own difficulties.

Text A   Angel on a Doorstep

Close Study of the Text

1. ... he wasn't his usual sunny self. (Para. 1)

5

Meaning: ... he was not cheerful and happy as usual.

self: a particular or typical part of one's nature

Similar expression: be oneself—in one's usual state of mind

2. ... seemed in no mood for talking. (Para. 2)

   Meaning: ... it seemed that he didn't want to spend time talking with me.

3. It took slow, careful questioning to extract the story from him. (Para. 3)

   Meaning: I asked him with care and bit by bit, painfully, he told me what had happened.

   extract from: to get information or response from (someone) with difficulty

4. With six children and another on the way. (Para. 4)

   Note: Here *on the way* means the woman has a baby developing in her body. She is pregnant.

5. "I was a stranger and you took me in." (Para. 11)

   Meaning: You received me as a guest.

   Note: The writer here cites from *the Bible*, persuading Ben to be kind-hearted to the poor family.

6. "Don't you mean she took *me* in"? (Para. 12)

   Note: In his anger, Ben refers to another meaning of "take someone in"—instead of "receive," Ben means, "she deceived me."

7. ... playing on my sympathies. (Para. 15)

   Meaning: ... making use of my feelings to take advantage of me.

8. ... he had been on a different route, covering for another milkman. (Para. 21)

   Meaning: ... he went to a different area, delivering bottles of milk for a milkman who was absent for some reason.

   cover for: to do work for someone who is ill or away

9. ... I didn't have the foggiest idea what I was crying about. (Para. 29)

   Note: Haven't the foggiest idea is an informal and emphatic way of saying someone does not know or understand something.

10. "Heck no,"... (Para. 31)

   Note: "Heck" is an exclamatory word expressing slight irritation or surprise. "Heck no" vividly implies that Ben was not happy in that his kind heart was misunderstood by the author.

Text-related Information

The Angel Gabriel (Para. 27): In the new testament of *the Bible*, Gabriel is the archangel who told Virgin Mary that she would be the mother of Jesus (See Luke I, 26~38). He is more frequently regarded as one of God's chief messengers.

In the text, the woman seems to regard Ben as a present-day angel who has showered blessings upon her family.

Text B   The Woman Who Would Not Tell

Close Study of the Text

1. ...trying not to be sick as she thought of what she had seen... (Para. 6)

   Meaning: ...she tried hard not to vomit when she remembered the wounded soldier...

2. The man's papers Bettie found in the attic established his identity. (Para. 7)

   Meaning: The man's documents told Bettie who he was.

3. ... 11th Vermont Volunteers... (Para. 7)

   Meaning: ...the 11th Regiment of volunteers from the state Vermont...

4. ...James Van Metre's wife fanned the spark of life that flickered in Henry Bedell. (Para. 8)

   Meaning: ...James Van Metre's wife gradually drew the critically wounded Henry Bedell back from the verge of death. Bedell recovered his health bit by bit.

   Note: Notice the metaphor employed in the sentence. "The spark of life" and " flicker" are enough to tell us the wounded officer was in a critical position.

5. The infection...flared up... (Para. 10)

   flare up: (of a disease or injury) to return suddenly or become painful again

6. He brushed aside Bettie's thanks. (Para. 19)

   brush aside: to refuse to pay attention to or consider (something)

7. ...Dr. Osborne brought Bedell through the crisis. (Para. 20)

   bring through: to save (someone) from (danger, crisis or trouble)

Text-related Information

All that I hated was the war. (Para. 1)

The war: the American Civil War, 1861, 4~1865, 5.

Text C   Mama and the Garfield Boys

╔══════════════════════════════════════╗
Close Study of the Text
╚══════════════════════════════════════╝

1. ...and I, along with several other students, wet my pants. (Para. 1)

   Meaning: ...several other students and I were so scared that our pants became soaked with urine.

2. Having your mother as a member of your school's faculty had its advantages. (Para. 3)

   Meaning: If your mother were a faculty member in your school, you could benefit generally from it.

3. I managed to stay unmarked by the Garfield brothers,... (Para. 4)

   Meaning: I tried my best to escape the attention of the Garfield brothers so that they could not look for an occasion for a fight.

4. I spent the next morning daydreaming... I was certain that's where I'd go. (Para. 21)

   Note: The whole paragraph is what the child is daydreaming in his mind. He is sure that the end of the world was coming for him. He imagines how the Garfield brothers will inflict a terrible revenge upon him and how they will celebrate his death. He even begins to make arrangements for his life in heaven. Notice the writer deliberately assumes a boy's tone while narrating the story. Vivid examples appear here and elsewhere in the story.

5. "...I ain't got no car to take 'em nowhere." (Para. 36)

   Note: The employment of two negatives in one sentence is very common in English uneducated speech. The meaning of the combination of two negatives seems to be positive or affirmative, but, in fact, this is only a special way of stressing the negative, the speaker repeating the negatives only because she believes that this will make her negative meaning clear and unmistakable, that one negative alone might not be heard. This use of double negatives is not allowed in the speech of educated people. The writer is using this structure to show the educational background of the family. The above sentence actually means: "I don't have a car to take them anywhere."

6. They were always at her beck and call. (Para. 56)

   be at someone's beck and call: be bound to obey someone's orders, to come and go, all the time

Unit 2　Parents and Children

Suggestions for Teaching

1. The knowledge of word-formation and context clues when employed together as skills helps students guess the meaning of unfamiliar words. Firstly, let students look at the word itself to see if it is made up of smaller words, or if it has a prefix or suffix that hints at its meaning. They should then look through the whole paragraph—or at least the sentences before and after the word—for clues to its meaning.

Giving them the basic knowledge of word formation or word building will greatly increase their ability to recognize new words in reading and speed up the growth of their vocabulary.

（1）**Teach Students to Analyze Compound Words**

Components	Formed words
door+step	doorstep
middle+aged	middle-aged
new+comer	newcomer
milk+men	milkmen
house+hunting	house-hunting
grand+mother	grandmother
great+aunt	great-aunt
farm+house	farmhouse
head+quarters	headquarters
blood+stained	blood-stained

（2）**Encourage Students to Memorize Prefixes**

（en- becomes em- before p, b, m; en- becomes el- or er- before l, r.）

（in- becomes im- before p, b, m; in- becomes il- before l; in- becomes ir- before r.）

Prefixes	Meaning	Examples
anti-	against	antitank
bi-	two	biannual, bicycle
com-	with	comrade
dia-	through, across	diameter, diagram

dis-	not	disagree
en-	in	enclose
ex-	former, out of, away from	extract
de-	from, the opposite of	depart
in-, im-	not	inactive, impossible
kilo-	a thousand times	kilometer
macro-	large	macrocosm
micro-	small	microscope
mis-	wrong	misbehavior
non-	not	nonconformity
pre-	before	predicate, predestined
per-	fully	perfection
re-	again	rearrange
un-	with an opposite meaning	unload, unlock

(3) Encourage Students to Memorize Suffixes

Suffixes used to form nouns from verbs	Verbs	Examples
-ment	abandon	abandonment
	agree	agreement
-ation	inform	information
-tion	appreciate	appreciation
	educate	education
	predict	prediction
-sion	divide	division
-ance	guide	guidance
	reassure	reassurance

Suffixes used to form nouns from adjectives	Adjectives	Examples
-ness	kind	kindness
-y	difficult	difficulty
-ence	different	difference
-ous	courage	courageous

Suffixes used to form adjectives from nouns	Nouns	Examples

10

-ful	fear	fearful
	thought	thoughtful
	wonder	wonderful
-less	breath	breathless
	value	valueless
-al	emotion	emotional
-tive	creation	creative
	imagination	imaginative

Suffixes used to form verbs from adjectives or nouns

	Adj. or n.	Examples
-en	quick	quicken
	length	lengthen
	strength	strengthen

（4）**Encourage Students to Memorize Roots**

Root	Meaning	Examples
aer-, aero-	air	aeroplane, aerocamera, aeroview, aerology
agri-	field	agriculture
anthro-	man	anthropologist
aqua-	water	aquarium
astro-	star	astronaut
bene-	well, good	benefit, benevolent
bio-	life	biology
-ced, -ceed, -cess	go	precede, recede, predecessor
dic-, dict-	speak	dictate, contradict, predict
geo-	earth	geography
mono-	one	monologue
-nym	name	anonymous
psycho-	mind	psychology
viv-, vit-, vig-	life	vivify, vitality, vigorous

2. Synonyms or near-synonyms may on the one hand avoid repetition, while on the other employing for each situation the most suitable choice. Ask students to find synonyms in the text and analyze the similarities and differences. By so doing, their consciousness of word relations will be enhanced.

3. Phrasal verbs look simple enough. They are, usually, combinations of simple verbs and members of a set of particles (*on*, *up*, *out* etc.).

 It is as easy for English-speakers to learn them as it is difficult for foreign learners to master them. This is because a phrasal verb may have a meaning which is simply the sum of its parts, but may also have a meaning which bears little apparent relation to those parts. The verbs of this latter type are so important in the spoken language that training in this respect cannot be ignored.

4. In a narrative, the time at which each event happens or at least the sequence in which all events are arranged are usually introduced clearly by the writer. But differences exist in the way to make that clear between English and Chinese. In Chinese, the adverbial, prepositional expressions are always used to specify the time or the sequence; the verb itself does not do that. In English, however, the time or the sequence can be indicated through the tense of the verbs, with or without extra use of adverbial or prepositional phrases. Due to the influence of their mother tongue, Chinese students are generally quite insensitive to the changes in the tense of English verbs, so that they will more often than not fail to grasp what really happens if no specific adverbial or prepositional phrases are supplied. Therefore, special training in this respect is absolutely necessary.

 There is a main tense—the simple past tense in narration. Usually a change in the tense of the verb can be found when the author gives background information.

 Sometimes the simple present tense is also adopted in narration. In that case, a vivid effect is targeted.

 Texts A and **B** adopt the simple past tense as the basic tense. In the two texts, the present tense is sometimes used for the writing time and the past perfect tense for the previous time. But in **Text C**, the present tense employed as the basic tense creates a vivid effect.

5. In **this unit**, the authors show the love of family members through examples. Firstly, one general example is given as an introduction. Then two or more examples follow to strengthen the idea.

 When reading and writing, students will need to know the difference between a general idea and a specific detail. Therefore, while reading they should be able to detect which part is the main idea and which the supporting details. In their own compositions,

12

they should support their general statement with details and examples.

Here is a group of terms in which each is more specific than the previous one:

creature

animal

horse

race horse

The following are groups of sentences with the lower levels supporting the upper levels:

My father enjoys taking his vacation in Florida.

Dad enjoys both fresh and saltwater fishing there.

He fishes for carp in the lakes.

He loves to fight the tarpon in Tampa Bay.

My father loves me very much.

My father was extremely patient to me.

For my father, no subject was off-limit.

My father told me how to behave like a lady.

My father explained to me how to handle a relationship with a boy.

The prom dress was special.

The prom dress was decorated with yards and yards of dotted swiss in red, white and blue.

When I wore the dress, I looked like Scarlet O'Hara.

Students need to be trained with a variety of groups of words and statements before they begin to see exact differences.

Text A   A Simple Act of Love

Close Study of the Text

1. ... when I'd breathlessly fill him in on my day. (Para. 1)

   fill (someone) in on (something): to supply information to (someone)

   e. g. : The secretary filled me in on what happened at the meeting that I couldn't attend.

2. ... no subject was off-limits. (Para. 1)

Meaning: ... any subject was allowed to be talked about.

off-limits: not to be entered or patronized by a designated class of individuals

Note: "off-limits" is used figuratively here, meaning "forbidden, not allowed".

3. "Keep the conversation neutral,"... (Para. 1)

   Meaning: "When you are talking together, don't show your emotional feelings about him,"...

   neutral: without any feelings on either side of a question

   Note: The father reminded his daughter to be tactful and not to give the impression that she is pursuing the boy.

4. Terry and I went steady for over a year,... (Para. 2)

   go steady: to date someone on a regular basis, often with an intent to marry

   e. g. : Mary went steady for three years before she found somebody else.

5. "... the hard part is getting rid of him." (Para. 2)

   Meaning: "... the most difficult thing to do is to break off a love relationship with a person when you realize that he is not what you thought."

6. ... I was ready to spread my wings. (Para. 3)

   Meaning: ... I was prepared to try something new and difficult so as to gain more experience.

   Note: "Spread one's wings" is used figuratively, meaning "to do something new and rather difficult or move to a new place to gain wider experience." When a young bird is ready to fly, and leave the nest, it "spreads its wings."

7. It was no dream job. (Para. 3)

   Meaning: It was neither an ideal job nor one I had dreamed about.

8. Many of my charges... (Para. 3)

   charge: a person for whom one is responsible

9. ... teaching jobs were tight in 1974,... (Para. 4)

   Meaning: ... it was difficult to obtain a teaching job in 1974,...

10. Everyone ... stranded me on the school grounds. (Para. 6)

    Meaning: I was unable to leave the school because the gate was locked.

    be stranded: to be put in a helpless position.

11. ... they were wearing gang insignia. (Para. 9)

    Meaning: ... a badge or decoration which shows that a person belongs to a particular group or gang.

12. "... She's kinda cute!" (Para. 12)

Meaning: "... The girl is rather good-looking. "

kinda = kind of: to some extent, inf.

13. I didn't tell him about my ordeal; I didn't want to worry him. (Para. 20)

   Meaning: I didn't let my father know of my unpleasant experience, because I was afraid he would be very much concerned about me.

14. ...I still look to him for wisdom, guidance and reassurance. (Para. 22)

   look to: to depend on (someone) (to do something)

   e. g. : She looked to her boss to give support to her project.

Text B   Mystery of the White Gardenia

Close Study of the Text

1. Calls to the florist were always in vain—it was a cash purchase. (Para. 1)

   Meaning: I failed to get the name of the sender every time I telephoned the florist, because the giver always bought the flowers by cash. (If the sender purchased by order or credit card, he would have had to leave his or her name and address.)

2. My mother contributed to these imaginings. (Para. 3)

   Meaning: Mother gave me some other possibilities that followed the general line of the things I was imagining.

   contribute to: to say or to do (something) to help make something successful

3. ... so he wouldn't have to venture down his icy steps. (Para. 3)

   Meaning: ... so that the old man wouldn't have to risk going down his steps, which were covered with slippery ice and were difficult and dangerous to walk on.

4. ... it might be a boy I had a crush on... (Para. 3)

   Meaning: ... the sender might be a boy whom I fell in love with...

5. When I finally went to get the glass cleaner, my mother knew everything was all right again. (Para. 4)

   Meaning: When I finally got the glass cleaner to erase Emerson's quotation scribbled on my mirror by my mother, my mother was relieved to know that I had totally recovered from the unsuccessful love affair.

6. My feelings ranged from grief to abandonment, fear and overwhelming anger that my dad was missing some of the most important events in my life. (Para. 6)

   Note: Mixed feelings crowded into the girl's heart after her father's death, mainly because her dad would certainly be absent from those important occasions, causing those upcoming activities to become meaningless to her.

7. But my mother, in the mist of her own grief, would not hear of my skipping any of those things. (Para. 6)

   Meaning: Although my mother was still sad over my father's death, she just could not tolerate the fact that her daughter would miss the upcoming activities.

8. It made me feel like Scarlet O'Hara, but it was the wrong size. (Para. 7)

   Meaning: Just like the leading lady in *Gone with the Wind*, I looked beautiful and dignified in the prom dress, except that its size didn't fit me.

9. She wanted her children to feel loved and lovable, creative and imaginative, imbued with a sense that there was magic in the world and beauty even in the face of adversity. (Para. 9)

   Meaning: She hoped that her children would feel her mother's love and that they would be able to love, to create and to imagine. She wanted them to cherish the belief that they were living in a world of miracles and they could discover the bright and beautiful aspects of life even when they were faced with difficulties.

Text-related Information

1. **Emerson** (Para. 4)

   Ralph Waldo Emerson (1803~1882): American philosopher, essayist and poet, whose philosophy was known as transcendentalism. His best known essays include *"Compensation,"* *"Self-Reliance"* and *"The Over-Soul"* in which he stressed such values as intellectual freedom, integrity, self-reliance and realism.

2. **Scarlet O'Hara** (Para. 7): the main character in the film *Gone with the Wind*.

Text C   My No. 1 Priority

Close Study of the Text

1. It's like being in heaven, like being a god, only the place is here and now. (Para. 8)

   Meaning: That Tommy leaned his head on my chest and fell asleep was a heavenly delight to me, making me feel like a god in heaven, except that the time and place were on earth.

2. "...I don't think either of us landed a punch." (Para. 11)

Meaning: "...I don't think we really hit each other."

3. I also felt neglected, as many fathers do when life revolves around the new baby and Mommy. (Para. 14)

Meaning: Besides this I felt I didn't get the needed attention of my wife. Mommy was chiefly concerned with the new baby and the baby became the focus of her life.

Note: It is easy to understand the feelings of a father who finds it difficult to play a role in the family when he is unable to take care of the baby and when the baby occupies his wife's attention.

4. Time with Tommy has been my biggest investment success. (Para. 17)

Meaning: I spent most of my time with Tommy and was greatly rewarded.

Note: "Investment" refers to the spending of time or effort on something in order to make it a success.

5. ...and then dress up as that person and tell about his or her accomplishments. (Para. 17)

Meaning: ...and then put on special clothes to role-play that historic figure and give an account of his or her achievements.

6. But the few years between five and 15... these years go by astonishingly fast. (Para. 22)

Meaning: But the short period during which your child grows up is nothing short of an instant.

Note: By this sentence, the author emphasizes how important and precious it is to build up "an extraordinary relationship of sharing" between father and child.

7. No billionaire can turn his surly 16-year-old into a devoted, hold-your-hand youngster. (Para. 23)

Meaning: It is too late for a wealthy man to ask his bad-tempered child whom he neglected when the child was young to be concerned about him and to love him.

Note: 1. "Hold-your-hand" is a gesture symbolizing a child's trust in parents.

　　2. In this paragraph, using three examples of parallel structure, the author tells us that neither wealth nor fame can bring about an intimate relationship between parents and children.

8. Time spent with Tommy isn't a distraction from the main event. It is the main event. (Para. 23)

Meaning: To spend time with Tommy is not something that turned my attention away from what I was concentrating on, but was rather the whole of my life.

Text-related Information

1. **Amelia Earhart** (Para. 17)

   Amelia Earhart (1898~1937): an American aviation pioneer. In 1928, she became the first woman to cross the Atlantic in a solo flight by air. In 1937, she attempted to make a round-the-world trip during which her plane vanished in the South Pacific.

2. **Thomas Jefferson** (Para. 17)

   Thomas Jefferson (1743~1826): Chairman of the committee which drafted *The Declaration of Independence*, ambassador to France (1785~1789), secretary of state (1790~1793) under Washington and third President of the U. S. A. (1801~1809).

3. **Richard M. Nixon** (Para. 17)

   Richard M. Nixon (1913~): 37th President of the U. S. A. (1969~1974), the first American President to resign from the office because of political scandals.

Unit 3   Encouragement

Suggestions for Teaching

1. Essentially, **elegant variation** is possible because English writers employ the concept of **semantic field** when they write. *Semantic field* refers to the range of expressions or words (*semantic*) that occur in the same area (*field*).

   It would be useful if the various expressions for the same idea could be called *synonyms* as well as *elegant variations*. But the latter is a more complex concept involving *semantic field*.

   In the examples below, the *italics* are elegant variations as well as synonyms, while the **bold italics** are elegant variations only.

   (1) Hera, for her part, while ultimately submitting to the will of *Zeus*, kept *the father of gods and men* under close and constant observation, and was never accommodating enough to reconcile herself with *her husband*'s new attachments. She had been forever on the run, trying to keep track of Zeus and devise ways of revenge not always on *the all-conquering god*, but rather on his unfortunate mistresses.

   The synonyms above emphasize one aspect or another of Zeus.

   (2) Because force is held in reserve and **control is not complete**, we can call ourselves a "democracy." True, **the openings and the flexibility** make such a society a more desirable place to live. But they also create a more efficient form of control.

   In the above example, the **bold italics** are taken from the semantic field and serve to explain one aspect of **incomplete control**. The elegant variations are in different parts of speech or structures.

   (3) Sally waited a few minutes after her mother **left the living room for the bedroom** before **following her example**.

   In the above example, the elegant variation is neither a synonym nor drawn from the semantic field. Rather, it consists of a summary of the actions.

2. The best means of helping students retain new words is to teach them to draw the network of an associative field centered on a term that has specific meanings in the text. This drawing will show clearly the various relationships between the specific term and the other related words.

In an associative field, everything connected with the central word—its collocations[①], situational sets, semantic sets and other associative ideas—can all be included, thereby forming a network.

Situational sets: Situational sets are cohesive chains of lexical relationships in discourse. For example, *university*, *lecture room*, *lectern*, *library* form a situational set. They are groups of words that are associated because of the subject of the text, its purpose or its construction; they are words related to a particular situation. The words in situational sets form one kind of element in the associative field.

Semantic sets: Semantic sets are words linked by such relationships as synonyms (sofa, couch, divan), antonyms (big, small; tall, short; rich, poor), coordinates (oak, elm, ginko), superordinates (上限词) (horse, animal; carp, fish; rice, grain), subordinates(下限词) (fruit, pear; meat, pork; area of study, English), and stimulus-response pairs (关系组合)(accident, car; baby, mother). They contribute to the chains of associations and are another way of bringing words together.

3. It is more important for students to recognize certain sentence structures in reading and to use them in writing effortlessly than it is for them to remember only the forms of the sentence structure. Techniques that enhance recognition and production are to be centered on the function of the structure rather than on its form; that is, on the searching for appropriate structures to fit the particular occasion. That is why sentence structure may be best taught if the structure is connected with its function.

For example, the concept of the "superlative degree" can be expressed by sentence structures of positive degree, of comparative degree and, of course of the grammatical superlative degree. He is *as* sympathetic a man *as* ever breathed. (= He is *more*

---

①   May be defined either broadly or narrowly. If broadly, it refers to the association of lexical items that regularly co-occur in a certain situation, whereas the narrow definition puts a restriction on the sorts of language that can follow what precedes it. Unless otherwise stated, "collocation" in this book will follow the second, narrow definition.

sympathetic *than* any other man that ever breathed. = He is *the most* sympathetic man that ever breathed.)

The sentence structures "Nothing is more... than" and " Nothing is so... as" both express the concept of the superlative degree. *Nothing* can be replaced by *no*, *nobody*, *nowhere*, *little*, *few*, *hardly*, *scarcely*, etc..

4. Transitional sentences are vital in any piece of writing. In narration, they alert the readers to the change of episodes, and fix the time when that episode happens. Students ignore them. However, from time to time, this may lead to a certain lack of comprehension. The teaching of transitional sentences is important and effective for clarity.

In **Text A**, three stages of time are depicted. Below are the transitional sentences with key words in *italics*.

As I was giving a master class for young pianists in Saarbrucken, West Germany, *in September 1985* ,...

How happy and proud *the first praise* I remember receiving made me feel!

At 16, I was in the midst of a personal crisis arising from differences with my music teacher.

Beethoven's kiss miraculously lifted me out of my crisis and helped me become the pianist I am *today*.

5: **Text A** is a narrative and is organized with flashback. **Text B** is an argumentative article and **Text C** an expository essay, both with many narrative parts. They are organized by one general statement plus examples.

Text A   Beethoven's Kiss

Close Study of the Text

1. master class (Para. 1)

   Meaning: a lesson where an expert in an area gives advice to very talented students.

   e.g.: Master classes frequently take place in public or are broadcast on TV.

2. ...if given a pat on the back. (Para. 1)

   Meaning: ...if he was praised.

3. I praised him before the whole class for what distinguished his playing. (Para. 1)

   Meaning: In the presence of all students, I praised him for his distinctive playing skill.

   distinguish: to be a mark of character, point out the difference

4. He immediately outdid himself, to his amazement and that of the group. (Para. 1)

   Meaning: He played better than usual at once, which greatly surprised himself and other students.

   outdo: to do more or better than

5. A few words brought out the best in him. (Para. 1)

   Meaning: He performed as well as he was able/ He used his best efforts to play after hearing a few words of praise.

   best: one's greatest, highest or finest effort, state or performance

6. At 16, I was in the midst of a personal crisis arising from differences with my music teacher. (Para. 3)

   Meaning: The conflict between my music teacher and me came about because I disagreed with my teacher's views.

   arise from: to result from, come about because of

   e. g. : The country's present difficulties arise from the reduced value of its money.

7. I put all my heart into playing Beethoven's "Pathetique" sonata and continued with Schumann's "Papillons." (Para. 3)

   Note: "Put one's heart into doing something" stems from "put (one's) heart and soul into" which means: to enjoy (something such as an activity) so much that one works hard at it. In the context, the phrase means: do one's utmost.

8. Nothing in my life has meant as much to me as von Sauer's praise. (Para. 4)

   Meaning: von Sauer's compliment was the most valuable thing in my life.

   mean: to be of importance or value to

   e. g. : Your advice means a great deal to me.

   Note: Notice the superlative concept implied in the sentence.

Text-related Information

1. **Emil von Sauer** (Para. 3) (1862~1942): German composer and pianist, Liszt's student.
2. **Liszt** (Para. 3)

   Franz Liszt (1811~1886): Hungarian composer and pianist.

3. **Bach** (Para. 3)

   Johann Sebastian Bach (1685~1750): German musician and composer.

4. **Beethoven** (Para. 3)

   Ludwig van Beethoven (1770~1827): German composer who lived in Vienna. His works include nine symphonies, 32 piano sonatas, five piano concertos, a violin concerto, etc..

5. **Schumann** (Para. 3)

   Robert Alexander Schumann (1810~1856): German composer, whose most characteristic music is for the piano.

Text B   Words that Work Miracles

Close Study of the Text

1. Words that work miracles. (Para. 1)

   work: to produce or obtain as a result of effort

2. "Maybe when I'm a hundred, I'll get used to having everything I do taken for granted,"... (Para. 1)

   Meaning: "Perhaps when I'm 100 years old, I will not care whether my husband praises me or not for anything I have done,"...

   Note: Although this is a real conditional sentence, "maybe" serves the function of a subjunctive form. The sentence is SIMPLY a complaint from a young homemaker.

3. Yet we must bask in the warmth of approval now and then or lose our self-confidence. (Para. 2)

   Meaning: But every so often it is necessary to receive someone's positive reaction towards us, otherwise we lose our belief in our own abilities.

   or: otherwise

4. Praise is the polish that helps keep his self-image bright and sparkling. (Para. 6)

   Meaning: Just as polish makes a surface shine, praise enables us to keep a positive and optimistic mental picture of ourselves.

   Note: The structure is equal to a metaphor, which compares praise to polish.

5. When you add to his self-esteem, you make him want to like you and to cooperate with you. (Para. 7)

   Meaning: If you raise his self-respect, he will be pleased with you and cooperative with you.

6. A new minister... decided against criticizing his congregation for its coolness towards strangers. (Para. 9)

   Meaning: The in-coming minister decided not to criticize his congregation for being unfriendly.

   congregation: people who are attending a church service or regularly attend a church service

7. ... giving his people a reputation to live up to. (Para. 9)

   Meaning: ... so that his congregation will behave in a manner worthy of that image.

   live up to: to behave according to; to be as good as expected or desired

   e. g.: Do you always live up to your principles?

8. The congregation thawed. (Para. 9)

   Meaning: His people became kinder and friendlier.

   thaw: (of a person) to become friendlier, less formal, etc.

9. Praise helps rub off the sharp edges of daily contact. (Para. 11)

   Meaning: Through praise, we can avoid unpleasant conflicts in our daily life.

10. The spouse who is alert to say the heartening thing at the right moment... (Para. 11)

    Meaning: The husband or wife who is quick to give encouraging words when they are appropriate...

11. "That question went through me like a knife," the mother said. (Para. 14)

    Meaning: "That question deeply stirred my feelings causing me pain," the mother said.

12. As artists find joy in giving beauty to others, so anyone who masters the art of praising will find that it blesses the giver as much as the receiver. (Para. 16)

    Note: 1. The "as... (so)" structure usually appears in proverbs. For example: As you sow, so shall you reap; as the twig is bent, so grows the tree.

    2. "As" in these cases means "in the way that you (verb)"; "so" means "that is the way that you (verb)".

Text-related Information

Lord Chesterfield (Para. 8)

Philip Dormer Stanhope, 4th earl of Chesterfield (1694 ~ 1773): English statesman and author. He was famous for "Letters to his Son".

Text C Profits of Praise

Close Study of the Text

1. Praise is like sunlight to the human spirit; we cannot flower and grow without it. (Para. 4)

   Meaning: We need praise just as a flower needs sunlight. With praise, we become confident and successful.

   Note: The writer mixes simile and metaphor in the sentence. Praise is likened to sunlight, while people are implied flowers which require sunlight to thrive.

2. ... or to a lonely salesman fishing out pictures of his family. (Para. 5)

   fish out: to bring (something) up from somewhere (often with a certain difficulty)

   e. g. : He fished out a notebook from his schoolbag.

3. It's strange how chary we are about praising. (Para. 6)

   Meaning: It's odd that we are so cautious about giving praises.

4. That is why some of the most valued pats on the back are those which come to us indirectly, in a letter or passed on by a friend. (Para. 6)

   Meaning: Since we adopt a defensive attitude towards words of praises, we receive the most valuable compliments in the form of a letter or through a friend instead of receiving them directly from the giver of praise.

   Note: "Pats on the back" is a gesture symbolizing someone's approval or praise.

5. When one thinks of the speed with which spiteful remarks are conveyed, it seems a pity that there isn't more effort to relay pleasing and flattering comments. (Para. 6)

   Meaning: People are quick to insult others and to repeat the insults from others to those they insulted. It is regrettable that they put little or no effort in passing on words of praise.

   spiteful: ready to say or do nasty things to those one dislikes; malicious

6. "Our praises are our wages. " (Para. 8)

   Meaning: "The praises we receive are the reward paid for our work. "

   Note: The implied message is: Our effort needs praise and approval.

7. Since so often praise is the only wage a housewife receives, surely she of all people should get her measure. (Para. 8)

   Meaning: A housewife receives no money for her work. Because she does not, she should be constantly praised.

Note: Notice the humorous tone in the sentence. No one feels it strange that a husband does not pay his wife for the housework she has done.

8. To give praise costs the giver nothing but a moment's thought and a moment's effort... (Para. 11)

Meaning: Complimenting a person is a piece of cake, requiring neither our time nor our effort...

Section Two   Mind and Action

Unit 4   Happiness

Suggestions for Teaching

1. Students should be encouraged, when they face long sentences, to look for the main thought, and to put off all the other parts of a sentence. (This is actually the practice among native speakers.)

Examples from the text book:

(1) (A) *The only answer (that can be given) is that* [*as all these exterior provisions are found to be inadequate*] *the defect must be remedied*, [*by so contriving the interior structure of the government as that,*] *and its several constituent parts may,* [*by their mutual relations,*] *be the means of keeping each other in their proper places.*

(B) [*Considered primarily as a means of spoken communication,*] *language has been regarded*, (*both traditionally and in modern linguistics,*) *as a system* (*for translating meanings in the speaker's mind into sounds, or conversely, for translating sounds into meanings in the hearer's mind.*)

Show students that by moving or eliminating subordinate parts of a sentence, they can grasp the basic sentence structure and then make the meaning clearer.

(2) (A) *That the individual should be free to do this was enhanced and reinforced by the life styles of the indigenous cultural groups already inhabiting the land.*

(B) *As one's ability to obtain a better home increases the individual's level of aspiration changes.*

Point out that the long-subject sentence is a fairly normal part of complex college texts. You may ask the students to bring in examples from their own reading.

(3) (A) The Federalist *has a quality of legitimacy, of authority and authenticity, that*

gives it the high status of a public document, (one to which, as Thomas Jefferson put it, "appeal is habitually made by all, and rarely declined or denied by any" as to "genuine meaning" of the constitution.)

(B) *Regardless of the differences in what constitutes the home, owning one is part of the American Dream, (visual proof that one has succeeded in achieving some of the dream.)*

After learning the function of appositives in the sentence, the students may find the sentence meaning easier to figure out. The form "noun/pronoun + modifier" serves as the appositive of either subject or object of the sentence.

(4) *It's certain that the connection of these economic fears about education would not necessarily have to last. If experts came along with other explanations and ways for improving the American economic position, the interest in education might indeed decrease.* On the other hand, however, *increasingly Americans are seeing that our failure to prepare our young people for productive and responsible adulthood has (terrible economic as well as social) implications for America's success (in the world economy of the future.)*

Students have long been accustomed to fill-in-blank exercises about the subjunctive mood. But some students can neither recognize it easily in longer sentences nor use it to express ideas. More practice in discourse may help: you may devise your own exercises.

2. The comparative idea may be shown through the following ways:

(1) comparison or contrast, or antithesis (one idea opposed to another: hot/cold, for example): these may appear as two sentences or two parts of one sentence, e. g. :

—It (to be unhappy) took no courage or effort.

True achievement lay in struggling to be happy.

—Books are the best of things if well used;

if abused, among the worst.

(2) comparative indicators: these are the words or expressions: *but the opposite is true, but it's truer to say, but on the contrary, whereas, while,* etc.. They generally appear at the beginning of a second sentence or as the second part of the sentence, e. g. :

—We assume it's a feeling that comes as a result of good things that just happen to us, things over which we have little or no control.

But the opposite is true: happiness is largely under our control. It is a battle to be waged and not a feeling to be awaited.

—You think me idle, but on the contrary, I am very busy.

—We are becoming stronger and stronger, while/whereas our enemy is getting more exhausted as the war drags on.

—Wise men love truth, whereas fools shun it.

(3) fixed sentence patterns, *e. g.* :

—*If* the desert can be called a sea, (*then*) the camels are its ships.

—*As* bees love sweetness, *so* do flies love decay.

These three comparative procedures are useful tools when students are comparing or contrasting in their writing. Remember to remind students that the vital element is the function beneath the structure of the sentences.

3. From general statement to specific example:

In both reading and writing, it is helpful for students to distinguish between the general ideas and the specific details. In reading, they will quickly grasp the main idea of a passage; in writing, they will supply details to support a general statement. You may find general statements and specific examples in texts, and devise more exercises for students.

4. Information

The Federalist: The **Federalist Papers** are a series of 85 articles advocating the ratification of the United States Constitution. Seventy-seven of the essays were published serially in *The Independent Journal* and *The New York Packet* between October 1787 and August 1788. A compilation of these and eight others, called **The Federalist**, was published in 1788 by J. and A. McLean. The Federalist Papers serve as a primary source for interpretation of the Constitution, as they outline the philosophy and motivation of the proposed system of government. The authors of the Federalist Papers wanted to both influence the vote in favor of ratification and shape future interpretations of the Constitution. According to historian Richard B. Morris, they are an "incomparable exposition of the Constitution, a classic in political science unsurpassed in both breadth and depth by the product of any later American writer." The articles were written by Alexander Hamilton, James Madison and John Jay.

Text A　A Simple Truth about Happiness

╔═══════════════════════════════════╗
Close Study of the Text
╚═══════════════════════════════════╝

1. As much as she loved him, she explained, it wasn't easy being married to someone so unhappy. (Para. 1)

   Meaning: She loved her husband, but to live in harmony with a cheerless person makes life difficult for her.

   (as) much as: although; even though

2. ... put into words what I had been searching for—the altruistic, as well as the personal, reasons for taking happiness seriously. (Para. 2)

   Meaning: ... to explain, from a selfless and a personal angle, why people are so serious about happiness.

   put into words: to express (something) in words

   as well as: in addition to

   altruistic: showing concern for the happiness and welfare of others rather than for oneself; selfless

3. ... owes it to our spouse, our children, our friends to be as happy as we can be. (Para. 2)

   Meaning: ... we feel it is our duty to be as happy as possible because we think our spouse, our children or our friends deserve this.

   owe it to someone to do something: to feel obliged or bound to do something for someone or oneself

4. ... I reveled in my angst. (Para. 3)

   Meaning: I took great pleasure in my worries.

   revel in: to take great pleasure or delight in (something)

   angst: a feeling of anxiety or apprehension often accompanied by depression

5. ... I was taking the easy way out. (Para. 3)

   Meaning: ... it would have been more difficult to try to be happy, but I was being unhappy because it was less trouble.

6. ... work at happiness... (Para. 4)

   Meaning: ... to really try to obtain/reach happiness...

   to work at: to give thought to, energy to, etc.

7. It is a battle to be waged and not a feeling to be awaited. (Para. 5)

Meaning: Happiness is not something that we can trust to chance. We have to fight for happiness before we have it in hand.

8. ... he was one of those lucky few for whom everything goes effortlessly right. (Para. 7)

Meaning: ... he was one of a small number of persons who are so lucky that everything turns out as they wish.

9. "Whenever I enter a room, all I see is hair." (Para. 14)

Meaning: "Each time that I enter a room, hair is the only thing that attracts my attention."

Note: This is a vivid and humorous example illustrating what the author calls the "Missing Tile Syndrome." According to the author, we worry about what we don't possess, while we seldom focus on what we do possess.

10. ... happiness is a byproduct of something else. (Para. 18)

Meaning: ... happiness is something that is obtained while pursuing other goals in life.

byproduct: a substance obtained during the manufacture of some other substance

11. ... something permanent transcends us and that our existence has some larger meaning can help us be happier. (Para. 19)

transcend: to go beyond the range of human experience, belief, etc.

existence: way of life

Note: "something permanent transcends us" and "our existence has some larger meaning" are actually the writer's definition of "a spiritual or religious faith" and "a philosophy of life" (Para. 20). In other words, happiness derives from lofty sentiments. Only by aiming at lofty goals can we experience happiness.

12. Whatever your philosophy, it should encompass this truism... (Para. 20)

Meaning: No matter what view you have upon the problems of life, it should include this self-evident truth...

13. As with happiness itself, this is largely your decision to make. (Para. 20)

Meaning: Whether you will experience happiness or not depends, to a great extent, on the choice you make. In this context, it's up to you to "choose to find the positive in virtually every situation" or "choose to find the negative." Happiness has much to do with the attitude you adopt towards life.

Text B　The Secret of True Happiness

```
❖❖❖❖❖❖❖❖❖❖❖❖❖❖❖❖❖❖❖❖❖❖❖❖❖❖❖❖❖❖❖❖❖
  Close Study of the Text
❖❖❖❖❖❖❖❖❖❖❖❖❖❖❖❖❖❖❖❖❖❖❖❖❖❖❖❖❖❖❖❖❖
```

1. year-round-sun (Para. 1)

   Meaning: The area is bathed in sunshine all the year round.

   year-round: lasting throughout the year

2. ... equate happiness with fun. (Para. 2)

   Meaning: ... claim that happiness means fun/happiness is equal to fun.

3. These rich, beautiful individuals have constant access to glamorous parties, fancy cars, expensive homes, everything that spells "happiness." (Para. 4)

   Meaning: These wealthy, beautiful persons frequently attend exciting parties; they can afford expensive cars, homes, etc.. In other words, they can enjoy anything that means so-called "happiness."

   have access to: to be able to reach or use (something)

4. ... will do what all the other parties, cars, vacations, homes have not been able to do. (Para. 5)

   do: to bring us happiness

5. The way people cling to that belief that a fun-filled, pain-free life equals happiness actually diminishes their chances of ever attaining real happiness. (Para. 6)

   Meaning: If people are unwilling to abandon the belief that happiness means to have a lot of fun or to enjoy themselves without making any effort, it is very likely that they will never experience true happiness.

   cling to: to continue to believe in the value or importance of something even though the belief may no longer be valid or useful

6. ... he is afraid of making a commitment. (Para. 8)

   Meaning: ... he is frightened of faithfully continuing with a relationship.

7. Marriage has such moments, but they are not its most distinguishing feature. (Para. 8)

   Meaning: You may sometimes have fun or have some exciting experiences after marriage, but all this (fun, adventure, excitement) is not typical of marriage.

8. ... are deciding in favor of painless fun over painful happiness. (Para. 9)

   Meaning: ... are deciding to enjoy themselves without suffering in any way instead of trying to obtain real happiness by making sacrifices.

in favor of: on the side of

9. I don't know any parent who would choose the word "fun" to describe raising children. (Para. 9)

Meaning: No parent would say bringing up children is a lot of fun.

10. But these forms of fun do not contribute in any real way to my happiness. (Para. 12)

Meaning: But these fun things or activities do not actually bring me any true and enduring happiness.

contribute to: to give or add something to something

11. ... that least permanent of things. (Para. 12)

Note: In the text, the writer has many times reminded us that fun is but a momentary happy feeling when compared with true happiness which is abiding.

12. ... is one of the most liberating realizations we can ever come to. (Para. 13)

to come to a realization: to realize; to understand

Note: In this paragraph, "one of the most liberating realizations" refers to a degree of understanding that, in its highest form, helps us overcome mistaken ideas about true happiness and lead a better life.

13. The moment we understand that fun does not bring happiness... (Para. 14)

the moment *conj*. : as soon as; at the time when

e. g. : The moment I saw you, I realized that you were angry with me.

14. life-transforming (Para. 14)

Meaning: completely changing one's life so that it will be much better or much more successful

Text-related Information

1. **the land of Disney** (Para. 1): refers to Disneyland which is located at Anaheim, 25 miles south of Los Angeles, California, U. S. A.. Designed by Walt Disney (1901~1966), the creator of Mickey Mouse, it opened on July 17, 1955.

2. **Hollywood** (Para. 1): a section of Los Angeles, best known as the center of the American film industry.

3. **racquetball** (Para. 11): A game played on a four-walled handball court by two or four players with short-handled rackets and a hollow rubber ball 2 inches (5. 7 centimeters) in diameter.

Text C   The Terribly Tragically Sad Man

Close Study of the Text

1. ... pick up after... (Para. 1)

   Meaning: to tidy up

   e. g. : I refuse to pick up after children who are old enough to keep their own things in order.

2. ... much less... (Para. 8)

   Meaning: and certainly not; not to mention

   e. g. : I didn't even speak to him, much less discuss your problems with him.

3. Sometimes he had to pick up things and put them away—even things that didn't belong to him. (Para. 12)

   put away: to store (something), as in a box or space

4. ... one of the best packages I've put together. (Para. 43)

   Meaning: ... one of the best lives I've ever designed.

   package: a group of objects, plans, or arrangements that are related and offered as a unit

Text-related Information

1. **Ferrari** (Para. 6): a brand of expensive Italian-made car.
2. **Frisbee** (Para. 11): A trademark used for a plastic disk-shaped toy that players throw and catch. This trademark sometimes occurs in print meaning a throw-and-catch game played with this toy.

Unit 5   Approaches to Reading

Suggestions for Teaching

1. In English writing the topic sentence alerts the reader to what to expect in the passage. The other sentences develop the paragraph in different ways: by giving examples or details to illustrate the main idea, by expanding upon it with related ideas, or by expressing an emotional reaction to the main idea.

   Ask students in all of their subsequent reading to locate the topic sentence and main idea while reading. That will increase their comprehension dramatically.

   Below are the main ideas in the passages given:

   (1) How happy and proud the first praise I remember receiving made me feel! or How happy and proud I felt when I received my first praise.

   (2) The praise I received at 16 helped me overcome a personal crisis with my music teacher.

   (3) The effects of praise can be great indeed.

   (4) Discarding the illusion of perfection, I realized our family life was wonderful.

   (5) The first secret is gratitude.

2. A successfully-written topic sentence usually contains an opinion that will be proved or supported in the paragraph, or a statement of intent that the writer will explain in detail in the paragraph. Therefore a topic sentence

   —should be the most general sentence in the paragraph.

   —should be the most important sentence in the paragraph.

   —cannot be a simple statement of fact because there are no controlling ideas that need development.

   —will be the primary part that ensures a unity and completeness of the paragraph.

Text A   Comprehension Skills

Close Study of the Text

1. ... found ourselves absorbed in a display of old wedding gowns. (Para. 2)

find oneself + adj. /adv. : to discover, realize, that one is

e. g. : He found himself alone with a strange woman.

be absorbed in: to give all one's attention to (something, or doing something)

2. The things the author saw have fallen into two groups... (Para. 4)

   fall into: to be divided into (kinds); belong to (a class)

3. As a demonstration of obedient purposelessness in the reading of 99% freshmen we found this impressive... (Para. 7)

   obedient: doing or willing to do what one has been asked or ordered to do by someone in authority

   Note: By "obedient purposelessness" the writer means that these students were reading without purpose, without looking for the general idea of a chapter, and without bothering about the central idea. They expected that their teachers would explain it to them. The word "impressive" is ironic; Perry is not favorably impressed, because the way the students read is not helpful to them.

4. ... they had all settled into the habit of leaving the point of it all to someone else. (Para. 7)

   Meaning: ...all of them had become used to letting their teachers tell them the purpose of what they were reading.

   settle into: to become used to

   leave to: to allow something to remain to be dealt with by (someone)

   point: purpose or usefulness

5. If this purposelessness in study exists among students like those at Harvard, what must be the case with other students elsewhere? (Para. 8)

   Meaning: If almost all Harvard freshmen, who are supposed to be outstanding students, read without purpose, what may we expect from those students who are considered less capable than Harvard students? The reading habits of these other students must be terrible.

6. The inefficient reader plods straight through the material, often with wandering attention because his goal is only to "read the lesson." (Para. 9)

   plod: to work or do something slowly and continuously in a tiring or boring way

   wandering: moving away from the main idea and/or beginning to think of other things

   Note: The writer is talking about the consequences of "obedient purposelessness." When reading without purpose, students find it hard to read with concentration, which will inevitably impair their reading efficiency.

7. Contrast the careful attention to detail, the search for visual imagery of the stu-dent...

(Para. 9)

Note： This is a elliptical sentence. The implied message is that the student with a purpose—making a drawing—is actively involved with the text.

8. ... which seems to have a bearing on this special topic. The student then settles down to read carefully for detail. (Para. 9)

have a bearing on： to influence; to be relevant to

settle down： to begin giving one's whole attention, as to work

9. The student who thus reads with purpose has achieved a comprehension impossible to the student who merely "reads. " (Para. 9)

Meaning： The student who reads with purpose is in possession of a power of understanding which is unfamiliar to students who read without purpose.

10. When he was recovering from a spell of illness, he wired a friend of his recovery and remarked that he had just taken a long horseback ride. (Para. 10)

recover from： to begin to feel better after an illness

spell： a period of time during which an activity or condition lasts

wire： to telegraph

Note： This anecdote is meant to tell us that the requisite background knowledge is the key to a good understanding of new material.

11. The friend wired in reply, "How is the horse?" (Para. 10)

Note： The friend pretends to worry about the horse, since "Taft was one of the fattest of our Presidents. " He weighed around 160 kilos.

12. It is partly a matter of chance whether readers happen to have a fact like this stored up in their heads, but there is more to it than chance. (Para. 12)

store up： to save a supply of (something or things) for the future

Note： By "there is more to it than chance," the writer means that having the background information does not necessarily enable a reader to understand a story. What counts is, as he explains in the next sentence, whether the readers "realize that they have it" and "use it. "

13. ... the ability to make full use of the backlog of real and vicarious experience which almost every reader possesses. (Para. 13)

Meaning： ... since almost all readers have both direct and indirect experience, they should make the best use of what they have stored up in their heads to enrich their understanding of what they are reading.

backlog： reserve; accumulation; supply

vicarious: experienced by reading or watching someone else do something

❧ Text-related Information

1. **Stars and Stripes** (Para. 2): (*used with a singular or plural verb*) the flag of the United States, consisting of 50 white stars (one for each state) on a blue field in the upper left-hand corner, and a body of 13 horizontal stripes alternately red (7) and white (6), representing the original 13 states that united to form the country.

2. **Harvard** (Para. 7): Harvard University, centered at Cambridge, Massachusetts. The oldest American college, Harvard College was founded (1636) with a grant from the Massachusetts Bay Colony and named (1638) for its first benefactor, John Harvard. Supported largely by private gifts, Harvard's expansion into one of the world's great universities began during the administration (1869~1910) of university president Charles W. Eliot, when the elective system was introduced and graduate education was developed. Besides Harvard College, the university has many graduate schools.

3. **Taft** (Para. 10): Taft, William Howard (1857~1930), the 27th President of the United States (1909~1913), whose term was marked by antitrust activity and the passage of the Payne-Aldrich Tariff Act (1909). He later served as the chief justice of the U. S. Supreme Court (1921~1930).

Text B   How to Find Time to Read

❧ Close Study of the Text

1. The chances are you will never attempt that... (Para. 1)

   (The) chances are... (that)...: It is likely (that)...

   e. g. : Chances are the girl has already heard the news.

2. ...in fiction over which you wish to linger. (Para. 1)

   to linger over: to spend time with (something or doing something) in order to enjoy it

3. Multiplied by 7, the days of the week, the product is 31,500. (Para. 2)

   Meaning: If this number is multiplied by 7...

   multiply something by something: to combine two numbers by adding one of them to itself as many times as the other number states *e. g.* : If you multiply 6 by 5 the answer is 30.

4. Nearly all of the practicing doctors today were brought up on his medical textbooks. (Para. 4)

Meaning: Almost all of the doctors who are practicing medicine received their medical education by studying his textbooks.

practicing: actively engaged in a specified career or way of life

practicing doctors: people who work as doctors

bring up: to raise, or educate

5. His greatness is attributed by his biographers and critics not alone to his profound medical knowledge and insight... (Para. 5)

attribute... to...: to believe (something) to be the result of (something)

e. g. : He attributes his success to working hard.

The car accident was attributed to faulty brakes.

6. Osler arrived at his solution early. (Para. 6)

arrive at: to reach, to come to, to work out

7. If research kept him up to 2:00, he... (Para. 6)

keep up: to prevent (someone) from going to bed at the usual time

8. Osler read widely outside of his medical specialty. (Para. 7)

outside of: in areas other than

specialty: the subject of one's study or work, or a particular skill

9. Indeed, he developed from this 15-minute reading habit an avocational specialty to balance his vocational specialization. (Para. 7)

Meaning: The habit of reading 15 minutes per day gradually helped him strike an adequate balance between his side interests (or hobbies) and his profession.

avocational: of a subordinate occupation pursued in addition to one's vocation esp. for enjoyment

vocational: providing skills and education that prepare someone for a job or profession

10. Every day, the enlisted men put in an hour of drill and formations. (Para. 9)

enlisted men: soldiers who volunteer for the army

put in: to devote; to spend (a period of time)

formation: an arrangement of people, aircraft, ships, etc.

11. No universal formula can be prescribed. (Para. 11)

Meaning: There is no method that can be applied everywhere.

formula: a plan or method for doing something well

12. Then all additional spare minutes are so many bonuses. (Para. 11)

bonus: anything pleasant in addition to what is expected

13. Last night an uninvited guest turned up to make five for bridge. (Para. 11)

uninvited guest: a guest who calls without an invitation

turn up: to arrive or be found, often unexpectedly

make: to count as

e. g. : Will you make a fourth at bridge?

bridge: a card game for 4 players (who play in pairs) during which one partner looks on as "dummy" while the other partner plays the cards for both. The dummy's cards are placed face up on the table.

Note: Obviously, the uninvited guest is unnecessary for a 4-player card game.

14. I had the kind of paper book at hand to make being the fifth at bridge a joy. (Para. 11)

at hand: near; within reach

Note: As the host, the writer naturally let the self-invited guest make a fourth at the card game, while he himself was getting pleasure from reading a paper book within his reach.

Text-related Information

1. **Sir William Osler** (Para. 4): (1849~1919), Canadian physician. A renowned medical historian, he was also the most brilliant teacher of medicine in his day, at McGill University (1875~1884), the University of Pennsylvania (1884~1889), Johns Hopkins (1889~1904), and Oxford (from 1905). His many observations include those on blood platelets and on the abnormally high red blood cell count in polycythemia. He wrote *Principles and Practice of Medicine* (1892), one of the most prestigious medical texts of modern times.

2. **McGill University** (Para. 4): a private university in Montreal, Canada, founded by the legacy of James McGill (1744~1813), a Montreal fur merchant and philanthropist. It opened in 1829.

3. **Sir Thomas Browne** (Para. 7): (1605~1682), English physician and writer known for the richness of his prose in works such as *Religio Medici* (1642), an attempt to reconcile Christian faith with scientific knowledge.

Text C The Learning Revolution
Relearn how to read—faster, better, more easily

╔══════════════════════════════════════╗
║ **Close Study of the Text**
╚══════════════════════════════════════╝

1. And we're not talking about super reading techniques at thousands of words a minute. (Para. 1)

   Note: The "super reading techniques" (also called "speed reading") are designed to train readers to read an entire page at a glance. The author outlines the procedures when he discusses the "moving pen or finger" technique, but his purpose is to apply this technique to skimming.

2. Even the writing style of newspapers makes it easy to glean the main points. (Para. 4)

   glean: to collect (esp. information) in small amounts

3. So you can either read the summary or devour the whole story. (Para. 4)

   devour: to read (a book or magazine) quickly and with great eagerness

4. Advertisers flag your attention with headlines and pictures. (Para. 5)

   flag: to mark (something) so it can be found easily among other similar things

5. Very simply, you've cracked the newspaper code. (Para. 6)

   crack: to solve something difficult esp. after a lot of thought

6. ... the chapter amplifies it... (Para. 9)

   amplify: to add to the information given in (something); to give fuller information, additional details, etc. , about

7. Then reflect on your brain's fantastic ability to take in all that information instantly. (Para. 12)

   reflect on: to consider (something) carefully and at length

   take in: to fully understand (something, esp. spoken words)

8. That's your brain's magical ability to "photograph" a complete picture. (Para. 12)

   Meaning: Your brain's amazing ability enables your eyes to record a full view of what you have seen.

9. If you own the book, use it as a dynamic resource. (Para. 15)

   dynamic: (usually) very active and forceful

   Note: Of course, a book cannot become dynamic until it is read by readers in a dynamic way. What the writer is emphasizing here is that readers should make a creative and flexible use of the book.

10. The physical act of writing or typing will help embed them in your brain's memory-vaults—learning through the sense of touch as well as sight. (Para. 15)

physical: connected with the body

Note: "The physical act of writing or typing" refers to "learning through the sense of touch as well as sight".

embed. . . in. . . : to fix (something) firmly in (something)

vault: a room, esp. in or under the ground floor of a large building, that is used to store things safely

Note: The expression "Brain's memory-vaults" is coined by the author to give emphasis to the word "memory" and also to indicate the ability of the brain to remember.

Text-related Information

1. **The *New York Times*** (Para. 2): a daily newspaper sold all over the United States, but in general only to those considered (or who hope to be considered) one of a highly educated and influential group. It is generally considered a liberal newspaper.

2. **The *Los Angeles Times*** (Para. 2): an American daily newspaper which is regarded as a powerful voice of Republican conservatism.

Unit 6　The Younger Generation

1. The organizational patterns are also common modes of thinking. In **Test 1**, the answers are as follows:

   (1) **Time sequence**

   (2) **Transition**

   (3) **Comparison and Contrast**

   (4) **Enumeration**

   (5) **Cause and Effect**

   (6) **Example/Illustration**

   (7) **Classification**

   (8) **Space relationship**

   (9) **Description**

   (10) **Process**

   These groups, in the order which the patterns are presented in the text, are:

   Time sequence: meanwhile, at first, before, after that, then, soon, finally, at last, now

   Space relationship: right, up, down, in front of, where

   Process: first, second, next, then

   Example/Illustration: for example, for instance, in other words, another example, in addition, thus, as an illustration

   Enumeration: to begin with, then, first, second, next, finally, also, furthermore

   Classification: first, second, third

   Comparison and Contrast: like, similarly, likewise, however, but, nevertheless, on the other hand, in contrast

   Cause and Effect: as a result, because, this led to, so that, thus, therefore, consequently

   Description: be, refer to, be called

   Transition: also, moreover, in addition, then, first, however, but, on the other hand, on the contrary

   Please note that certain expressions—*first, second, third; however*, and so on—appear in more than one group. This is the case because their purpose shifts as the trend of the passage.

Note also that *at last* **always** implies the speaker's relief:

> *We walked for hours and at last we arrived.*
>
> *The lecturer talked on and on. At last he shut up.*

The word *finally* may or may not express relief. It is the common way of ending a series however.

For **Test 2**, dealing with passages in the reading skill sections of the *Student's Book*, the following patterns of organization apply:

(1) illustration

(2) cause and effect

(3) contrast

2. Compound words are formed mostly following three general principles:

noun+noun: farmhouse

adj.+noun: newcomer

noun+participle: bloodstained, house-hunting

3. Teaching sentence structure by its function may help students grasp more than the surface meaning, for the same idea may be expressed by different sentence structures and sentences with different surface meanings may have the same purpose. For example, the following imperative, interrogative and declarative sentences express the same idea—asking to open the window:

> Open the window. —the most direct of the three, used with close friends and relatives
>
> Would you please open the window? —a politer way of making the same request
>
> It's rather hot here. —a roundabout way, used especially when the speaker is in an unfamiliar place

4. In **Text C**, the function of the first two paragraphs is to present the argument and put the readers on the same footing with the author. The questions in the first paragraph help to make the voice milder and close the distance between the arguer and the reader.

The argument is actually put forward through the two questions: Shall we voice our objections? Or shall we accept the behavior on the theory that in this way at least we avoid secrecy and deceit? The author's argument is essentially a compromise or combination of the two opinions expressed in the two questions: wise parents should give freedom to their children while supplying them with necessary guidance.

5. The process of writing a paragraph is basically the same for writing all paragraphs:

(1) Choose the subject: be certain you know about what you write.

(2) Narrow the subject to a topic that will be of interest to your audience.

(3) List details about your topic.

(4) Limit the details to the most important ones you want to communicate.

(5) State the main idea of the paragraph in your topic (first) sentence.

(6) Outline the main points of the paragraph.

(7) Write the paragraph, using the details you have listed.

Text A   New-New Generation (新新人类)— A Special Lifestyle

Close Study of the Text

1. On their delicate faces is a very cool expression—they are confident and do things in their own way. (Para. 2)

cool: calm and self-controlled

do something in one's own way = go one's own way: to do what one wants and how one wants rather than doing what everyone else does or expects

2. Xu and his peers, however, are fully immersed in the international milieu thanks to the technological advances that have narrowed the gap between China and the rest of the world. (Para. 4)

be immersed in: to give all one's attention to (something such as study, work, music)

milieu: environment; social surroundings

thanks to: on account of; owing to; because of

3. ...and the names of Japanese and South Korean singers and film stars on their lips... (Para. 5)

Note: If something is on everyone's lips, it means that a great many people seem to be interested in it and are talking about it.

45

4. Their excuse is the rebellious mindset of their generation. (Para. 6)

   Meaning: The explanation they give for their not observing those rules is that to be disobedient is the very spirit of the "New-New Generation."

   mindset: attitudes or opinions resulting from earlier experiences

5. I feel like I'm exchanging ideas with the sculptor. (Para. 13)

   feel like: (of persons) seem to be

   exchange... with...: to share (words, ideas, etc.) with (someone), as in conversation

6. Leaving blind idolatry behind them... (Para. 14)

   idolatry: excessive attachment or devotion to something

   blind idolatry: the act of admiring someone or something in an unreasoning way

7. ... he had to repeat the year's work. (Para. 15)

   Meaning: ... he failed to go up to the next grade and was obliged to stay down.

8. ... and sensual desires. (Para. 17)

   sensual: interested in, related to, etc., giving pleasure to one's own body, as by sex, food, or drink

9. Content includes the bar scene, excessive drug and alcohol intake, and sex. (Para. 17)

   Meaning: What their works reflect includes drinking in the bar, taking drugs and indulging in excessive drinking, and in having sex.

10. Not bothering with how their literary works are received... (Para. 18)

    bother with: to take trouble concerning (something or someone)

11. ... please woo me openly. (Para. 18)

    woo: esp. *old use* (of a man) to seek the affection of (a woman) with intent to try to persuade (her) into love and marriage

12. ... most of them will cast off this life and return to a normal lifestyle. (Para. 20)

    cast off: to free oneself from (something unwanted)

Text-related Information

1. **Generation Y** (Para. 3): Americans born between 1979 and 1994 have been labeled Generation Y. Generation Yers, also referred to as the "Eco-boomers," "Millennium Generation," or "Generation M," differ significantly from past generations. Generation Yers are as young as ten and as old as 25. At 78 million strong, they are more than three times the size of Generation X. They have been portrayed as a materialistic and cynical

generation, but also as a generation of idealists intent on changing the world.

2. **Generation X** (Para. 3): the group of Americans born between 1961 and 1981, also known as the thirteenth generation of America. They live in the present, like to do experiment, and are looking for immediate results. They are selfish, and cynical, and depend greatly on their parents. They question authority and feel like they carry the burden of the previous generations.

3. **McDonald's** (Para. 9): the U. S.-based world fast-food giant.

4. **Henry Moore** (Para. 10): (1898~1986) British sculptor whose works, mostly semi-abstract human figures, are characterized by smooth, organic forms.

Text B　An Insider's Guide to Teen-speak

Close Study of the Text

1. Only later do you discover that... (Para. 3)

   Note: When adverbial expressions with the word only come at the beginning of sentences, inversion is used. This is a somewhat literary structure, although the expression "only later" + inversion appears on occasion in spoken English.

2. I am assured by friends whose children are now ambassadors and bank presidents that, at some point, it ends. (Para. 4)

   Meaning: My friend's children, who once practiced Teen-speak in their childhood, have grown into ambassadors and bank presidents. This fact makes me confident that children will, at some stage of their growth, get away from Teen-speak. To practice Teen-speak is a stage that children have to go through.

   point: time; stage

   it: Teen-speak

3. But whether that day comes before or after the Nobel Prize is not clear. (Para. 4)

   that day comes before or after the Nobel Prize: ... the time when children stop using Teen-speak arrives before or after they are awarded the Nobel Prize / become famous

   Note: Notice the humorous tone in the sentence and in the whole text. In the eyes of the writer, Teen-speak, though a headache to parents, is not that unpleasant. Implied in the complaints about Teen-speak is a mother's loving care for children and her wish to better communicate with children.

4. The keys to understanding them are tone, duration and pitch—a little like Chi-

nese (Para. 5)

duration: time during which something lasts or exists

pitch: (music and speech) degree of highness or lowness

Note: Tone, duration and pitch play an important role in the language of Chinese. Different degrees of these three factors decide upon the meaning. The same is true with Teen-speak. To have a better understanding of their language, you have to understand those three aspects. Underneath this comparison lies the fact that most Americans do not understand Chinese.

5. Most parents encounter the tonal dimension of teen language... (Para. 6)

    tonal dimension: the aspect of tone

6. ... but in this case the briefest version has the most devastating intent. (Para. 7)

    Meaning: ... but in this example, because "yeah" lasts for the shortest time, it has the strongest impact on the parent.

    devastating: confounding, stunning, frustrating

7. But before you're overcome with guilt, you should know that "my life" only refers to the next 45 minutes. (Para. 8)

    overcome: to feel so helpless, surprised, or embarrassed that one cannot think clearly

    Note: This sentence tells us that we should never take Teen-speak at face value. "My life" doesn't mean "my whole life," but rather a short period of time. In a word, Teen-speak remarks never mean what they seem to.

8. Asking questions about school gets you another wave of Teen-speak. (Para. 10)

    Meaning: Asking teenagers about their performance at school will bring about another large group of Teen-speak remarks.

9. Don't venture any further into the subject of school, because the next step is foolhardy:... (Para. 11)

    Meaning: To take the risk of asking additional questions about school is useless or unwise.

    foolhardy: foolishly brave, or taking unnecessary risks

10. "I don't know when it's due,"... (Para. 12)

    due: expected (to happen, arrive, etc.) at a particular time

11. All teenagers occasionally slip back into ordinary speech.   (Para. 13)

    Meaning: Now and then all teenagers conduct conversations in a normal way, meaning what they say.

12. If they catch you translating when you should just be listening, it's an incredible victory

for their side. (Para. 13)

Meaning: Sometimes you might as well take their speech as it is. If they see you trying to find an implied meaning in their remarks, they will regard it as a surprising success.

catch someone doing something: to come unexpectedly upon (someone) doing something (esp. something wrong); surprise or detect

13. As a reward, they get to say "You never listen to me!" (Para. 13)

Meaning: In return for parents' misunderstanding their remarks, teenagers will say "You never pay any attention to what I say."

Note: In this example, the writer seems to humorously remind us of the fact that it is impossible for parents to gain the upper hand when coping with such a complicated language as Teen-speak.

Text-related Information

The Nobel Prize (Para. 4): Any of the several international prizes awarded annually by the Nobel Foundation for outstanding achievements in the fields of physics, chemistry, physiology or medicine, literature, economics, and the promotion of world peace.

Text C   Coexisting with Teenagers

Close Study of the Text

1. Shall we voice our objections? (Para. 1)

   voice: to express (esp. an opinion or feeling)

2. Or shall we accept the behavior on the theory that in this way at least we avoid secrecy and deceit? (Para. 1)

   secrecy: the act of keeping something (information, opinions) from others

   deceit: behavior that is deliberately intended to make people believe something which is not true

   Note: This is another choice which is justified by the following hypothesis: If parents accept children's behavior they don't like, children will be frank with parents, telling them everything and not misleading them.

3. Do we, because a 16-year-old insists that "it's done," serve cocktails to youngsters at a birthday dance? (Para. 2)

   Meaning: "It is commonplace to serve cocktails to youngsters..."

   be done: to be considered polite; be the usual custom

   cocktail: a drink, esp. an alcoholic one, made by mixing two or more liquids together

4. "Someone's liable to spike the punch!" (Para. 2)

   Meaning: If you don't serve cocktails, someone will probably add alcohol to the punch and make it much stronger than cocktails.

   liable to: likely to do, happen, or experience something

   spike: to make (esp. a drink) stronger by adding alcohol

   punch: a cold or hot drink made by mixing fruit juices, pieces of fruit, and sometimes wine or other alcoholic beverages

5. Do we, to prove our broad-mindedness, laugh at—and thus encourage—the 14-year-old's off-color stories or ignore his locker-room language... (Para. 2)

   broad-mindedness: willingness to listen sympathetically to the views of others even though one does not agree with them; having a liberal and tolerant mind

   off-color: verging on the indecent; sexually improper

   locker-room: relating to, or suitable for use in a men's locker room, esp. of an earthly or sexual nature

   Note: The writer lists three examples in paragraph 2 to consider whether it is feasible to make compromises with children over matters we don't approve of.

6. Others, however, may have been confused by warnings against filling their children's mind with their own thinking. (Para. 3)

   Meaning: Other parents have no idea of what to do because they were told that to fill the minds of their children with their own ideas or opinions may change their individuality.

7. Or attempting to "mold them in their own image." (Para. 3)

   mold them in their own image: bring up children in such a way that they will be exactly like their parents

8. Or they may not even tricks but will announce, "If I can't do this in front of you, I'll just do it behind your back!" (Para. 4)

   resort to: to make use of (something or to do something, often something bad) in order to gain an advantage, often when everything else has failed

9. The adult wish to get a clear picture of the youngster's social scene today has prompted an

increasing number of surveys. . . on such matters. . . (Para. 5)

get a clear picture: to have a better understanding of

prompt: to be the cause of (an action, feeling or thought)

Note: The adult wish is the subject of the sentence. Adult is used as an adjective here.

10. . . . whether or not lights should be left on during parties. (Para. 5)

   Note: Parents have good reason to worry about this, since anything may happen after the lights are turned off during parties.

11. . . . where they seemed aware that their own impulses might get the best of them. (Para. 6)

   impulse: a sudden, strong desire to do something

   get the best of: to defeat (usu. someone)

12. . . . and keeping to a reasonable bedtime during the week. (Para. 7)

   keep to: to behave exactly according to (something such as a promise or plan)

13. At other times they may have to point out in no uncertain terms. . . (Para. 9)

   in no uncertain terms: in clear and unambiguous language

14. . . . youngsters will experiment with new forms of behavior in ways that parents may not like. (Para. 10)

   experiment with: to try different methods and ideas (when doing something)

15. Adult sanction for inappropriate behavior, however, may just add to adolescent confusion. (Para. 10)

   Meaning: Youngsters may become more bewildered if their parents permit them to behave in an unsuitable manner.

16. But it is quite possible to encourage individual thinking. . . (Para. 11), they form elegant variations

   individual thinking = to think for themselves (Para. 11)

17. We must give them both "roots and wings. " (Para. 11)

   Note: Both "roots" and "wings" are used metaphorically, with "roots" meaning "a strong foundation (in one place)" and "wings" indicating "to fly away" or "to think for themselves".

Section Three　Humans and Nature

Unit 7　Humans and Animals

Suggestions for Teaching

1. An awareness of article structure will greatly enhance the students' comprehension skill. Every type of writing has its own general structure, and it is because of this that a specific structure helps you to understand what you are reading.

    Both *expository prose* and *argumentation* generally contain three parts: *introduction*, *body* and *conclusion*.

    The introductory part usually begins with several general statements to call the readers' attention to the topic or to bring readers to the same stand as the author himself. Then it narrows to one specific statement, the thesis statement, which will include one or more points to be elaborated in the body.

    The body carries out the plan set up in the introduction. Each part of the body will explain, define, clarify or illustrate one point made in the thesis statement. The beginning of each part may indicate what the final point of the paragraph will be or it may not if the topic is complicated.

    The conclusion usually summarizes or reaffirms the thesis of the article. It may also contain a suggestion or a prediction based on material in the article.

    The structure may be clearly seen in the following diagram:

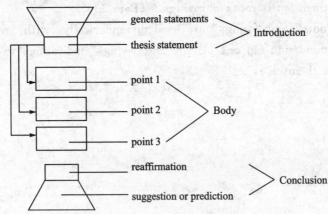

The structure is of course flexible, but the basic elements will always be found.

2. **Text A** is a typical example of argumentation. It can be taken as a model to teach students the way to read and write an argumentative essay.

　　Text B is an amusing story describing how Montmorency, a dog given to fighting cats, is changed into a dog afraid of cats.

3. A successfully-constructed thesis statement is the basis of a well-organized article. Therefore, constantly help your students recognize the important words in a thesis statement that are going to shape and control the whole article. You must explain to them the way in which those words determine the logical relationships between the parts of the article. This is both a helpful tip in reading comprehension and useful advice for preparing a paper.

　　A well-defined thesis statement indicates or predicts the type of discourse:
　　(1) Objective report
　　　　—To take a TOEFL Test, three simple steps must be followed.
　　　　—George Bush advocated a four-step approach to reducing Federal expenditures.
　　　　These kinds of thesis statements will call for an objective tone and produce an expository essay.
　　(2) Personal "is" thesis statements (with or without a definition)
　　　　—Rehearsing for a play is a strenuous activity that demands endurance and coordination.
　　　　—The Student Union is a great help to college students.
　　　　This kind of thesis statement comments personally on a central quality or characteristic of a subject.
　　(3) "Should be" thesis statements
　　　　—The problem of students cheating during examinations should be remedied by administrative action.
　　　　This type of statement will probably list the types of administrative actions that can be taken.

　　There are also causal statements (x leads to/causes y), comparison thesis statements (x resembles/is similar to/likey) and a few others. Each kind of statement leads respectively to a different type of article.

Text A   Canine Crisis

Close Study of the Text

1. For ages the word has been going around that the dog is man's best friend. (Para. 1)

   for ages: for a very long time

   word: news; information

   go around/round: (of news, disease, etc.) to spread round (a place or group)

2. But I contend that having a dog for pet is so expensive and annoying that I can do without such a friend. (Para. 1)

   contend: to argue, assert

   having a dog for pet: the gerund serves as the subject of the clause introduced by so... that...

   do without: to live or continue (an activity) in spite of lacking (something, someone, or doing something)

   Note: This sentence should be regarded as a sort of topic sentence for the following paragraphs in which a great many examples and reasons are presented to prove how "I can do without such a friend." Another point worthy of our attention is the writer's clever use of the structure of "so + adj./adv. + that" for the effect of exaggeration. This effect naturally gives a humorous tone to the whole article, warning us "that the author is quite serious about the topic but has chosen not to be solemn about it".

3. Providing for the dog's needs is so expensive that the animal should be an income tax deduction. (Para. 2)

   provide for: to supply necessary things such as food, clothing, and shelter for (someone, a time, or life)

   income tax: a tax on the net income of an individual or a business

   deduction: an amount taken away from the total.

   Note: In the U.S., one's income is taxed at a certain rate. This gives a base figure for the tax. However, one may take away from that certain expenses (deductions) for children, for charitable donations, and so on. The author is implying that a dog is as expensive to maintain as a child.

4. There's the medical bill for shots to keep the mongrel healthy. (Para. 2)

shot: the injection (of a drug) from a needle

5. Unless it's kept in the house, a female must be given "preventive maintenance," a ten-to twenty-dollar investment. (Para. 2)

   "preventive maintenance": an elegant and humorous euphemism for "contraception measure (of certain kind)," which is, in turn, a euphemism for "spaying," the act of removing part of a female animal's sex organs to prevent contraception.

   Note: In this paragraph, the writer regularly uses long, formal or technical words or expressions (such as "income tax deduction," "medical bill," "preventive maintenance," or "investment") to deliberately play up the seriousness of so commonplace a matter as keeping a dog. Playing with these words and expressions is largely responsible for the humorous effect that permeates the whole article.

6. Don't think you can buy a case of Ken-L-Ration and be done with it. (Para. 2)

   Ken-L-Ration: a popular brand name of dog food

   be done with: to be finished with (something or someone)

7. For about thirty dollars' worth of materials, a weekend's work, and a smashed thumb, you can build a leaky, 5'×4'×4' plywood box yourself. (Para. 2)

   smash: to hit violently

   leaky: made or in a state so as to permit water to enter or run out

   Note: This sentence explains the "heavy price" we have to pay. Notice that although the dollar amount is smaller, the work will require at least two days ("the weekend") and physical injury ("smashed thumb"), all in order to obtain a poor-quality finished product ("leaky").

8. Only those who can afford mink can really afford a dog. (Para. 2)

   mink: the highly valued brown fur skin of a small animal (a mink) somewhat larger than a squirrel

   Note: Exaggeration ("hyperbole") is used in the sentence to intensify the humorous effect. The price of a dog cannot be compared with that of the priceless mink, unless the dog is of a very rare breed.

9. A dog is such a nuisance that no one in his right mind would want to own one. (Para. 3)

   Meaning: Only mad people would keep an annoying dog.

   Note: "No one in his right mind" is a variant expression for "not in one's right mind" which means "mad," "insane," or, commonly, "crazy."

10. They inquire about holes reported dug in neighbors' flower beds, prize cats maimed and bleeding, and pet chickens and ducks sent to their eternal reward. (Para. 3)

Note: 1. "Holes reported dug" is a highly abbreviated, although common, structure for "holes which were reported as a complaint to the police as having been dug (by a dog)." "Sent to their eternal reward" stems from "go (or pass/pass on) to one's reward," an euphemism for "to die." Here the expression implies that pet chickens and ducks were killed.

2. Composed of three cases, this sentence is a typical example of *a trinomial*. A trinomial is a set of three. Three is frequently found in English. God, for example, is termed the *Trinity*, or *Three-in-One*. *Faith*, *Hope* and *Charity* identify the three major (cardinal) virtues. *Aglaia*, *Euphrosyne*, and *Thalia* are the sweet Graces in Greek mythology. Julius Caesar's famous expression is *I came*, *I saw*, *I conquered* (*veni*, *vidi*, *vici*). In Shakespeare's *King Lear*, the old king has three daughters, while in his *Macbeth*, there are three witches. In daily life, English-speaking children often count to three before they start a game (ready, set, go), and they have three wishes (as in fairy tales) or cherish three dreams. For our purposes, a trinomial has a rhetorical function. As a rhetorical device, it serves to build up, by the listing of three cases or examples, a climatic tension or effect, mainly for force or emphasis. In addition to this the listing of three examples is considered sufficient to illustrate a point or to persuade others to accept your idea. In this sentence, the device is again employed to exaggerate the image of a dog as a troublemaker. This sentence is not the first one of its kind in this text. It looks familiar to careful readers since the same structure has appeared in the first three paragraphs:

—"A dog can be handy as a night watchman around the house, as a pointer and retriever on a hunting trip, as a guardian and playmate for the children." (Para. 1)

—"For about thirty dollars' worth of materials, a weekend's work, and a smashed thumb, you can build a leaky, 5'×4'×4' plywood box yourself." (Para. 2)

—"Have you eased your bare feet into slippers fetched by a slobbering basset hound, seen a living room demolished by a toy-retrieving boxer, tried to read a newspaper chewed to wet confetti by an obedient Boston bull?" (Para. 3)

Without doubt, trinomials are an important and effective weapon in the writer's arsenal of persuasive rhetorical devices.

11. Neither a fire-breathing mother-in-law nor a nagging spouse will prove more annoying to man than a dog. (Para. 3)

   Note: The comparative structure actually performs the function of a superlative: among all nuisances to man, a dog is the most annoying. However, the byproduct of this unique comparison should not be ignored. The dog is not the only target of the writer's complaint. Because they are put side by side with a dog, innocent mothers-in-law and spouses are unavoidably victims of the writer's sense of humor. The sentence itself exemplifies the advantage of this unique structure. The comparative pattern of this type enriches the connotation of the superlative structure.

Text-related Information

They might consider me as cruel as the Russians, who—possibly attempting to solve their own canine crisis—shot Fido into orbit.

Note: On November 3, 1957, the former Soviet Union sent its second artificial earth satellite *Sputnik* 2 aloft, with a dog aboard. Fido (*faithful*), a once common name for a dog, is used instead of *Laika*, the actual Russian name. The dog was sent to space obviously not because the Russians wanted to "solve their own canine crisis," but rather because they were testing the possibility of manned space programs. The purposeful distortion of the Russians' intention helps the writer successfully bring his article to a humorous climatic end.

Text B   About Montmorency

Close Study of the Text

1. ... not very picturesque on the whole... (Para. 1)

   picturesque: having the quality of being like, or of being fit to be, the subject of a painting; pretty and interesting in an old-fashioned way

   on the whole: taking everything into consideration

2. ... Montmorency made an awful ass of himself. (Para. 2)

   make an ass of oneself: to behave stupidly so that one is ridiculed

3. I do not blame the dog, because I suppose that it is his nature. (Para. 3)

Note: This is the first time in this passage that we learn the real identity of Montmorency. This sudden surprise we feel mainly results from personification. The introducing of this figure of speech, which gives the gender and a human name to the dog, lends a human touch to Montmorency and a vividness to Jerome's description of the animal. The fact that Jerome does not disclose the real identity of Montmorency until the third paragraph proves that to catch readers unprepared is an indispensable element of a comic effect. Moreover, the association of the dog with the successful French marshal Montmorency (see **Text-related Information** below) is ironic, given the anticlimax at the end of the story.

4. Dogs of this kind are born with about four times as much wickedness in them as other dogs are, and it will take years of patient effort on the part of mankind to improve their character. (Para. 3)

on the part of: proceeding from, done by

Note: No one can be sure whether the wickedness of this breed of dogs is four times as much as that of other breeds. This seemingly exactitude, together with the expression "it will take years of patient effort on the part of mankind to improve their character," works in the same way as a hyperbole to create a comic effect.

5. A solemn peacefulness reigned over everything. (Para. 5)

reign over: to be influential; prevail

6. ... and a yelp of pain rang out. (Para. 7)

ring out: (of a voice, bell, or other sound) to sound loudly and suddenly

7. ... including the hall-porter, which gave the terrier the chance to enjoy an uninterrupted fight of his own with an equally willing Yorkshire terrier. (Para. 8)

uninterrupted: continuous; without a break or interruption

willing: ready or eager to do something

equally willing: the Yorkshire terrier is eager to "enjoy an uninterrupted fight," also

8. A crowd collected in the street outside, and wanted to know who was being murdered. (Para. 10)

collect: to come or bring together from a variety of places or over a period of time

Note: The reference to a murder when applied to a dog fight implies a great deal of uproar and adds to the humor.

9. ... I do not reproach Montmorency for being quarrelsome with cats... (Para. 12)

reproach... for: to scold (someone) gently; express disappointment in (someone) because of (a fault or doing something wrong)

10. ... —the cry of a stern warrior who sees his enemy given over to his hands—and flew after his prey. (Para. 12)

give over to: to yield (someone or something) to (someone)

11. It had a calm, contented air about it. (Para. 14)

Meaning: The cat seemed to be quiet and satisfied with itself.

air: appearance; manner

12. It trotted quietly on until its would-be murderer was within a yard of it.... (Para. 15)

would-be: desiring, professing, or having the potential to be

13. ... backing down the High Street... (Para. 22)

back down: to go down (while facing an opposite direction)

14. ... and took up an unimportant position in the rear. (Para. 26)

take up: to hold; to occupy

rear: the back part

Note: 1. In British English, "in the rear" indicates the back part of something, while "at the rear" refers to something that is behind and beyond. In American English, "in the rear" and "at the rear" is commonly used interchangeably for both.

2. This ending of the text is another example of Jerome's unexpectedness. To build up this comic anticlimax, the writer painstakingly selects his words and expressions and lists examples to conjure up the image of "the bravest dog." Firstly, the dog's name reminds us of the famous French marshal Montmorency, who was brave and skillful in warfare. Then the writer shows us by one vivid example (of the dogfight) how dogs of Montmorency's breed behave wickedly towards other dogs. And lastly, the writer compares the dog to a stern warrior who "sees his enemy given over to his hands." Jerome is purposely ambiguous in his description of the cat: although "large," it seems to be in poor physical shape ("It had lost half its tail, one of its ears and a fairly large proportion of its nose"). At the same time, however, it is "muscular-looking." We suspect that the "calm, contented air" comes from being unaware of the danger posed by Montmorency. This splendid image of a brave and belligerent dog is gradually weakened ("the look of that cat" and Montmorency's apology) and eventually shattered when we see Montemorency, with his tail between his legs, turning away from "his victim."

~~~

╔══════════════════════════════════╗
║ **Text-related Information**   ║
╚══════════════════════════════════╝

1. **Jerome K. Jerome:** (1859~1927), English writer and drama critic. He is noted for his humorous novel ***Three Men in a Boat*** (1889) and his play ***The Passing of the Third Floor Back*** (1907).
2. **Montmorency:** Duc Anne de (1493~1567), French marshal. A politically powerful nobleman, he successfully fought in numerous battles against Spain, the Huguenots, and the Holy Roman Emperor Charles V.

Text C   Old Ranger

╔══════════════════════════════════╗
║ **Close Study of the Text**   ║
╚══════════════════════════════════╝

1. ...put Old Ranger in the stable and keep him penned up until the danger period was over. (Para. 3)

   pen up: to enclose or imprison (someone or an animal) in a small space
2. ...that Mr. Epperly's children might slip out and feed him and get bit. (Para. 3)

   slip out: to leave quietly without being noticed
3. I decided to wait for the gloom. (Para. 13)

   gloom: darkness or near darkness

   Note: The boy was waiting for the sunset so that Old Ranger could not see him take aim.
4. While I waited for the gloom, the burning started in my pocket. (Para. 14)

   Note: A one-dollar (paper) bill could not possibly burn his pocket. It was a guilty conscience that was tormenting the boy's heart.
5. I had a feeling there was something nasty about it. (Para. 14)

   nasty: mean, unpleasant, or offensive
6. That would set the folks to worrying again. (Para. 16)

   set...to doing something: to cause someone to start doing something
7. I tried to think up how I could explain to my mother... (Para. 17)

   think up: to invent (usu. an excuse)
8. I could not decide how I could ever explain with a good face that in my pocket I had a one-dollar bill I had been given to shoot Old Ranger. (Para. 17)

Note: "With a good face" stems from "put on a good face," which means to try not to show how disappointed or upset one is about the situation. Similar phrases are "put a brave face on (a bad situation)" or "put on a brave face". Here his conscience was troubling him again, because he failed to shoot Old Ranger as told. The boy did not think that he deserved the one-dollar bill.

9. They would pucker up to cry when they saw me. (Para. 20)

   pucker up: (usu. of someone's face or mouth) to (cause to) tighten into folds. Here, to show the first stage of tears

   e. g. : The girl puckered up her lips for a kiss.

10. "But," she added, "if it was to do over..." (Para. 22)

   do over: to do (something) again; repeat or remake (something)

11. Old Ranger let go with a great howl that rolled and rocked across the ridges, and the Epperlys came bounding. (Para. 25)

   let go with: to shout or express something wildly

   bound: to move quickly with large steps or jumps

12. They alternated between my neck and Old Ranger's and I don't know to this day which of us got the most hugging. (Para. 25)

   alternate between: to change from (one thing, esp. a state) to (another thing)

   Note: They hugged the boy's neck and Old Ranger's in turn, showing their gratitude to the boy and their fondness for Old Ranger.

13. We started for the schoolhouse, feeling rich, with a whole dollar to spend. (Para. 29)

   Note: "A whole dollar" might seem trivial today, but, for the boy and the children, it was a large sum of money ("I had never had a one-dollar bill all my own"). The story is set in the distant past: "the schoolhouse" suggests "a little red schoolhouse" in the countryside. Moreover, the boy "walked through two miles of woods" to reach it. Today, when there is community busing, the children from several small communities are driven to a large "district" or "county" school.

Unit 8   Seasons

```
◇◇◇◇◇◇◇◇◇◇◇◇◇◇◇◇◇◇◇◇◇◇◇◇◇◇◇◇
  Suggestions for Teaching
◇◇◇◇◇◇◇◇◇◇◇◇◇◇◇◇◇◇◇◇◇◇◇◇◇◇◇◇
```

1. **Tone, unity** and **coherence**

Identifying the author's *tone* is, on occasion, as important to the comprehension as understanding the literal meaning. In ironic essays, for example, the author may be expressing a meaning totally opposite from the surface meaning. Three examples:

"You make a better door than a window." (*said to a child standing in front of a television set*)

"That film should have received the 'golden alarm clock award'." (*of a slow-moving film at a festival*)

"Daddy, why is that woman smiling at you?"

"Shut up," I explained.

In the first example, the speaker is saying that the child is blocking the view: the speaker is unable to see. In the second, the meaning is that the movie caused the speaker to fall asleep. In the third, the woman is either "making a pass" at the father (=flirting with him), or is a woman of whom the father does not want his son to be aware. In literature, Jane Austen is the most famous (and extensive) user of irony. Recognizing the tone, is, therefore, always necessary, and occasionally crucial. Students must be helped to recognize the tone.

Unity and *coherence* are the two sides of the same coin, the former referring to the content (the author does not wander) and the latter to the way the form holds together (the author does not ramble).

2. Collocations are simply narrowly defined in the student's book. Collocations supply restriction on which sorts of language can follow from what has preceded: by remembering collocations, students become aware of certain lexical restrictions and certain lexical possibilities. They will see, for example, that a certain word can only modify one type of thing not another. Collocations are as useful for teaching writing as they are for teaching comprehension.

3. In **Text A**, the coming of autumn and the departure of summer cause the author to feel sad about the quick passage of the time and the passing of youth. Two basic tenses are used in this article. The present tense is used for the description of the author's feelings right now and the past tense is employed for reminiscence about the past.

The author of **Text B**, in contrast, has chosen language of great energy and exuberance, and underlines this energy through his opening punctuation: the two exclamation points (!) indicate, first, joy at the arrival of spring, and, second, amazement that the weather is so poor ("... anticlimax!"). As can be seen in the article, this author is optimistic and holds a deep respect of and sense of wonder about nature.

In **Text C**, we find many words and sentences revealing the author's feeling towards summer.

... perfect stillness...

... had come lazily to a stop...

June was far away, September a distant blur.

We were free just to be ourselves, to build forts, to moon around the neighborhood with a head full of fantastical schemes.

What I miss is summertime, the illusion that the sun is standing still and the future is keeping its distance. On summer afternoons, nobody got any older. Kids didn't have to worry about becoming adults, and adults didn't have to worry about running out of adult-hood. You could lie on your back watching clouds scud across the sky, and maybe later walk down to the store for a Popsicle. You could lose your watch and not miss it for days.

In the author's youth, summertime was slow and contained an illusion that the future was far away, whereas now, as an adult, city time is about a fast rhythm of life and permits no fun.

Text A   Song of Autumn

Close Study of the Text

1. It all Happens so quickly: the days turning shorter, the leaves going red on the dogwood tree, the sunlight slanting through the windows at a different angle. (Para. 1)

   Note: "Happens" is capitalized possibly to startle or surprise the reader in the same way the writer is startled or surprised to notice the onset of autumn. Follow: *turning*, *going*, *slanting*. Their "present" form implies that we see it "happening" before our eyes.

2. And you're aware that your summer clothes feel all wrong—the color too light, the shoes too bare. (Para. 2)

all: altogether; completely; wholly

light: not deep or dark in color; pale

bare: without any clothes or not covered by anything. Here, not covering enough

Note: 1. It is not simply your summer clothes that feel all wrong. It is you who feel wrong in summer clothes. The writer here employs a figure of speech called synecdoche. Synecdoche involves the substitution of the part for the whole, or the whole for the part. In this case, "summer clothes" is used to represent the wearer.

2. Both light-colored clothes and "bare" (= "open") shoes are traditionally for summer wear. The message the writer wants to emphasize here is that autumn has silently and suddenly come upon us even before we feel it and have the time to take off our summer clothes and put on autumn ones.

3. "You" in this passage is the American, general "you." In British English, this would be "one (notices)." Whether the American "you" is general or specific depends on the context:

You must study hard if you want to succeed. you=everyone must if they...

You should study hard if you... you=you yourself.

However, nothing prevents the first sentence from being a "specific you."

3. Porches start to look emptier, and the air is no longer as fragrant with the smell of steaks sizzling on a grill. (Para. 2)

sizzle: to make the hissing sound of frying fat

grill: a frame of metal bars on which food is cooked over a fire

Note: Summer is the usual time for outdoor barbecues in western countries, usually in the backyard, or on an outdoor patio or balcony. Friends are often invited, grills are set up outdoors, and sausages, steaks and/or (ham) burgers are cooked. "Hamburgers" refer to ground beef originally prepared in the German city of Hamburg.

4. ... we catch our last glimpse of the brilliant light of that high, bold season we call summer. (Para. 3)

catch a glimpse of: to see... very briefly and not very well

5. It begins with putting away bathing suits that smell of chlorine and getting out sweaters

and jackets. (Para. 4)

put away: to store (something), as in a box or special space

smell of: to have an odor like that of (something causing the odor)

Note: Starting from this paragraph, there appear at least six parallel sentences beginning with "It begins with". By these parallel sentences the writer presents the scenes that symbolize the changing of summer into autumn. Parallelism is regularly employed in the listing of facts, ideas, events, etc.. It is often used with repetition to emphasize the equal importance and weight of the parallel parts.

6. ... with packing lunches and driving in car pools. (Para. 4)

car pool: a joint arrangement by a group of private automobile owners (here probably parents) in which each in turn drives his/her own car and carries other passengers (here, school children)

7. It begins with loading the car with stereos and clothes and beanbag chairs and driving your teenager off to a new life in some distant dormitory. (Para. 5)

load with: to make (something) full or heavy with (a weight)

beanbag: any of various pellet-filled bags used as furniture (such as a chair or couch); originally, a small bag filled with dried beans tossed back and forth between children as a game

drive off: to (cause to) leave for (a place), as in a vehicle

8. ... and I can pinpoint its origins. (Para. 7)

pinpoint: to find or describe the exact nature or cause of

9. I was eight years old and home the first week of school with a strep throat. (Para. 7)

strep = streptococcus: any of various rounded bacteria that occur in pairs or chains causing illness

10. "Oh, the days dwindle down to a precious few—September, November!..." (Para. 7)

dwindle (down) to: to reach (something such as a quantity that is much smaller) little by little

Note: "A precious few" is an imitation of "a chosen few" (a few people who have been selected for favor or special privilege)

11. This year marks her 85th changing of summer into fall. (Para. 9)

Note: This elderly friend actually uses the change of seasons to be mark of her life. "The 85th changing of summer into fall" implies that she is reaching the age of 85.

╔══════════════════════════════════╗
║   **Text-related Information**   ║
╚══════════════════════════════════╝

1. **Labor Day** (in the United States and Canada) falls on the first Monday of September. For historical political reasons, this holiday honoring workers is celebrated on this day to distinguish it from the socialist International Labor Day (May1ˢᵗ) celebrated worldwide. May 1ˢᵗ in the United States and a number of Catholic Countries is referred to by religious citizens as Lady's Day (or Mary's Day).

2. **"September Song"** was first sung in a Broadway musical by an elderly singer who has fallen in love with a younger woman. He describes his aging in ways similar to the ending of a year, and asks her to share his "precious few" remaining days. It is a very touching song.

Text B   Spring Diary

╔══════════════════════════════════╗
║   **Close Study of the Text**   ║
╚══════════════════════════════════╝

1. *March* 20. It is officially spring! (Para. 1)

   Note: March 20 is the day of the Vernal or Spring Equinox. "Officially" is used because our calendar tells us that spring arrives on that day.

2. ... the air is raw and chill. (Para. 1)

   raw: (of weather) cold and wet

   chill: cold

3. I recall Henry van Dyke's observation that the first day of spring and the first spring day are not always the same thing. (Para. 1)

   observation: a remark

   Note: There is the difference between "the first day of spring" and "the first spring day". The former is March 20, officially designated as the first day of spring, whereas the latter loosely indicates the first day which brings to us the real feeling of spring. Not every Spring Equinox answers our expectation of a bright and beautiful spring day. Hence, the writer's use of "anticlimax." Better weather had preceded this day.

4. Before the females arrive, each male stakes out a homestead, and then with spectacular aerobatics defends and holds as much of the territory as possible. (Para. 2)

stake out: to claim ownership of or a particular interest in (something)

homestead: a house with the land and outbuildings around it

aerobatics: the performance of stunts in the air, as with an airplane

Note: Both "homestead" and "aerobatics" are used figuratively, vividly describing how male redwing blackbirds build nests to welcome the females and how they fly around to defend their territory. In this paragraph, as in the rest of this text, the writer's frequent employment of such figures of speech as simile, metaphor and personification adds greatly to the vividness and liveliness of the description of spring.

5. The air rings with their wild xylophone calling. (Para. 3)

   ring with: (of a place) to be filled with the sound of (something such as a bell)

   xylophone: a musical percussion instrument consisting of a mounted row of wooden bars, each longer than the preceding, played by striking with two small mallets

   Note: The chirps of blackbirds are metaphorically likened to the sounds made by the xylophone.

6. The time of baby squirrels is at hand. (Para. 4)

   Meaning: The time for the birth of baby squirrels is near.

   at hand: near; within reach

7. I see gray squirrels stripping off the dry bark of cedar limbs... (Para. 5)

   strip off: to remove a thin covering of (a material) little by little

8. I wonder if there is some untaught wisdom... (Para. 5)

   untaught: natural, spontaneous, in-born

9. In the breeding season the starlings' mimicking of other birds reaches its peak. (Para. 8)

   starling: the common bird (with black, brown-spotted plumage) which nests near buildings and is a good imitator of sounds

   mimic: to imitate; to ridicule by imitating; mock

10. ...and caught the different shades of green in new grass clumps and young leaves... (Para. 9)

    catch: to notice or manage to see something briefly

    shade: a slightly different version of the same color

11. ...the peculiar illumination before a summer thunderstorm brings out special details and alters a whole landscape. (Para. 9)

    Meaning: Before a summer thunderstorm, the unusual sunlight presents in detail everything one sees, and the whole landscape taking on a new look.

illumination: the strength of light

12. ... an old saying took on added meaning: "to see it in a *new* light." (Para. 9)

saying: well-known phrase, proverb, etc.

take on: to seem or begin to have (a quality, form, or appearance)

Note: "To see it in a new light" generally means "to regard or understand something or a person in a fresh, different or more favorable way." In this context, the italicized *new* refers to the unusual quality of the sunlight. The author is playing with meaning.

13. A long soaking rain before daybreak, and earthworms are stranded everywhere on the inhospitable cement of sidewalks, in imminent danger of early birds or drying sun. (Para. 10)

stranded: lacking what is necessary to leave a place or to get out of a situation

inhospitable: (of places) not forming a shelter; not suitable to stay in

imminent: which is going to happen very soon

Note: The lives of earthworms are endangered because very soon they will be eaten by early birds or scorched to death by the blazing sun.

14. And, in a way, I am dealing in treasure. (Para. 11)

in a way: to some degree

deal in: to buy and sell; trade in (something such as goods)

15. Yet the world's most valuable animal is the earthworm—a humble burrower, nature's plowman! (Para. 11)

plowman: a person who uses a farming tool with a heavy blade (usually pulled by horses) to turn over the earth in a field for planting

Note: The reason the writer puts the value of the earthworm above that of a silver fox or a racehorse or the other animals is that the earthworm performs a function necessary to daily human life.

Text-related Information

Henry van Dyke: (1852~1933), American clergyman and writer. He was a prominent pastor of the Brick Presbyterian Church, in New York City (1883~1890), and a professor of English Literature at Princeton (1900~1923). His many writings include poems, essays and short stories, mostly on religious themes.

Text C　When the Sun Stood Still

```
◇◇◇◇◇◇◇◇◇◇◇◇◇◇◇◇◇◇◇◇◇◇◇◇◇◇◇◇◇◇◇◇◇◇◇◇
```
Close Study of the Text
```
◇◇◇◇◇◇◇◇◇◇◇◇◇◇◇◇◇◇◇◇◇◇◇◇◇◇◇◇◇◇◇◇◇◇◇◇
```

1. When the Sun stood still... (title)

   stand still: to stay in the same position without moving

2. We are well into summer now here in the city. (Para. 1)

   well into: far into; past the beginning of

3. ... and try to find a way to cram a vacation in somewhere. (Para. 1)

   cram in: to force or pack (things or people) tightly in a space

4. The calendar was a blank. (Para. 2)

   Note: This refers both to the space left in the square of each day on the calendar because there were not any arrangements made for the days, and to the feeling that one did not have to know what day it was.

5. Every day the hills of Lagunitas pressed in and the light pressed down. (Para. 3)

   press in: to surround; advance steadily

   the light pressed down: the sunlight felt heavy upon us

6. ... September a distant blur. (Para. 4)

   blur: something whose shape is not clearly seen

   Note: "Blur" is use figuratively here to indicate September was still far away, being vague and indistinct in the mind.

7. ... good students or goof-offs... (Para. 4)

   goof-off: one who evades work or responsibility

8. ... to moon around the neighborhood with a head full of fantastical schemes. (Para. 4)

   moon around: to wander without aim, activity, or interest (around a place)

9. Minutes were as big as plums, hours the size of watermelons. (Para. 5)

   Note: The writer cleverly compares an abstract concept to tangible fruits, vividly telling us how ample and how "delicious" their time was when they had nothing to do.

10. ... and adults didn't have to worry about running out of adult-hood. (Para. 6)

    run out of: to have no further supply of; lack (something)

11. You could lose your watch and not miss it for days. (Para. 6)

    Note: Since time seemed to stand still, a watch had become meaningless.

12. They're on city time. (Para. 7)

Meaning: My children lead a fast tempo of city life.

13. He's a city child, a child whose fun is packed into short, hurried weekends. (Para. 8)

    pack into: to crowd (an activity) into (time)

14. It won't be long before an hour—once an eternity—is for him, too, a walk to the grocery store, three phone calls, half a movie. (Para. 8)

    eternity: endless time; time without limits

    grocery store: a store where food and small items for the house are sold

    Note: There is an implied comparison between the value of time in the city and time in town. Time in a small town in the past seemed endless with nothing to do, whereas in the city time is measured by the activities that can be crammed into it.

15. ... to anchor kids to the earth, keep them from rocketing too fast out of childhood. (Para. 9)

    rocket: to go up fast like a rocket

    Note: The writer here humorously reinterprets the purpose of long school vacations. However he thinks that children should temporarily abandon the fast tempo of city life in order to have more time to enjoy 'to the full' their childhood. In this way, they could "carry their summertime with them into adulthood."

Text-related Information

Popsicle: the trade mark used for flavored, colored water frozen into a rectangular shape on one or two flat handles.

Key to Exercises

Unit 1

Text A

Pre-reading Focuses

1. See *Teacher's Book*, 3.

Post-reading Focuses

I. Reading Comprehension

1. (1)~(4) b d c d   (5)~(8) a d b d

II. Micro-writing Skills Practice

1. (1) sympathize   (2) extractions   (3) stupidity   (4) embarrassed
   (5) exclamation   (6) recognition   (7) repetition   (8) announcer
   (9) indignation   (10) rejoicing

2. (1) the next time Ben delivered milk to my home.
   (2) the day she got back.
   (3) The year Hongkong returned to the embrace of the motherland,
   (4) the evening she checked in at a hotel.
   (5) every time I listen to this love song.
   (6) the second time Ben saw the poor woman.
   (7) the next time you are doing your exercises.
   (8) the morning they set off.
   (9) any time you like.
   (10) the day he decided to give her the milk as a Christmas present.

3. (1) when   (2) then/once   (3) had   (4) same   (5) them

    (6) whose   (7) wrote   (8) later   (9) stood   (10) either

III. Functional Training

1. the happy mood

—Ben's jovial conversation

—lightened up

—arrived with a tremendous smile and a glint in his eyes

—grinning

the unhappy mood

—wasn't his usual sunny self

—seemed in no mood for talking

—was gloomy

—was distraught at his stupidity for allowing this bill to grow so large

—his anger seemed worse

—He bristled as he talked about...

—he replied indignantly

2. Adverbial clauses:

—When Ben delivered milk to my cousin's home that morning, (he wasn't his usual sunny self.)

—(He bristled) as he talked about the messy young ones who had drunk up all his milk.

—But when Ben left, (I found myself caught up in his problem and longed to help.)

—"When someone has taken from you, (give it to them, and then you can never be robbed.)"

—(We'd joke about it) when he'd come.

—Before I knew what was happening, I started to cry, and I didn't have the foggiest idea what I was crying about.

Coordinate clauses:

—It was late November 1962, and (as a newcomer to Lawndale, Calif, I was delighted that milkmen still brought bottles of milk to doorsteps.)

Prepositional phrases:

—In the weeks that my husband, kids and I had been staying with my cousin while house-hunting, (I had come to enjoy Ben's jovial repartee.)

—On a sunny January morning two weeks later, Ben almost ran up the walk.

Noun phrases:

—Today, (however, he was gloomy as he dropped off his wares from his wire carrier.)

—The next time I saw him, (his anger seemed worse.)

—The next time Ben delivered milk, (I told him I had a way to make him feel better about the $79.)

—Every time I'd ask the question, (it seemed he lightened up a bit more.)

—Then, six days before Christmas, (it happened.)

Text B

Pre-reading Focuses

3. (1)~(5) a b a c b   (6)~(10) b c b a a

Post-reading Focuses

I. Reading Comprehension

1. (1)~(5) T F F F T   (6)~(10) F T F T T

II. Micro-writing Skills Practice

Sample

By 1850, when the total population of the country exceeded twenty-three million, the total number of slaves was 3,200,000. In South Carolina and Mississippi slaves exceeded the whites in number. Only a minority of Southerners held slaves. Political and economic power was concentrated in a small group of Southern slave owners.

III. Functional Training

Adverbial clauses:

—(I heard it many times as a child,) whenever my family visited Aunt Bettie in the old house in Berryville, Virginia.

—When Aunt Bettie told me about her first sight of the bearded man in the stained blue uniform, (she always used the same words.)

—As his strength returned, (Bedell told Bettie about his wife and children in Westfield, Vermont.)

—(And Bedell listened) as she told him about her brothers and about James.

Noun phrases:

—One hot day in late September (Dick Runner, a former slave, came to Bettie with a strange report.)

—Early the next morning (she set off.)

—Three days later (Bedell was hobbling on a pair of crutches that Dick had made for him.)

Text C

Post-reading Focuses

I. Reading Comprehension

(1)～(5) F O F O O　　(6)～(10) O O F O F

Unit 2

Text A

Pre-reading Focuses

1. (1)～(5) h a f b c　　(6)～(10) d e g j i

2. See *Teacher's Book*, 4, 5.

Post-reading Focuses

I. Reading Comprehension

(1)～(5) c a c c d　　(6)～(9) c a d c

II. Micro-writing Skills Practice

1. (1) neutrality　(2) breath　(3) enthusiast　(4) retriever　(5) engrossing
　(6) counselor　(7) custody　(8) simplicity　(9) naivete　(10) disturbance

2. —low-income, schoolyard, teenager, shoplift, flashlight, handbag, off-limit, pocketbook, extraordinary

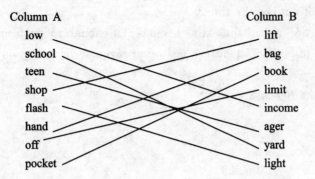

Column A

low
school
teen
shop
flash
hand
off
pocket

Column B

lift
bag
book
limit
income
ager
yard
light

3. (1) Having worked..., After working...
   (2) Having put down..., After putting down...
   (3) Used...
   (4) Lost...
   (5) ...arriving...
   (6) Having...
   (7) Not having received...
   (8) Seen...
   (9) ...permitting...
   (10) Granted...

4. (1) looks   (2) was   (3) different   (4) remembered
   (5) had   (6) for   (7) grandfather   (8) play

III. Functional Training

1. (1) synonyms or near-synonyms for *say*: counseled, gave him daily progress reports, was joking, warned, reassured, called out, shouted
   (2) synonyms or near-synonyms for *walk*: headed towards, quickening my pace, jogged across the grass

2. (1) Several evenings later I stayed after school to rearrange my classroom. Finished, I *turned out* the light and closed the door. Then I *headed towards* the gate. It was locked! I *looked around*. Everyone—teachers, custodians, secretaries—had gone home and, not realizing I was still there, stranded me on the school grounds. I *glanced at* my watch—it was almost 6 p.m.. I had *become so engrossed in* my work

75

that I hadn't noticed the time.

After checking all the exits, I found just enough room to *squeeze under* a gate in the rear of the school. I *pushed my purse through* first, *lay on* my back and slowly *edged through*.

(2) See *Teacher's Book*, 3.

3. (1) b   (2) a

Text B

Pre-reading Focuses

2. (1)~(5) b a c b a   (6)~(10) c b a c b

Post-reading Focuses

I. Reading Comprehension
(1)~(4) b c c b   (5)~(8) c b a c

II. Micro-writing Skills Practice
Sample

If there be (is) a universal complaint from men about their fathers, it is that their dads lack patience. I remember one rainy day when I was about six and my father was putting a new roof on his mother's house, a dangerous job. I wanted to help. He was impatient and said no. I made a scene and got the only spanking I can recall. He has chuckled at that memory many times over the years, but I never see the humor.

III. Functional Training
1. (1) Clause

    ...if there was someone for whom I had done a special kindness who might be showing appreciation.

(2) Noun phrase

Perhaps the neighbor I'd help when she was unloading a car full of groceries.

(3) Sentences

Or maybe it was the old man across the street whose mail I retrieved during the winter so he wouldn't have to venture down his icy steps.

(4) ... it might be a boy I had a crush on or one who had noticed me even though I didn't know him.

2. They first retell some less important examples in their daily life and then come to the singular most significant event to form the climax for the whole story.

Text C

Post-reading Focuses

I. Reading Comprehension

1. (1) vanished   (2) pajamas   (3) sulked   (4) affection
(5) figure   (6) envious   (7) articulate   (8) limousine

2. (1)～(4) F F T F   (5)～(8) T F T T

Unit 3

Text A

Pre-reading Focuses

1. As I was giving a master class for young pianists in Saarbrucken, West Germany, in September 1985, I felt that one student would do even better if given a pat on the back. I praised him before the whole class for what distinguished his playing. He immediately outdid himself, to his amazement and that of the group. A few words brought out the best in him.

2. See *Teacher's Book*, 4.

Post-reading Focuses

I. Reading Comprehension

(1)～(4) F F T F   (5)～(8) F F T T

II. Micro-writing Skills Practice

1. (1) personalities   (2) survivor   (3) reception   (4) potency   (5) distinguished
   (6) amazement   (7) miracles   (8) magician   (9) marvels   (10) enriched

2. (1) 我最大的心愿就是出国留学。
   (2) 这个问题比(所有)其他的问题都重要。(这是所有问题中最重要的问题。)
   (3) 我从未见过比简更漂亮的姑娘。(简是我见过的最漂亮的姑娘。)
   (4) 没有人比他的儿子更文雅的了。(他儿子是最文雅的人。)
   (5) 没有比健康更宝贵的东西。(健康是最宝贵的东西。)
   (6) 世上再也没有比这更难的了。(这是世上最难办的事。)
   (7) 谚语：瞎莫过于视而不见。
   (8) 我还没读过比这更好的小说。(这是我读过的最好的小说。)

3. (1) teacher   (2) instead   (3) the   (4) better   (5) favorably
   (6) above   (7) waits   (8) comment   (9) it

III. Functional Training

1. *Sample*

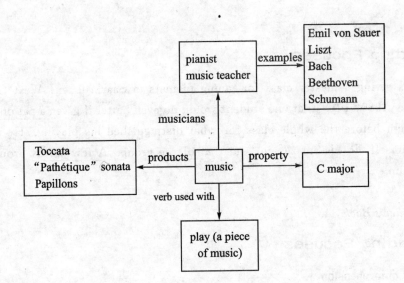

2. (1) **Comparative**：
   —...one student would do even *better* if given a pat on the back.
   —He immediately *outdid* himself.

Superlative:

—A few words brought out *the best* in him.

—I worked *as hard as* I could and was richly rewarded when he kissed me and said, "Thanks, son, you did very well."

—*Nothing* in my life has meant *as much* to me *as* von Sauer's praise.

—Soon I in turn will pass it on to the one who *most* deserves it.

(2) a. A few words of praise from me brought out *the best* in him.

   After I said a few words of praise, he immediately *outdid* himself.

   b. Nothing is more important than music in my life.

Text B

Pre-reading Focuses

1. See *Teacher's Book*, 5.

2. *praise:*

Nouns:

—compliment, encouragement, approval, words of praise, reassurance, appreciation

Verbs:

—say the heartening thing, giving praise, commend

congregation:

—members, visitors, his flock, his people, the ice-cube members warmhearted human beings

Post-reading Focuses

I. Reading Comprehension

(1)~(5) c b d a c   (6)~(10) d b c a c

II. Micro-writing Skills Practice

Sample

   Each of us has built up beliefs about ourselves. Unconsciously, our pictures of who we are have been formed by past experiences. Our successes and failures, what others have told us and what we think people believe about us all help form our self-image.

III. Functional Training

(1) **for comparative**:

—"If Bill would compliment me once in a while, he'd make my life much *happier*."

—He suddenly likes other people *better*.

—He is *kinder and more cooperative* with those around him.

—Yet it is perhaps in the home that the value of praise is *less appreciated* than elsewhere.

for superlative:

—*Nowhere* is this *truer than* in marriage.

—The spouse who is alert to say the heartening thing at the right moment has learned one of *the most important* requirements for a happy family life.

(2) Nobody is more important than her in my life.

Text C

Pre-reading Focuses

1. See *Teacher's Book*, 5.

Post-reading Focuses

I. Reading Comprehension

(1)～(5) a c b d a   (6)～(10) d a b a b

II. Micro-writing Skills Practice

1. (1) higher, faster   (2) greater   (3) younger, more experienced

   (4) the most crowded   (5) less   (6) later

   (7) the shortest   (8) the politest, polite, politer

III. Functional Training

Interrogative:

Do you ever tell your laundry manager how pleased you are when the shirts are done just right?

Do you ever praise your paper boy for getting the paper to you on time 365 days a year?

Imperative:

Let's be alert to the small excellences around us.

(So, let's be alert to the small excellences around us—and comment on them.)

Text A

Pre-reading Focuses

1. (1) This woman enabled me to put into words what I had been searching for—the altruistic, as well as the personal, reasons for taking happiness seriously.

  (2) The notion that we have to work at happiness comes as news to many people.

  (3) We assume it's a feeling that comes as a result of good things that just happen to us, things over which we have little or no control.

  (4) He spoke of his love for his beautiful wife and their daughters, and of his joy at being a radio talk-show host in a city he loved.

  (5) Finally, the belief that something permanent transcends us and that our existence has some larger meaning can help us be happier.

Post-reading Focuses

I. Reading Comprehension

(1)~(4) d c b a   (5)~(8) c d b a

II. Micro-writing Skills Practice

1. (1) The girl's condition has *worsened* since I last saw her.

  (2) He gave his men orders to *behead* the prisoner.

  (3) He *enslaved* his captives.

  (4) They have decided to *strengthen* the foundation by using more cement.

  (5) They should *deepen* that hole.

  (6) There is no need to *belittle* your rival's achievements.

  (7) How can I *thicken* this soup?

  (8) They *widened* the main street by 5 yards.

  (9) The blacksmith is *straightening* the piece of metal.

(10) Tom's carelessness with the gas *endangered* all their lives.

2. (1) complaints (2) philosophers (3) assumption (4) pursuit
   (5) revels (6) occurrence (7) permanent (8) ungrateful
   (9) essence (10) sufferers/suffering

3. (1) ...I knew...
   (2) ...would be no moonlight.
   (3) ...would not take place in it.
   (4) ...should have failed in the last exam.
   (5) ...could be seen shining at night.
   (6) ...would undergo...
   (7) ...be large or small.
   (8) ...would have helped us.
   (9) ...would have to step on the gas.
   (10) ...would help us to solve these problems.

4. (1) father (2) children (3) third (4) dog (5) works
   (6) women's (7) house (8) garden (9) relatives (10) family

III. Functional Training

1. —spouses, children, divorced, marriage, wife, the birth of our son, remarried, family life, what was wrong with, daughter, a previous marriage, ex-wife, shared custody

2. See *Teacher's Book*, 2.
   (1) —...it (to be unhappy) took no courage or effort.
      True achievement lay in struggling to be happy.
      —We assume it's a feeling that comes as a result of good things that just happen to us, things over which we have little or no control.
      But the opposite is true: happiness is largely under our control. It is a battle to be waged and not a feeling to be awaited.
      —We all know people who have had a relatively easy life yet are essentially unhappy.
      And we know people who have suffered a great deal but generally remain happy.
      —We tend to think that being unhappy leads people to complain,

but it's truer to say that complaining leads to people becoming unhappy.

—If you choose to find the positive in virtually every situation, you will be blessed, and if you choose to find the awful, you will be cursed.

(2) We tend to think that it's a feeling that comes as a result of good things that just happen to us, things over which we have little or no control, but it's truer to say that happiness is largely under our control. It is a battle to be waged and not a feeling to be awaited.

The contrasted meanings are realized by the use of antonyms (words of opposite meaning) and the conjunction *but*.

Text B

Pre-reading Focuses

1. (1) The way people cling to the belief that a fun-filled, pain-free life equals happiness actually diminishes their chances of ever attaining real happiness.

(2) Understanding and accepting that true happiness has nothing to do with fun is one of the most liberating realizations we can ever come to.

(3) Buying that new car or those fancy clothes that will do nothing to increase our happiness now seems pointless.

(4) We now understand that all those rich and glamorous people we were so sure are happy because they are always having so much fun actually may not be happy at all.

2. (3) The main idea sentences:

c) The truth is that fun and happiness have little or nothing in common.

d) Fun is what we experience during an act. Happiness is what we experience after an act. It is a deeper, more abiding emotion.

f) The way people cling to the belief that a fun-filled, pain-free life equals happiness actually diminishes their chances of ever attaining real happiness.

h) The single life is filled with fun, adventure, excitement. Marriage has such moments, but they are not its most distinguishing features.

j) More difficult endeavors—writing, raising children, creating a deep relationship with my wife, trying to do good in the world—will bring me more happiness than can ever be found in fun, that least permanent of things.

k) Understanding and accepting that true happiness has nothing to do with fun is one of the most liberating realizations we can ever come to.

3. (1)~(5) f i g h k   (6)~(10) b j a m e

Post-reading Focuses

I. Reading Comprehension

(1)~(5) T T T T F   (6)~(10) T F T F T

II. Micro-writing Skills Practice

Sample

While happiness may be more complex for us, the solution is the same as ever. Happiness isn't about what happens to us—it's about how we perceive what happens to us. It's the knack of finding a positive for every negative, and viewing a setback as a challenge. It's not wishing for what we don't have, but enjoying what we do possess.

III. Functional Training

1. —marriage, raising children, bachelor resists marriage, dating, making a commitment, single life, couples, infant children, parent, grandchild

2. —Many intelligent people still equate happiness with fun.

   The truth is that fun and happiness have little or nothing in common.

   —Fun is what we experience during an act.

   Happiness is what we experience after an act.

   —Going to an amusement park or ball game, watching a movie or television, are fun activities that help us relax, temporarily forget our problems and maybe even laugh.

   But they do not bring happiness, because their positive effects end when the fun ends.

   —These rich, beautiful individuals have constant access to glamorous parties, fancy cars, expensive homes, everything that spells "happiness."

   But in memoir after memoir, celebrities reveal the unhappiness hidden beneath all their fun: depression, alcoholism, drug addiction, broken marriages, troubled children, profound loneliness.

   —If fun and pleasure are equated with happiness, then pain must be equated with unhappiness.

   But, in fact, the opposite is true: more times than not, things that lead to happiness involve some pain.

—The single life is filled with fun, adventure, excitement.

Marriage has such moments, but they are not its most distinguishing features.

Text C

Pre-reading Focuses

2. (1)~(6) a b a b a c

Post-reading Focuses

I. Reading Comprehension

(1)~(5) T F F F F　　　(6)~(10) T T F F T

III. Writing Guidance

(1) (4)—Fun and happiness have little or nothing in common.

(2) (3) (5)—Things that lead to happiness involve some pain.

Unit 5

Text A

Post-reading Focuses

I. Reading Comprehension

(1)~(4) b c a b　　　(5)~(8) d c d c

II. Micro-writing Skills Practice

1. (1) comprehensible　　(2) absorption　　(3) impression　　(4) combinations

　　(5) precedence　　　(6) inflexible　　　(7) failings　　　(8) variation

　　(9) presentations　　(10) exemplified

2. (1) Thanks to the sudden rain, we came home wet (ironic). /Because of the sudden rain...

　　(2) We help them out of sympathy for their national independence movement.

　　(3) Criticism is necessary in that it helps us to correct our mistakes.

(4) She took the law course at her teacher's suggestion.

(5) The driver was fired for careless driving.

(6) Owing to their lack of experience, they didn't do the work well enough.

(7) They were obliged to wear thick, high boots, for fear of poisonous snakes.

(8) We must not relax our efforts on account of the great success already achieved.

(9) Many soldiers died on the march either from starvation or from severe wounds.

(10) Because of his knowledge of this country, Thomson was appointed as our guide.

3. (1) slow   (2) words   (3) nouns   (4) pronouns

   (5) verbs   (6) adverbs   (7) sentence   (8) Other

   (9) readers   (10) less   (11) eyes

III. Functional Training

2. —Here is a simple example of the most common kind of thought relationship:

—Now examine the same sentence parts arranged in a different way:

—Here is another sentence:

—Once more, observe the same facts but in a fourth relationship:

—William G, Perry has reported a study done with fifteen hundred Harvard freshmen to determine their habits of study when presented with a typical chapter in a history text. In presenting his results, Perry has this to say:

—Suppose, for example, that a student is studying a chapter about life on Southern plantations.

—Contrast again the procedures of the student who wants to compare the way of life of a southern plantation with that in colonial New England.

—Or, again, the method used by a student whose responsibility is to report on one very specific topic: the duties of the mistress of a plantation.

—The following is a story told by Helen Taft Manning about her father...

Text B

Pre-reading Focuses

2. (1) <u>300 words a minute</u>   (2) <u>4,500 words 126,000</u>   (3) <u>20 books</u>

   (4) <u>before he went to sleep</u>   (5) <u>1,000</u>

Post-reading Focuses

I. Reading Comprehension

(1)~(5) T T F T F   (6)~(10) T F F F T

II. Micro-writing Skills Practice

Sample

A person with a rate of less than 150~250 words per minute almost always reads word by word. This method is so slow and inefficient that it actually hinders comprehension. In learning to read by meaningful word groups, a person enables his brain to function much closer to its capacity and almost invariably improves comprehension.

III. Functional Training

—If the average reader can read 300 words a minute of average-type reading, then in 15 minutes she/he can read 4,500 words.

—Multiplied by 7, the days of the week, the product is 31,500.

—Another multiplication by 4, the weeks of the month, makes 126,000.

—And a final multiplication by 12, the months of the year, makes 1,512,000.

—In one year of average reading by an average reader for 15 minutes a day, 20 books will be read.

Text C

Pre-reading Focuses

2. (1)~(4) a b a c   (5)~(8) a b a b

Post-reading Focuses

I. Reading Comprehension

(1)~(5) F T F T T   (6)~(10) T F F T F

II. Micro-writing Skills Practice

Main idea: The principles for reading a newspaper apply to nonfiction reading.

I. An introduction presenting the main purpose

II. Three-part formula giving you a clear guide

III. Other types of <u>pointers</u> supplying additional help

Conclusion: Select the <u>needed</u> parts to read.

Unit 6

Text A

Post-reading Focuses

I. Reading Comprehension

(1)~(4) a b b c   (5)~(8) c a b c

II. Micro-writing Skills Practice

1. (1) stipulation   (2) eruption   (3) impulse   (4) reflects   (5) observant

   (6) originality   (7) isolated   (8) accessible   (9) acquaint   (10) overwhelming

2. —necklace, skateboard, on-line, internet, outside, mindset, classmate, downtown,
   shopkeeper, lifestyle, artwork, nationwide, full-length, intake

3. (1)~(5) D C D D C   (6)~(10) D D C D C

4. (1) me   (2) me   (3) mother   (4) criticize   (5) wall
   (6) low   (7) both   (8) over

III. Functional Training

1. <u>subordinate</u>:   decoration—necklaces, beads, rings
   <u>coordinate</u>:   necklaces—beads, rings
                            necks—wrists, noses, ears
   <u>superordinate</u>:   on-line, e-mail—internet
   <u>antonym</u>:   delicate—cool
   <u>stimulus-response</u>: their elders—these young people

2. **appearance**
   —They dye their hair different colors, wear necklaces around their necks, beads on their

wrists and rings in their noses and ears.

—They put temporary tattoos with the words "Hello Kitty" on their chests and various small decorations on their clothes.

—They wear black or brightly colored vests and overalls, and shoes with broad toes and very thick soles

—On their delicate faces is a very cool expression.

—Japanese and South Korean Fashion.

—With their dyed hair, baggy South Korean clothes, and the names of Japanese and South Korean singers and film stars on their lips, Zhang Yu, 16, and her classmates are often mistaken for Japanese or Koreans.

—Zhang said the shoes she was wearing were the latest fashion and hard to find anywhere else in Beijing.

way of thinking

—Xu and his peers, however, are fully immersed in the international milieu thanks to the technological advances that have narrowed the gap between China and the rest of the world. They often neglect the past, focusing instead on the future.

—Leaving blind idolatry behind them, this younger generation has begun to concentrate on their own feelings while observing what is happening around them.

—I like doing things my own way rather than following others. I'm disgusted by the fixed life-pattern others try to impose.

lifestyle

—They are often seen riding skateboards, dancing in discos, and enjoying themselves in bars.

—Having mastered computer skills, they are used to communicating on-line or through e-mail. With the aid of the Internet, they have access to much more information than the older generation.

—Collecting posters, seeking information about Japanese and South Korean singers and stars, listening to CDs, spending more than 100 yuan on music concerts and talking about Japanese and South Korean films or TV shows are important parts of the New-New Generation's lives.

—While pursuing Japanese and South Korean lifestyles, the New-New Generation also adopt foreign things, such as McDonald's food and foreign films. In their eyes, the world is a colorful kaleidoscope.

—The sense of lacking mental or spiritual balance, and of being unconcerned and impulsive, are frequently displayed in their works. Content includes the bar scene, excessive drug and alcohol intake, and sex. The works often describe marginalized people, including those who lack fixed jobs and vagrants who lead isolated lives.

3. (1) the first para.

—They are a new kind of young people.

—Description.

(2) the second para.

—These young people are called the "New-New Generation."

—Enumeration.

(3) the 4th para.

—The New-New Generation is the most significant transitional generation since the mid-20th century.

—Cause and Effect.

(4) the 15th para.

—Han Han is an example of the younger generation.

—Time sequence.

Text B

Pre-reading Focuses

The following appear in the texts and should be checked:

☑ Teen-speak is a different language in that it has different tone, duration and pitch, and hence different meanings.

☑ Teen-speak will be naturally abandoned when the children are old enough.

Post-reading Focuses

I. Reading Comprehension

1. (1) ambassador (2) awesome (3) pitch (4) version (5) parka
   (6) venture (7) due (8) incredible

2. (1)~(4) F F T T (5)~(8) F F T F

II. Micro-writing Skills Practice

Sample

I have two kids—my daughter is 19, my son is 17. Growing up, they treated me with proper awe. I was powerful, brilliant, infallible. Such canonization did not prepare me for life with a teenager.

III. Functional Training

1. —speak ordinary adult English

 —conduct conversations

 —practice Teen-speak

 —an English vocabulary

 —tone, duration and pitch

 —the tonal dimension of teen language

 —punctuation

 —ordinary speech

Their use in the texts adds a serious and academic atmosphere to the whole article. But the article is actually written in an ironic tone. Beneath the complaint is the mother's love for her daughter and her anxiety to better understand her.

2. —*Don't bother me.* (directly expressing reluctance)

 —*Did somebody cut off your legs?* (The sentence structure is ironic, and the diction is harsh.)

 —*I deeply resent the authority you have over me, but I acknowledge it and will take out your stupid garbage.* (a milder way of expressing reluctance than (a) and much milder than (b))

 —*Out of affection for you and respect for your age, I will take out the garbage.* (an even milder way to express reluctance)

 —*Okay.* (showing acceptance)

Text C

Pre-reading Focuses

1. See *Teacher's Book*, 4.

Post-reading Focuses

I. Reading Comprehension

(1)~(4) T F T F　　(5)~(8) T F T T

Unit 7

Text A

Pre-reading Focuses

1. (2) ☑ exaggerated

   ☑ humorous

   (3) The structure of the article and the organization of paragraphs are different.✔

Post-reading Focuses

I. Reading Comprehension

(1)~(4) a c a a　　(5)~(8) b a d c

II. Micro-writing Skills Practice

1. (1) eternity　　(2) frequency　　(3) denial　　(4) maintained　　(5) deducted

   (6) Prevention　(7) invested　　(8) sleepers　(9) guard　　(10) exaggeration

2. (1) There were so many people waiting for the bus that they decided to walk.

   (2) Jane had such a bad headache last night that she couldn't sleep.

   (3) George is such a good teacher that his students learn French very fast.

   (4) Paris is such an unusual city that many tourists visit it every year.

   (5) Last night it was so hot that Tom couldn't sleep.

   (6) Her husband is so wealthy that nobody knows exactly how much money he has.

   (7) She is so eager to enter Oxford University that she studies day and night.

   (8) Elizabeth is such a pretty girl that Hernando has fallen in love with her.

   (9) Elvis Presley was such a popular singer that he is still remembered and revered today.

   (10) The sun is so far from the earth that it takes eight minutes for its light to reach us.

3. (1) lover   (2) canine   (3) those   (4) dogs   (5) whatever
   (6) predict   (7) before

III. Functional Training

1. —man's best friend
   —handy as a night watchman around the house
   —as a pointer and retriever on a hunting trip
   —as a guardian and playmate for the children
   —having a dog for a pet

2. —the <u>animal</u> (a general term to emphasize the species of animal the dog belongsto as contrasted to human beings, another species)
   —a <u>female</u>
   —a <u>Chihuahua</u> (to name a particularly small, elegant and expensive breed, as opposed to the "big mutt" in the following sentence: a large dog of no particular breed, a mongrel)
   —a big <u>mutt</u> (see preceding)
   —<u>basset hound</u> (this, and the two names following are particular breeds of dogs with the emphasis on their most unattractive features)
   —a toy-retrieving <u>boxer</u>
   —an obedient <u>Boston bull</u>
   —<u>mutts</u>
   —<u>pooch</u> (a slang term, often of endearment)
   —<u>Rex</u> (a possible name for the dog)

3. **ideas of equality:**
   —A dog can be as particular about food as a French connoisseur.
   —Only those who can afford mink can really afford a dog.
  ideas of comparative:
   —Neither a fire-breathing mother-in-law nor a nagging spouse will prove more annoying to man than a dog.
  Change the listed sentence under comparative into the structure of equality:
   —A dog can be as annoying as a fire-breathing mother-in-law or a nagging spouse.
   —Only those who can deal with a fire-breathing mother-in-law or a nagging spouse can really deal with a dog.

—They all create a degree of superlative, implying that the dog is the most troublesome creature in the world.

4. —For ages the word has been going around that the dog is man's best friend.

—But I contend that having a dog for a pet is so expensive and annoying that I can do without such a friend.

—Providing for the dog's needs is so expensive that the animal should be an income tax deduction.

—There's the medical bill for shots to keep the mongrel healthy.

—And dogs have to eat.

—(a dog-house) They're expensive.

—A dog is such a nuisance that no one in his right mind would want to own one.

—Consider the dog owner blessed with a dog that fetches-slippers, rubber toys, newspapers.

—And dogs make noise.

—Cops are frequent visitors to dog owners' homes.

—Suspect: your pooch!

—Dogs are pests.

Text B

Pre-reading Focuses

1. Narration.

2. (1) A dog.
   (2) ☑ a fox-terrier

Post-reading Focuses

I. Reading Comprehension

(1)～(4) T T T F   (5)～(8) F T F F

II. Micro-writing Skills Practice

Sample

A cat will love, comfort and caress you, but it will never truckle to you. People who prefer dogs are uncomfortable with fears that cats consider themselves superior to people. I enjoy the company of my superiors, so I like cats.

If my husband wants to get a dog someday, he will do so with my blessing. But my heart really lies elsewhere.

III. Functional Training

verbs showing the actions of a cat:

—the cat *sticks* its tail into the air, *arches* its back, and *rubs* itself against my trousers, lovingly and peacefully.

—a cat *darted out* from one of the houses in front of us, and began to *trot* across the road.

—It *trotted* quietly on until its would-be murderer was within a yard of it, and then it *turned round* and *sat down* in the middle of the road, and *looked at* Montmorency with a gentle, inquiring expression, that *said*:

—Then the cat *rose*, and *continued his trot*.

description of a fox-terrier (Montmorency's breed):

—Montmorency made an awful ass of himself.

—When Montmorency meets a cat, the whole street quickly knows about it, and the noise and disturbance are overpowering.

—Then he looked up towards the ceiling, and seemed, judging from his expression, to be thinking of his mother.

—Then he yawned.

—Then he looked round at the other dogs, all silent and noble-looking.

—Then without a word of warning, and for no possible reason, he bit the poodle's near front leg, and a yelp of pain rang out.

—So pleased was the fox-terrier with what he had done that he *determined* to continue.

—He sprang over the poodle and attacked a sheep-dog which woke up and immediately commenced a fierce and noisy battle with the poodle.

—...he had injured the Yorkshire terrier severely, and was now wearing an expression of complete innocence

—...he gazed up into her face with a look that seemed to say: "Oh, I'm so glad you've come to take me away from this terrible scene."

—Montmorency gave a cry of joy—the cry of a stern warrior who sees his enemy given over to his hands—and flew after his prey.

—Montmorency dashed after that poor cat at the rate of twenty miles an hour;

—Montmorency is not without courage; but there was something about the look of that cat that might have turned cold the heart of the bravest dog.

—Montmorency, putting his tail between his legs, came back to us, and took up an unimportant position in the rear.

Text C

Post-reading Focuses

I. Reading Comprehension

(1)~(5) T F F F F   (6)~(10) T F F T F

Unit 8

Text A

Pre-reading Focuses

1. (1) ☑ reminiscent
      ☑ melancholy

Post-reading Focuses

I. Reading Comprehension

(1)~(3) c a c   (4)~(6) a b d

II. Micro-writing Skills Practice

1. (1) turn /grow   (2) go/turn   (3) slants   (4) seems /feels
   (5) feel/seem   (6) look   (7) swings   (8) smell of/reek of

2. (1) (e)   (2) (h)   (3) (i)   (4) (d)   (5) (b)   (6) (f)   (7) (c)   (8) (a)   (9) (g)

3. (1) audible—which can be heard
   (2) fallible—who is likely to make mistakes
   (3) navigable—which is deep and wide enough for a ship to go through
   (4) plausible—which is likely to be true

(5) credible—which is able to be believed or trusted

(6) affable—who is friendly, kind, relaxed and easy to talk to

(7) amiable—who is pleasant and friendly

(8) tenable—which can be successfully defended against attack

(9) negligible—which is a very small or trifling amount

(10) edible—which is fit to be eaten

4. (1) coloring   (2) bathed   (3) recognized   (4) originate   (5) infinity
   (6) brilliance   (7) warm   (8) extension   (9) fragrance   (10) autumnal

5. (1) with being   (2) in taking   (3) X going   (4) in thinking/learning
   (5) with having   (6) at being   (7) in reading   (8) against being
   (9) with embezzling   (10) against being

6. (1) sits/lies   (2) turns   (3) schedule/time   (4) roll/curl
   (5) they   (6) as   (7) trunk

III. Functional Training

1. —the air is **no longer as fragrant** with the smell of steaks sizzling on a grill

—catch our **last** glimpse of the brilliant light of that high, bold season we call summer

—driving your teenager off to **a new life in some distant dormitory**

—coming back to your teenager's **empty room** and wondering **where the years went**

—the streets are **no longer filled with sounds of children playing**

—fall begins with the **melancholy** feeling that **something has been lost**

—"Oh, the days **dwindle down to a precious few**—September, November! ... "

—I knew it was about **loss,** and it made me **sad.**

—Maybe the **sadness** is the dim recognition that there are a **finite** number of summers and falls left in your life.

—... **with the last of summer all around me,** I want to extend my arms and **catch the warmth, the breeze, and the flowers** and draw it all inside myself, **where it could live forever.**

2. **Phase 1:**

—The days turning shorter, the leaves going red on the dogwood tree, the sunlight slanting through the windows at a different angle.

Phase 2:

—Then one day you notice that the garden seems quite still. And you're aware that your summer clothes feel all wrong—the colors too light, the shoes too bare. Porches start to look emptier, and the air is no longer as fragrant with the smell of steaks sizzling on a grill.

Phase 3:

—... for most of us the fall season begins just after Labor Day. It begins with putting away bathing suits that smell of chlorine and getting out sweaters and jackets.

3. —... the days turning shorter, the leaves going red on the dogwood tree, the sunlight slanting through the windows at a different angle.

—Porches start to look emptier, and the air is no longer as fragrant with the smell of steaks sizzling on a grill.

—If we listen carefully, we can almost hear the sound of a door closing.

—It begins with putting away bathing suits that smell of chlorine and getting out sweaters and jackets. It begins with the kids going back to school, with packing lunches and driving in car pools. It begins with saying "Hurry up or we'll be late" a dozen times a day.

—It begins with loading the car with stereos and clothes and beanbag chairs and driving your teenager off to a new life in some distant dormitory. It begins with coming back to your teenager's empty room and wondering where the years went.

—It begins with noticing how early the dark comes on and how, after dinner, the streets are no longer filled with sounds of children playing.

—Suddenly, a man's voice started singing on the radio next to my bed: "Oh, the days dwindle down to a precious few—September, November! ..."

—I didn't know who was singing or what the song was.

—An elderly friend tells me that some years ago she began numbering the seasons. It helps her to understand that each one is unique. This year marks her 85th changing of summer into fall.

The form "verb+ing" greatly enhances the dynamic and rhythmic effect of the language, and therefore stresses the author's feeling towards the quick passage of the time.

4. The friend's remark indicates that others feel the same melancholy, and even more so as

they age, when their own "autumn" (death) approaches. The remark also stresses the feeling of the "September Song," and the passage of time.

5. See *Teacher's Book*, 3.

Text B

Pre-reading Focuses

See *Teacher's Book*, 3.

Post-reading Focuses

I. Reading Comprehension

(1)~(5) T T F F F   (6)~(10) F T T F F

II. Micro-writing Skills Practice

1. (1) (c) (2) (e) (3) (a) (4) (b) (5) (d) (6) (f)

2. *Sample*

"*March* 20. It is **officially** spring! **What an anticlimax**! Gust-driven rain is slashing the trees under a sullen sky; the air is raw and chill. I recall Henry van Dyke's observation that the first day of spring and the first spring day are not always the same thing.

To me **spring** was marked this year by the return of the male redwing blackbirds, **who** came back with a rush a month ago. Almost overnight the dreary stretches of our winter swamp were filled with life. Everywhere, with scarlet epaulets flashing, the blackbirds have been singing and darting about, chasing each other, shooting up like rockets, whirling like pinwheels. Before the females arrive, each **male** stakes out a homestead, and then with spectacular aerobatics defends and holds as much of the territory as possible.

The air rings with **their** wild xylophone calling. **It** is an exultant, jubilant call, a fitting voice for a season of flowing sap and awakening life.

III. Functional Training

1. To me spring was marked this year by the return of the male redwing blackbirds, who **came back with a rush** a month ago.

   Almost overnight the dreary stretches of our winter swamp **were filled with life.**

Everywhere, with scarlet epaulets **flashing**, the blackbirds have been **singing** and **darting about**, **chasing** each other, **shooting up** like rockets, **whirling** like pinwheels.

It is an **exultant, jubilant** call, a fitting voice for a season of **flowing sap** and **awakening life**.

I once saw peas, planted in a flowerpot, **lift** and **thrust aside** a heavy sheet of plate glass laid over the top. Another time, when peas and water were tightly sealed in thick glass bottles, the germinating seeds **developed** pressures sufficient to **shatter** the glass.

Only a few weeks ago the frozen earth appeared hard and dead, yet now I see the beginning of **a flood of life that nothing can halt**.

As I walked up through the old orchard late this afternoon I looked back and caught **the different shades of green in new grass clumps and young leaves**, all suddenly **brilliant** in the sun, which had just **emerged** from behind a cloud. In the same way, the peculiar illumination before a summer thunderstorm **brings out** special details and **alters** a whole landscape.

As I stood there, an old saying took on added meaning: "to see it in a **new** light."

2. The words in verb+ing form highlight the immediacy of the actions, produce a dynamic effect, and underline the vitality of spring.

Text C

Post-reading Focuses

I. Reading Comprehension

(1)~(4) T F T F   (5)~(8) T T F T

II. Functional Training

1. **summer in the past**

—...a perfect stillness awaited us when we stepped out of school in June. We had no summer classes, no camps, no relatives to visit. The calendar was a blank.

—every day the hills of Lagunitas pressed in and the light pressed down. It was as if the planet had come lazily to a stop so we could all hear the buzzing of the dragonflies above the creek—and the beating of our own hearts.

—you could spend a quarter of an hour watching the dust motes in the shaft of sunlight from the doorway and wondering if anybody else could see them.

summer in the present

—An early morning alarm gets my daughter, Morgan, up for summer school. My son, Patrick, has gone off with his uncle, and my husband and I have to go to our jobs and try to find a way to cram a vacation in somewhere.

—He's a city child, a child whose fun is packed into short, hurried weekends. Even in summer his hours grow shorter and begin to run together, faster and faster. It won't be long before an hour—once an eternity—is for him, too, a walk to the grocery store, three phone calls, half a movie.

2. —We are well into summer **now** here in the city.

—**When I was growing up** in a small California town called Lagunitas

—**Every day** the hills of Lagunitas pressed in and the light pressed down.

—What **I miss is** summertime. . .

—**On summer afternoons**, nobody got any older.

—These busy kids I'm raising **today** don't know what summertime is.

These "time sentences" form a time line like this:

Now   past   now   past   now

3. (1) So you sat in Miss Parlett's class and dreamed of sleeping late and waking to the smell of <u>sizzling bacon</u> and <u>new-mowed grass</u>. And you <u>dreamed of</u> playing Monopoly on the screened-in porch that <u>remained cool on the hottest days</u> because it was <u>shaded by a huge elm tree</u>.

You <u>dreamed</u> about <u>wearing white shorts and halter tops</u>. And knowing the <u>pleasure</u> of walking <u>barefoot</u> on damp sand, on cool grass, on rain-soaked asphalt.

season: Summer; the author enjoyed this season.

(2) The early <u>snows</u> fall soft and white and seem to heal the landscape.

At such times, locked away inside wall and woolens, lulled by the sedatives of woodsmoke and candlelight, we recall the competing claims of nature. We <u>see</u> the branch and bark of trees, rather than the sugar-scented green of their leaves. We <u>look out</u> the window and <u>admire the elegance of ice crystals</u>, the <u>bravely patient</u> tree <u>leaning leafless into the wind</u>, the <u>dramatic shadows</u> of the <u>stooping sun</u>. We <u>look at</u> the structure of things, the geometry of branch and snowflake.

season: Winter; the author admires the scene as though looking at a picture or a play.

(3) In the <u>heat</u> of mid afternoon the women would <u>draw the blinds</u>, spread blankets on the floor <u>for coolness</u> and nap, while in the fields the cattle herded together in the

shade of spreading trees. Afternoons were absolutely still, yet filled with sounds.

Bees buzzed in the clover. Far away over the fields the chug of an ancient steam-powered threshing machine could be faintly heard. Birds rustled under the tin porch of the roof.

Rising dust along the road from the mountains signaled an approaching event.

season: Summer; the author feels relaxed and not pressured in this season of heat and sound.

Section One　Humans and Culture

Unit 1　The Westerner's Character

Suggestions for Teaching

1. In "real-life" material, devices to achieve unity and coherence are quite naturally used in various combinations; here we will artificially separate them for purposes of explanation.

   (1) The topic sentences

   A sharply refined topic sentence is the first step in establishing a coherent paragraph.

   e. g. : Unlike the Senate, who were narrow in their views, the President had a larger, idealistic vision of foreign policy.

   (2) Key function words

   One of the standard ways of showing the logical relationships of your parts is to use the number of key function words required.

   Here is a topic sentence for paragraph three with *key function words* :

   *The **third stage** of the argument reaches **deeper** levels.*

   The example below is the topic sentence for a paragraph:

   *The argument for the re-unification of Taiwan with the motherland has **three** levels, **each** deeper than the preceding.*

   (3) Key content words

   The repetition of key content words is also an important device. These words refer to key elements of the particular content of the essay and so establish the emphasis and definition of subdivisions.

   (4) Pronouns

   Pronouns, such as *this*, *that*, *it*, *he*, and *they*, are a necessary part of paragraph continuity. They also establish the logic of your transitions. In terms of use, *this* and *that* are chosen depending on the distance the writer assumes towards the topic.

   e. g. : China is surrounded by many countries. This has determined her foreign policy = the writer feels near to the issue.

That has determined her foreign policy = the writer feels a certain distance from the issue.

The pronouns *it*, *he* and *they* refer to the closest noun.

e. g. : I visited my father's sister and my mother's sister. She was sick = the mother's sister.

I bought some apples and took them to my relatives. They were expensive = the relatives were expensive.

Avoid the "free-floating" *it* (an *it* with no immediate reference).

e. g. : We walked along the river. Then we stopped for dinner. Then we visited friends. It was (What was? The river, the dinner, or the visit to friends?) very pleasant. = The entire day was very pleasant.

(5) Substitutes

The use of alternate words is of value within the paragraph in the same way that it is of value throughout the essay.

(6) Sentence structure

The repetition of sentence structures stresses the thought.

2. A text is realized in the form of sentences. Every sentence except the first exhibits some form of cohesion with a preceding sentence, usually with the one immediately preceding. Lexical cohesion (realized by word relations) is just one type; the other types of cohesion are:

(1) reference, such as

—Personal references: *I*, *me*, *mine*, *my*, *it*, *one*

—Demonstrative references: *this*, *these*, *here*, *now*, *then*

—Comparative references: *same*, *identical*, *similarly*, *otherwise*, *better*

(2) substitution, such as

—Nominals: *one*, *ones*, *same*

—Verbals: *do*

—Clausals: *so*, *not*

(3) ellipsis, or the omission of a word easily understood, as in "This is a fine hall you have here. I've never lectured in a finer."

(4) conjunctions, such as *but*, *accordingly*, *therefore*, *furthermore*, *on the contrary*, *in spite of that*

3. Associative field: In an associative field, we can enlarge the circle of a central word to include a central concept. Those words connected with the central concept may be situational sets (see Teacher's Book I, Unit 3, 2), semantic sets (see Teacher's Book I, Unit 3, 2), collocations and other associative ideas.

4. *Queer* is the key word in **Text A**. *Strange*, *odd*, and *peculiar* (with their respective meanings) are synonyms of *queer*.
   —A *queer* thing is one that is difficult to understand.
   —Something that is *strange* is unusual or unexpected, and makes you feel slightly uneasy or afraid.
   —If you describe someone or something as *odd*, you think that he/it/she does not follow the common expectation or common behavior.
   —A *peculiar* thing is unusual in an unpleasant way.

   In Text A, the author uses queer to refer to Americans, emphasizing those unusual traits of theirs that outsiders do not understand.

5. "," ";" or ":"
   The punctuation marks ***comma***(,), ***semicolon***(;), ***colon***(:)and ***period***(.)are used to show *voice pauses*. The longest pause is the ***period***, while the shortest pause is the ***comma***. These marks also serve certain grammatical and conceptual purposes.

   A ***comma*** separates items in a series: *I bought a book, a pencil, and an eraser.* Or *I came, I saw, I conquered.* It also separates closely associated or attributive clauses within a sentence: *Her boyfriend, (who is) a self-centered person, is no good.*

   Semicolons are used to list equal, related sentences or to list a (numbered) series of ideas:
   The messenger arrived in the village. He delivered his news quickly; the elders debated their decision passionately; (and) the townspeople awaited their fate anxiously.

   This reasoning was dominated by the following factors: 1) workers generally desire a higher standard of living; 2) as their salaries rise, the cost of the goods they produce rises; 3) salaries elsewhere must rise as the cost of goods rises.

   The ***colon*** is used to list information or an example at the end of a sentence, to connect two closely related thoughts, and to substantiate a statement:

A professional tennis match requires at least four participants: two players, a referee, and a ball retriever.

The government was unable to arrive at a policy: the alternatives all contained elements dangerous to economic stability.

The Council was opposed to war: only three of the nine members voted in favor.

Let us now turn to several examples for the differences among **comma**, **semicolon**, **colon**:

[1] Schoolchildren have adopted the fund as one of their favorite charities; their small contributions have enabled the fund to reach its target.

[2] I've just had some good news: I've been offered a job in a law firm.

In [1] we would need to insert *and* if we wished to replace the *semicolon* with a *comma*:

Schoolchildren have adopted the fund as one of their favorite charities, and their small contributions have enabled the fund to reach its target.

The last example above illustrates the conditions favoring the use of the *comma* to separate independent clauses in compound sentences:

(a) the parts are closely related semantically (both dealing here with the children's contributions to the fund);

(b) they are linked by a coordinator (in this case by *and*).

In [2], the *colon* serves its classic function of uniting two independent clauses, and serves also to substantiate *some good news*. The *colon* indicates a closer interdependence between the units separated than does the *semicolon*. Indeed, it sometimes indicates as close a relation as the *comma* does, but it is a different relation. The functions of the *colon*, common in formal English, can be summed up as follows: what follows (as in this sentence) is an explication of what precedes it or a fulfillment of the expectation raised (even if raised only by its own use). Thus:

I've just had some good news: I've been offered a job in a law firm.

Those who lead must be considerate: those who follow must be responsive.

When two independent clauses are regarded as being sufficiently related to or belong to one sentence, the relationship is shown by a *colon*. If the sentence is re-written with a *comma*, a conjunction of some sort must be introduced:

Those who lead must be considerate, while those who follow must be responsive.

To a native speaker, the loss of the *colon* indicates a loss of force in the idea.

Consider the example below:

> Taylor was, as always, a consummate actor, and with a few telling strokes he characterized King Lear magnificently.

Re-written with a *semicolon*, the sentence acquires more force:

> Taylor was, as always, a consummate actor; with a few telling strokes he characterized King Lear magnificently.

If we now examine the exercise passage after **Text A**, we see the following:

—(1) Americans are queer people: they can't play.

The colon may be considered to precede an example, or to provide substantiation.

—(2), (3) , (4) They used to open their offices at ten o'clock; then at nine; then at eight; then at seven.

The semicolons present a series.

—(5), (6), (7) They eat all night, dance all night, build buildings all night, make a noise all night.

The comma indicates closely associated clauses.

—(8) They try to, but they can't.

The comma joins two independent sentences.

—(9), (10) They turn football into a fight, baseball into a lawsuit, and yachting into machinery.

Same as (5), (6), (7).

—(11),(12) The little children can't play; they use mech anical toys instead. The groun-up people can't play; they use a mechanical gymnasium and a clockwork horse.

The semicolons display contrastiue relationship between the former and the latter sentences.

—(13),(14),(15) They can't swim: they use a float.   They can't run: they use a car. They can't laugh: they hire a comedian and watch him laugh.

Same as 1.

However, these three types of punctuation do not always follow the rules outlined above. They do not do so because the author is also emphasizing voice pauses for special effects.

(1) The comma is more commonly found than semicolon when the second clause is coordinated with *and* or when three or more clauses are coordinated. However, in the

following sentences:

—*They have a fierce wish to be sober; and they can't.*

—*They pass fierce laws against themselves, shut themselves up, chase themselves, shoot themselves; and they can't stay sober and they can't drink.*

the semicolon causes the voice to pause longer, and then drop.

(2) In the following examples, the first two sentences are punctuated by semicolon (showing parallel voice tones), but the latter three by colon. The shift of punctuation implies a shift in the stress of the tone.

—*(11) The little children can't play; they use mechanical toys instead. (12) The grownup people can't play; they use a mechanical gymnasium and a clockwork horse. They can't swim: they use a float. They can't run: they use a car. They can't laugh: they hire a comedian and watch him laugh.*

Text A   Americans Are Queer

Close Study of the Text

1. ... they rush up and down as Shriners, Masons, Old Graduates, Bankers—they are a new thing each day... (Para. 1)

   Meaning: ... they hasten from one gathering or reunion to another as members of certain fraternal society, old graduates or bankers, assuming different roles every day.

2. ... till eventually the undertaker gathers them to a last convention. (Para. 2)

   Meaning: ... until finally they are gathered by a mortician (funeral director) to the last meeting of their life, their funeral.

   Note: This implies that Americans keep on moving about, attending various gatherings or meetings until they die.

3. The last Americans who sat down to read died in the days of Henry Clay. (Para. 3)

   Meaning: Americans in the early 19th century were the last generation of Americans who took time out for real reading.

   Note: Here the author humorously conveys his idea that Americans had long ceased to do any serious reading.

4. All of the American nation is haunted. (Para. 4)

   Meaning: Americans suffer from persistent dread of getting drunk and they are obsessed

110

with a belief that they should practice temperance.

5. They have a fierce wish to be sober... They pass fierce laws against themselves...
   (Para. 4)

   Note: The first "fierce" means "eager or intense", while the second means "extremely severe and rigid".

   Additional examples: a fierce competition, a fierce attack, a fierce cold

6. They got this mentality straight out of home life in Ohio, copied from the wild drinking and the furious regret of the pioneer farmer. (Para. 4)

   Meaning: Their idea that "sobriety helps bring big success" came directly from the pioneering life in the west where the pioneers indulged in wild drinking and felt deep regret and sorrow when they became sober on the following morning.

   Note: Pioneer Americans were mostly pious Protestants who firmly believed in asceticism, therefore drinking too much was considered evil.

7. ... red specters, rum devils... poison hooch... (Para. 4)

   Note: The first two refer to the effects of a lifetime of drinking alcoholic liquors, that is, to *delirium tremens*, or *the DTs*. Because alcohol short-circuits the brain, one "sees" and believes that snakes are crawling about, or that bugs are dropping from one's eyes, or that pink elephants are dancing. "Poison" is used to modify "hooch" because the latter refers to "cheap or illegally made alcoholic liquor," which is likely to be poorly made or "poisonous."

8. It's a stimulant—the only one they are not afraid of. (Para. 5)

   Meaning: Work is like a stimulating drug to Americans, the only one that they do not have to fear (unlike drink).

   Note: "Stimulant" primarily refers to a "drug that quickens physical or mental activity and alertness." It also refers to "food or beverage that stimulates, like coffee, tea or alcoholic liquor in its initial effect." As the preceding paragraph talks about the American fear of alcohol, "stimulant" here has double meanings.

9. Foreign visitors come and write them up. (Para. 6)

   Meaning: Foreigners who visit the U. S. write detailed, critical articles about Americans.

   write sth. up: to make a full written record of sth.

   e. g. : write up the minutes of a meeting

   write the visiting Australian premier up

   Note: The author is Canadian.

10. Writers shoot epigrams at them. (Para. 6)

111

Meaning: Writers make a number of quick, witty remarks about Americans.

11. Equatorial Africa is dead sour on them. (Para. 6)

Meaning: African countries near the equator find Americans absolutely hateful.

be sour on sth. / sb. : (*Am colloq.*) to dislike or hate

dead: (adv.) absolutely, completely

e. g. : You're dead right.

Her comments were dead on the mark.

12. The Chinese look on them as full of Oriental cunning...Communism. (Para. 6)

Note: As a proof of how queer Americans are, the author builds up world criticism of Americans by attributing to them characteristics or stereotypes that Americans (and other Westerners) attribute to the peoples mentioned, thus creating a humorous and ironic effect.

13. That's their salvation. (Para. 7)

Meaning: Americans are unharmed by these criticisms because of their attitude of indifference to world opinion.

Note: This concluding sentence is intended as irony. Its superficial meaning is as stated above, but underneath the author implies that "Americans are almost beyond saving" because they never spare the time to reflect on what they are doing or have done.

Text-related Information

1. **Stephen Leacock:** (1869~1944) Canadian humorist and economist.

2. **General background:** the "can't drink" paragraph describes America in the 1920s and 1930s, both before and after the passage of the amendment to the constitution prohibiting the sale of alcoholic beverages. It would not be too far inaccurate to describe this period as "the age of alcoholism" because of the vast (illegal) use. Ernest Hemingway's *A Farewell to Arms*, the short stories of F. Scott Fitzgerald and Dorothy Parker, as well as such films as *The Lost Weekend* all deal with alcohol as a social phenomenon, accepted as a part of daily life.

3. **Shriner** (Para. 1): a member of a fraternal order, the Ancient Arabic Order of Nobles of the Mystic Shrine. This is an auxiliary of The order of Masons, another fraternal order.

4. **Mason** (Para. 1): a member of a widely distributed secret order (The Free and Accepted

112

Masons), having for its object mutual assistance and the promotion of brotherly love.

5. **Henry Clay** (Para. 3): (1777~1852) U. S. statesman and orator. He was the Secretary of State from 1825 to 1829 and a Senator from 1831 to 1842.

Text B   Tea Custom

Close Study of the Text

1. The trouble with tea is that originally it was quite a good drink. (Para. 1)

   Meaning: Tea, as a beverage, used to be fine, but its being good is where the problem lies. The British have tried to make it better!

   Note: The first sentence sets the ironic tone for the whole article. What is implied in the sentence is "if it were not good to begin with, then it could be spared being spoiled later."

2. So a group of the most eminent British scientists... to find a way of spoiling it. (Para. 1)

   Meaning: A number of famous British scientists consulted together... to figure out a way of ruining the drink.

   Note: The irony in this sentence shows itself in a "collocative clash," i. e. a combination of words which conflicts with the reader's expectations. Words such as "most eminent scientists," "put their heads together" and "complicated experiments" lead the reader to expect something of great value or of great scientific importance to be produced, but what comes after is "spoiling," a far cry from "achievement."

3. To the eternal glory of British science their labour bore fruit. (Para. 2)

   Meaning: Their hard work finally produced a result, giving credit to the everlasting honor and achievements of British science.

   Note: Again a sentence with acid sarcasm.

4. ... you are judged an exotic and barbarous bird without any hope of ever being able to take your place in civilized society. (Para. 3)

   Meaning: ... if you refuse a cup of tea, you will be considered a hopelessly uncivilized alien.

5. You must not refuse... if you have just had a cup. (Para. 6)

   Note: The author enumerates all these circumstances in which one cannot refuse tea not to be informative but to indicate, in a mocking manner, that you will never escape this practice since it is met in almost all circumstances.

113

Text C   Canadians' Temperament

Close Study of the Text

1. Americans... would tell... next time. (Para. 1)

   Note: 1. The two different attitudes towards a tenth-place winner bring home one of the major differences between the Canadians and the Americans. To the latter, who have a superpower mentality, only the first place is valuable—you are either a first place winner or nobody at all, other places simply do not count.

   2. "Tough luck" is "bad luck." Here "tough" is equal to "unfortunate."

2. In the world family of nations... a superpower. (Para. 2)

   Meaning: Canada's friendly ties with most developing nations is proof of the Canadians' modesty. Unlike citizens from a superpower, they are not proud or disdainful.

   Note: "A superpower" is likely to refer to the U. S.. The author, while writing this article, must always have this neighbor of Canada in mind.

3. ... a country of uncertain identity... and a hazardous future. (Para. 4)

   Meaning: Canada does not have her own defined personality, with her history yet to be clarified and her future full of risks and dangers.

4. ... take things as they are. (Para. 5)

   Meaning: ... accept whatever comes their way.

Unit 2　Intercultural Communication

1. As mentioned in the students' text, there are, generally speaking, three kinds of outlines: *a random outline*, *a topic outline* and *a sentence outline*. An outline can be useful to students both in their reading practice and writing activity.

   A random outline is informal; it may be no more than a mental outline, a random list of ideas or details of the subject jotted down as they occur to one. Such a list usually takes a more definite shape as one develops and refines one's plan. When planning a writing assignment, students may be encouraged to prepare a random outline first if they do not form any matured or complete ideas about the topic. But many of them believe that they should begin to write only after they have considered every detail of their composition. That is not necessarily true. In many cases, the procedure of preparing an outline, even a random one, helps students think deeper and clearer about their topics. One may say that, frequently, the ideas become clear as one begins to express them.

   The random outline may be turned into **a topic outline** by adding a title, by sharpening the thesis statement, and by arranging the ideas and facts on the right levels. One may also put in number and letter symbols. *The topic outline* might be the most useful form for first year students.

   A sentence outline is one that consists of sentences. This type of outline is helpful when one will write longer essays, because the sentences on each level remind one at all times of the close link between the subject, the content of the thesis statement and the main divisions. Sentences also help distinguish between the main divisions and subdivisions of the essay.

2. There are a few general rules for **a topic outline**:

   (1) Each item in the outline should be made up of a word, a phrase, or a dependent clause. In an outline, less is more!

   (2) The first word in each topic heading on any level should be capitalized.

   (3) No punctuation is necessary for an item on any level and grammar may be simplified: she (was) happy; (they) studied (the) problem; they (had the) right idea.

(4) Items on the same level should be logically equal and, as closely as possible, grammatically equal (*parallelism*). The following diagram illustrates outline parallelism for a typical article:

I.   Introduction (leading to the thesis)

II. Body Paragraph: On this line a phrase indicating the topic sentence

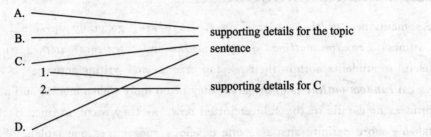

III. Body Paragraph: Phrase indicating the topic sentence

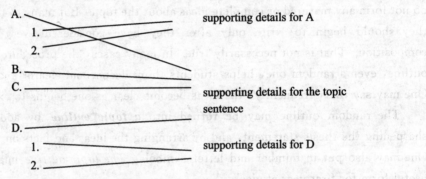

IV. Body Paragraph: Phrase indicating the topic sentence

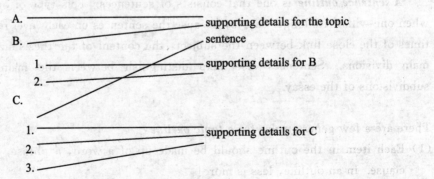

V. Conclusion: Phrase indicating concluding ideas

3. Here is a possible outline for Text A. This must be explained to the students with

illustration on the blackboard.

I.   Introduction

   A. The problem when talking with the Japanese

   B. The cause of the problem (thesis statement)

II. American-style conversation compared to tennis

   A. Conversation between two people

      1. Topic introduction

      2. Idea carrying through

   B. Conversation among more people

III. Japanese-style conversation compared to bowling

   A. Whose turn decided by relations

   B. No interruption to speaker's speech

IV. Conclusion

   A. Explanation of cross-conversation problems

      1. American activity

      2. Japanese inactivity

   B. Prediction

3. We often explain things or ideas by means of **comparison and/or contrast**. The pattern of *comparison and/or contrast* has two possibilities, but both are based on the same logical process. You explain one point by relating it to something that is similar (*comparison*) or to something that is different (*contrast*). It is also possible to use in a single paragraph *both* comparison *and* contrast.

In comparison and/or contrast patterns the two items being connected may both be equal parts of the topic: *The Colt's backfield is faster than the Ram's.* Or only one item may be the topic, with the second merely a means of describing or explaining the first: *The Colt's backfield reminds me of a well-tuned engine.*

Particularly in cases where the two items are equal parts of the topic, there are two basic ways in which the comparison/contrast may be made. In the first, all the details on one side may be separately presented, and then all the comparable details on the other: AAA/BBB. In the second, one detail from each side may be alternated with one detail from the other: AB/AB/AB.

Text A   Conversational Ballgames

```
◇◇◇◇◇◇◇◇◇◇◇◇◇◇◇◇◇◇◇◇◇◇◇◇◇◇◇◇◇◇
  Close Study of the Text
◇◇◇◇◇◇◇◇◇◇◇◇◇◇◇◇◇◇◇◇◇◇◇◇◇◇◇◇◇◇
```

1. ... my Japanese gradually improved to the point where I could take part in simple conversations. (Para. 1)

   Meaning: ... little by little, I improved my Japanese to such an extent that I could join simple discussions in Japanese.

   Note: "To the point where" means "up to/to the extent or degree of progress."

   e. g. : He admired his uncle, almost to the point of hero worship.

   He has reached the point where nothing seems to matter anymore.

2. We were unconsciously playing entirely different conversational ballgames. (Para. 3)

   Meaning: We were unknowingly handling conversations in completely different ways.

   Note: A metaphor is used in "conversational ballgames," with "conversations" likened to "ballgames."

3. I am just as happy if you question me, or challenge me, or completely disagree with me. (Para. 4)

   Meaning: If you ask questions or have doubts as to my view or do not agree with me at all, I will feel equally happy as when I hear your agreement.

   Note: "just as + adj. /adv." means "no less (than), equally."

   e. g. : The vice-president murmured a terse "no comment;" the other officials were just as tight-lipped.

4. No wonder everyone looked startled when... (Para. 10)

   Meaning: It is not surprising that everyone looked surprised...

   Note: "No/little/small wonder (that...)" means "it is not/hardly surprising (...)."

   e. g. : No wonder you couldn't find the book—it had fallen behind the chair.

   There are many cases of accounting scandals coming to light lately in the States. Small wonder that investors' confidence has plummeted.

5. ... the conversation fell apart... (para . 10)

   Meaning: the conversation did not continue.

   Note: "Fall apart" means "break off; break up; stop; fall into pieces; disintegrate."

6. This explains why it can be so difficult to get an American-style discussion going with Japanese students of English. (Para. 11)

Note： "Get + direct object + present participle" means "to bring (sb. /sth.) to the point at which he/it is doing sth. . ."

e. g. : I find it difficult to get the Chinese students talking in English.

7. Now that you know about. . . you may think that all your troubles are over. (para . 12)

   Meaning： Since you have some knowledge of the difference in conversational styles, you may think that you won't have any trouble at all handling conversations of different styles.

   Note： "Now (that)" introduces adverbial clause of reason, meaning "since. "

8. . . . it is no simple matter to switch to another. . . (Para. 12)

   Meaning： . . . it is by no means easy to suddenly change and begin playing another game.

Text B   Body Language—Nonverbal Communication

Close Study of the Text

1. If two young friends of the same sex walk with their arms around each other's shoulders or hold hands, would this be regarded by English-speakers as proper? (Para. 2)

   Note： English-speakers would probably consider them gay or lesbian.

2. Figures from a study offer interesting insight into this matter. (Para. 9)

   Meaning： One will reach a better understanding of the differences through the figures shown in a study, and these figures are interesting to look at.

3. They know that no harm is meant. . . (Para. 11)

   Meaning： They know that there is no ill intention towards their children.

   Note： Americans tend to feel that adults who fondle children are interested in them sexually.

4. It so happened that one of the teachers had a Latin-American background and knew about Puerto Rican culture. (Para. 17)

   Note： "It (so) happened that. . ." means "coincidentally" or "by chance. "

5. In a sense, all body language should be interpreted within a given context. (Para. 18)

   Meaning： When we look at body language from a certain point of view, we realize that it should be explained and understood in specific circumstances.

   in a sense： when considered from only one point of view

6. . . . it is generally advisable to use the nonverbal behavior that goes with that particular language. (Para. 19)

Meaning: ... usually it is wise to use the body language that matches the language in which one communicates.

Text C   The Customs and Language of Social Interaction
—Compliment

```
◇◇◇◇◇◇◇◇◇◇◇◇◇◇◇◇◇◇◇◇◇◇◇◇◇◇◇◇◇◇◇◇◇◇◇◇◇◇◇◇◇◇◇◇◇◇◇◇◇◇
    Close Study of the Text
◇◇◇◇◇◇◇◇◇◇◇◇◇◇◇◇◇◇◇◇◇◇◇◇◇◇◇◇◇◇◇◇◇◇◇◇◇◇◇◇◇◇◇◇◇◇◇◇◇◇
```

1. Personally I think it's one of the nicest in this block. (Para. 2)

   Meaning: In my opinion, it's...

   (see Text A, Unit 5, Book II, Note 16 about disjuncts)

2. Alternatively, compliments can be returned. (Para. 3)

   Meaning: One can also choose to praise the other party in return.

Section Two   Mind and Action

Unit 3   Self-improvement

Suggestions for Teaching

1. Reading rapidly—and well—is in large part a matter of training. Perhaps the first thing for students to learn is to let their eyes do the work. When one reads to oneself, there is no need to pronounce the words. Not only does this take too much time (a native speaker can **say** only 125 words in a minute, but can **read** up to 500 words a minute), it also defeats the purpose of reading (comprehension). When you pronounce as you read, you are reading for pronunciation, and are unable to talk about what you have read. Finally, students, because of their general background, should be able to read at even faster speeds than non-students. For example, the scanning rate of a college native speaker may approach 2,000 words per minute or more. Non-native speakers who read at half this scanning speed are doing quite well.

We must face the fact that most students, because of prior teaching, focus on one word at a time. To read at a faster rate by skimming, the student must leave out various materials. What material should the student leave out?

Let us say that average students wishing to skim a factual article of several thousand words should first read the opening paragraph or two at their fastest average rate. That means that they leave out nothing, but read at their top reading speed. They may read the whole of the first several paragraphs in order to get started, to find the idea of the article, the setting, a little of the author's style, the tone or mood, and so on. Frequently an author provides an introduction in the first few paragraphs, and this helps the readers form an overall impression of the article. But very shortly, if the students are to achieve a skimming rate of 500 words per minute or better, they must begin leaving out material. Hence, by the third or fourth paragraph they read only the key sentences, struggling to grasp the main idea of the paragraph; they may even skip the second half of the paragraph if they have found the main idea earlier. Perhaps they will read the key sentence and let their eyes jump down through the paragraph, picking up one or two important words, phrases, or numbers.

A somewhat faster way of skimming is **not** to read the opening paragraphs in detail, but rather to look only for the main purpose of the article.

Sometimes the key sentence will not be found in the first sentence of the paragraph. The student will then have to hunt around a little in the paragraph in order to find either the key sentence or several phrases or sentences which give the main idea of the paragraph. In skimming, students should attempt to find the main idea of every paragraph plus a few of the facts. They cannot, nor should they, hope to pick up all the facts in the article, but rather only some of them, some of the proper names, or some of the numbers.

The students' awareness of the main idea and paragraph organization helps them greatly in their skimming.

2. Intellectually mature readers usually read for the *literal* and *inferential* meanings of the text and try to form a *critical* evaluation as they do so. The more mature a reader is, the better she/he will achieve these three goals.

Literal reading refers to the understanding of the words, sentences, paragraphs and text at the level of the stated meaning. Ironic statements, humor, and metaphors are examples of various stated meanings.

Inferential reading refers to drawing conclusions, making generalizations, recognizing the author's purpose, and anticipating the outcome.

Critical evaluation refers to judging accuracy, distinguishing between fact and opinion, and making similar assessments.

Any given reader may, of course, be doing these three things, although unconsciously, in a blending process. But only after readers are proficient at the recognition of literal meanings will they perform better in the two higher levels of comprehension.

Text A Secrets of Straight-A Students

Close Study of the Text

1. They get high grades, all right, but only by becoming dull grinds, their noses always

stuck in a book. (Para. 1)

Meaning: It's true that they get high grades, but they pay the price of becoming boring hard-working students, who are always absorbed in books.

Note: "Their noses always stuck in a book" is an absolute construction, which is used to further explain "dull grinds."

2. Knowing how to make the most of your innate abilities counts for more. (Para. 5)

Meaning: It is more valuable and important to know how to give full play to the abilities that you are born with.

make the most of: to use fully; give full play to sth.

e. g. : George studied hard. He wanted to make the most of his chances of learning.

count: to be of value or importance

e. g. : Knowledge without common sense counts for little.

Quality is what counts most.

Take careful aim and make every shot count.

3. ... they never find out how to buckle down. (Para. 5)

Meaning: ... they never know how to set to work with concentration and determination.

buckle down: to set to work with vigor and determination

e. g. : Everyone's got to buckle down, to get ready for the press conference.

Buckle down to work now!

4. Top students brook no intrusion on study time. (Para. 8)

Meaning: Top students do not allow anything to get in the way of study.

brook: (*fml*) (usu. with a negative) to tolerate (sth.); allow

e. g. : I will not brook anyone interfering in my personal life.

Professor Liu is a strict teacher who brooks no nonsense from her students.

5. ... a cross-country runner who worked out every day. (Para. 9)

work out: to train the body by heavy physical exercise

e. g. : He works out three times a week to keep fit.

6. ... Domenica draws up timetable... so it isn't so overwhelming. (Para. 15)

draw up: to write out

overwhelming: too much or too great

e. g. : He won the election with an overwhelming majority of votes.

The temptation was overwhelming.

7. ... complete the writing in one long push over a weekend. (Para. 16)

Meaning: ... finish the writing by working hard for long hours over a weekend.

push: a vigorous effort

8. ... even the best students defer action sometimes. (Para. 17)

   Meaning: ... even the best students sometimes put off what should be done.

9. ... they face up to it. (Para. 17)

   Meaning: ... they accept and deal with the problem honestly and bravely.

   face up to sth.: to accept and deal with sth. unpleasant or demanding honestly and
       bravely

   e. g.: He must face up to the fact that he is no longer young.

       She's finding it difficult to face up to the possibility of an early death.

10. ... it comes down to late nights. (Para. 17)

   Meaning: ... it becomes a question of staying up late for several nights.

   come down to sth.: to be a question of sth.; be able to be summarized briefly

   e. g.: It comes down to two choices: you either improve your work or you leave.

       The whole dispute comes down to a power struggle between management and
       trade unions.

   a late night: a night when one goes to bed later than usual

   e. g.: I can't afford another late night this week.

11. It's a matter of showing intellectual curiosity. (Para. 22)

   a matter of sth. / doing sth.: a situation, question or issue that depends on sth. else

   e. g.: Success in business is simply a matter of knowing when to take a chance.

12. ... how the Chinese economy could be both socialist and market-driven, without
    incurring some of the problems that befell the former Soviet Union. (Para. 23)

   Meaning: ... how it is possible for the Chinese economy to be both socialist and market-
       driven and yet not suffer the problems that the former Soviet Union had
       encountered.

   incur: to cause oneself to suffer (sth. bad); bring upon oneself

   befall: (*formal and rare*: used only in the 3rd person) to happen to sb.

   e. g.: A great misfortune befell him.

Text-related Information

1. **GPA**: grade point average, a measure of scholastic attainment computed by dividing the
   total number of grade points received by the total number of credits taken.

2. **Albuquerque:** a city in central New Mexico.

Text B   The Power of a Good Name

```
Close Study of the Text
```

1. ... this time there was a damper on my spirits. (Para. 1)

   Meaning: ... this time I felt less cheerful.

   put a damper on sth. : (*infml*) to cause (an event, atmosphere, etc.) to be less cheerful, exciting; cause (a person, feelings, etc.) to feel less cheerful, less excited

2. ... the ugly shadow of racism was still a fact of life. (Para. 2)

   Meaning: ... there still existed a strong hostile atmosphere of racism.

   ugly: hostile or menacing; ominous

   e. g. : ugly threats, rumors

   shadow: a feeling of trouble

   e. g. : The war cast a shadow over daily life.

   a fact of life: thing that cannot be ignored, however unpleasant

   e. g. : We must all die some time: that's just a fact of life.

3. ... a patronizing store owner questioned whether they were "good for it. " (Para. 2)

   Meaning: ... a store owner with a sense of superiority asked whether they were able to repay the lent goods.

   patronize: to treat sb. as inferior; condescend

   e. g. : Don't patronize me! Tell me what you want to do!

   be good for: (of a person or his credit) to be such that she/he will be able to repay (a sum lent)

4. ... a good name could bestow a capital of good will of immense value. (Para. 7)

   Meaning: ... a good reputation could bring a person a great wealth of friendly and helpful feelings.

   bestow: to present (sth.) to (sb.) as a gift; confer

   good will: friendly, cooperative or helpful feelings

5. Compromising it would hurt... the transgressor... (Para. 8)

   Meaning: Bringing the good name into danger would be harmful to the person who committed the mistake.

   compromise: to bring sth. /sb. /oneself into danger or under suspicion by foolish behavior *e. g.*: He has irretrievably compromised himself by accepting money from them.

6. We had a stake in one another... (Para. 8)

   Meaning: Our interests were dependent on each other.

   stake: (usu. money, time, effort) invested by sb. in an enterprise or undertaking so that she/he has an interest or share in it

   e. g. She has a stake in the future success of the business.

7. ... it gave me the initiative to start my own successful public-relations firm in Washington, D. C.. (Para. 10)

   Meaning: ... it gave me the courage and willingness to establish my own public-relations firm in Washington, D. C. , which turned out quite successful.

8. If pride in a good name keeps families and neighborhoods straight, a sense of shame is the reverse side of that coin. (Para. 11)

   Meaning: If pride in a good reputation keeps families and neighborhoods honest and truthful, then a sense of shame keeps them from committing transgressions.

   the reverse side of the coin: the opposite or contrasting aspect of a matter

   e. g.: Everyone assumes he's to blame, but they don't know the other side of the coin.

9. ... encouraged by the pervasive profanity on television and in music, kids don't think twice about aggressive and vulgar language. (Para. 15)

   Meaning: ... because offensive words are said and heard everywhere on television and in Rap music, children thus don't feel the need for restraint and don't think carefully before they speak or act.

10. Many of today's kids have failed because their sense of shame has failed. (Para. 16)

    Meaning: Many children are unsuccessful in their life because they do not have a sense of shame.

11. I receive respect because of the good name passed on as my father's patrimony and upheld to this day by me and my siblings. (Para. 17)

    Meaning: I am respected because of the good reputation inherited from my father and maintained up till now by me and my brothers and sisters.

12. ... it was my family's good name that paved the way. (Para. 17)

    Meaning: ... what laid the foundation of my success was the good reputation of my family.

    pave the way: to create a situation in which sth. specified is possible or can happen

Text-related Information

Colin Powell (Para. 11): A black-American, five-star general in the U.S. army, and currently U.S. Secretary of State.

Text C   The Art of Smart Guessing

Close Study of the Text

1. Did you get too bogged down in the details trying to come up with the "exactly right" answer? (Para. 2)

   Meaning: Did you get stuck in the details trying to find the "100% correct" answer?

   get bogged down: (*usu. passive*) (cause sth. to) to become stuck and unable to make progress

   e. g.: Our discussion got bogged down in irrelevant details.

   bog down: to become stuck; to sink

   e. g.: The peace talks bogged down on the question of borders.

   come up with sth.: to find or produce (an answer, a solution, etc.)

2. ... did you focus on the two most important problems... then hazard a guesstimate? (Para. 4)

   Meaning: ... did you fix your attention on the two most important problems... and then venture to make an estimate by guessing?

   guesstimate: (a word created by blending or joining *guess + estimate*)

   n. an estimate arrived at by guesswork

   v. to estimate without substantial basis in fact or statistics

   More examples of blending: smog (*smoke+fog*); brunch (*breakfast+lunch*); chortle (*chuckle+snort*)

3. The law of averages is partly responsible. (Para. 13)

   Meaning: Guess work can be accurate partly because the extremes of your guesses (either too high or too low) will cancel each other out, resulting in an average which is close to the real figure.

   the law of averages: the principle according to which one believes that if one extreme occurs it will be matched by the other extreme, so that a normal average is maintained

4. But because of the law of averages, your mistakes will frequently balance out. (Para. 13)

Meaning: Because of the law of averages, your wrong guesses, which are either too high or too low, won't matter much because they cancel each other out.

balance (out): to offset each other; to be of the same value as (sth. opposite)

e.g. : My accounts balance out for the first time this year.

His lack of experience was balanced out by his willingness to learn.

This year's profits will balance out our previous losses.

High birth rates are often balanced out by high death rates.

Text-related Information

1. **The Mariana Trench** (Para. 2): the deepest point of the Pacific Ocean. A "trench" is a long, steep-sided valley on the ocean floor.

2. **Enrico Fermi** (Para. 9)(1901~1954): Italian-born American physicist who lived in the U. S. after 1939. He won a 1938 Nobel Prize for his work on artificial radioactivity caused by neutron bombardment. In 1942 he produced the first controlled nuclear chain reaction, in a squash court at the University of Chicago.

Unit 4　Friendship

1. The division of comprehension into literal, inferential, and critical components is intended to facilitate the teacher's task of improving students' reading rather than to imply sharp separations among the processes themselves. Actually, the students have long begun their higher levels of comprehension in Chinese and are by and large quite competent: essentially, we are teaching them to apply these skills to English unconsciously; we are attempting to improve and advance them.

   The skill of inference is one that we practice constantly in our daily reading, for very seldom are we presented with surface facts only, and even when we seem to be presented with surface facts only, we almost automatically look behind the simple facts in order to determine whether we should be inferring or not!

   The following apparently factual statements from **Text A** actually supply readers with important implied ideas:

   1) *The note scrawled in a greeting card to ask, "How's your back?"*

   The words were written quickly, as one would to a friend. Even though your note is short and written in a hurry, it shows you are concerned with the recipient's problems.

   2) *Whenever a friend moans about doing something dumb or embarrassing, I mention the time I stopped to mail letters on my way to the airport—and dropped my airline tickets in the mailbox!*

   If you find my deed more foolish than yours, you will not feel so sorry for what you yourself have done. The writer is sharing the feeling by giving a personal example.

   3) *Crossroad friends forge powerful links, links strong enough to endure with not much more contact than once-a-year letters at Christmas.*

   The bonds between crossroad friends are so strong that it lasts through the years even though they seldom contact each other. These types of friends do not depend on frequent meetings.

2. **Text C, Functional Training**

   Examples of *And* not following normal grammatical order to achieve special functional effects. *e. g.* :

(1) *It was the finest friendship anyone could have, a brilliant, pure friendship in which you would give your life for your friend.*

   <u>And</u> life seemed marvelous, it seemed full of sunshine, full of incredible, beautiful things to discover, and I looked forward so much to growing up with René.

   <u>And</u> then at the age of 14, his parents moved to the south of France, and we were in the east of France, which is 750 kilometres away... the south of France sounded like the end of the world.

   The two *and*s serve a dual purpose: together they illustrate a child's thinking process—"and then..., and then...," which the author then drops from # 13 onward when he is writing as an adult. Separately, the first *and* shows a continuity of happiness, and the second *and* shows how quickly that happiness can disappear, thereby enhancing the suddenness of the bad news.

(2) *I had other friends, but never did I achieve that kind of closeness. My world completely collapsed, and nothing was the same, people, the classroom, nature, the country, butterflies.*

   The listed items *people, the classroom, nature, the country, butterflies* does not use *and*: we would expect *people, ...the country, **and** butterflies*. When *and* is left out, a stronger emphasis is achieved mainly, in this case, because of the random, non-connected order: the reader feels the list is endless. Using *and* here would imply that those were the only things. Moreover, the absence of *and* obliges the reader to change the tone of voice, ending on a note of sadness and wistfulness.

Text A   How to Build Better Friendships

Close Study of the Text

1. I was surprised to find the church overflowing at her funeral. (Para. 1)

   Meaning: I was surprised that so many people came to attend her funeral that the church could barely contain them.

   overflow: to be more than filled with sth. ; be so full of sth. that the container runs over

2. Thinking I'd underestimated her achievements, I approached a man... (Para. 1)

   Meaning: I thought that I had set too low a value on what she had accomplished, so I went near to a man. . .

3. I left the church feeling awed at the loss felt by the people there. (Para. 3)

　Meaning: When I left the church, I was filled with respect and wonder at the grief and suffering felt by those who came to the church.

4. The experience flooded me with images of my own friends. . . who had drifted away. (Para. 3)

　Meaning: The experience filled my mind with images of my friends, of those who had once shared my joys and sorrows but who had casually gone away.

　flood sb. /sth. with sth. : (of a thought or feeling) to flow powerfully over (sb.), surge over (sb.); to arrive in great quantities

　e. g. : The corridors were flooded with girls. / The girls surged along the corridor.

　　Anxiety flooded his face. / Anxiety surged through his body.

　drift: (of people) to move casually or aimlessly

　e. g. : They used to be friends, but now they've drifted apart.

　　I didn't mean to be a teacher—I sort of drifted into it.

5. But friendships don't just happen. They have to be created and nurtured. (Para. 4)

　Meaning: Friendships don't just naturally come into being. They have to be created and helped grow and develop.

6. I've learned many lessons about friendship—sometimes the hard way. (Para. 5)

　Meaning: I have learned through my own experiences many dos and don'ts about friendship, sometimes in a painful way.

　the hard way: using the most difficult or least convenient method to do or achieve sth.

　e. g. : You never listen to good advice. You prefer learning the hard way (= through constant avoidable errors).

7. But aren't these small prices to pay for the pleasures of companionship? (Para. 8)

　Meaning: But when compared with the delight you get from friends' company, these losses are really rather small.

　pay a /the price (for sth.): to suffer a disadvantage or loss in return for sth. one has gained

　e. g. : Our troops recaptured the city, but they paid a heavy price for it in the numbers killed.

　Note: This is a rhetorical question that requires no answer. The negative form of a question is equal in meaning to a strong affirmative statement, only with a more emphatic effect.

8. But the seemingly trivial acts of caring are what keep friendships going. . . (Para. 9)

   Meaning: But the acts of caring, though they appear to be small and of little importance, are what really make friendships last. . .

9. . . . the talks that matter most tend to. . . (Para. 10)

   Meaning: . . . the talks that are most important are likely to. . .

   matter: to be important

   e. g. : It doesn't matter to me whether he comes or not.

   Does it matter if we're a bit late?

   tend to: to be likely to behave in a certain way or have a certain characteristic or influence

10. . . . the long meaning-of-life conversations. . . (Para. 10)

    Note: There is a simplification trend in modern English called "syntactic switch to frontal position." A case in point is the formation of compound words. Compounding, properly employed, can not only create quite a few new words, but also make a sentence concise, vivid and sometimes humorous. A compound adjective derives from elements such as adverbial phrases, infinitive phrases, prepositional phrases, phrasal verbs, attributive clause or even a sentence. The compound adjective "meaning-of-life" derives from a prepositional phrase "the long conversations about the meaning of life."

11. Risk being yourself. (Para. 11)

    Meaning: You should take the risk of showing your true feelings.

    be oneself: to be your normal or customary self

    e. g. : A few days after the operation, she had fully recovered and was herself/her old self again.

    You are not quite yourself when you rage like that.

    He's not himself today, and it's no improvement! (= He is usually not pleasant, but today he is more unpleasant than usual.)

    Note: You don't have to suppress your emotions, negative ones in particular, thinking that this will cause you to look "normal" to your friends. Rather than hide your weaknesses, you should be frank and honest with those you hope will become your friends.

12. . . . Erin's first impulse was to feign indifference. . . she blurted out how miserable she'd felt. (Para. 12)

    Meaning: . . . Erin had an urge to pretend to them that she did not care. But she felt so depressed that she suddenly told them almost despite herself how unhappy she had felt.

feign: to give a false appearance of

blurt out: to say sth. suddenly and (usually) tactlessly

13. Others can feel close to you only if you let them know you. (Para. 12)

   Meaning: Others will never feel intimate towards you unless you let them know what you are really like.

   only if: unless (the stated condition following) exists

14. ... it's endearing to admit your faults. (Para. 13)

   Meaning: ... telling your friends your weaknesses will result in their love for you increasing.

15. ... let them know the real—imperfect—you. (Para. 15)

   Meaning: ... let them know the real you who are imperfect.

16. Don't keep score. (Para. 16)

   Meaning: Don't record somewhere how much you have done for your friends and they for you.

   Note: "Keep score" is mainly used to record the number of points made by the players or teams in a game. Here it is used metaphorically: the "game" is friendship, while "the players" are you and your friend and the "score," how much you have given to and taken from each other.

17. Too often people get hung up on the duties of friendship... (Para. 16)

   Meaning: Very often people become emotionally upset because they continually think about what they and their friends should do for each other.

   be/get hung up on/about: (*slang*) to become emotionally upset or inhibited by, be obsessed by; become infatuated with

   e. g. : She never goes to parties. She is really hung up about meeting new people.

   He rarely finished his tasks on time. He gets hung up on petty details.

   For heaven knows what reason, he is hung up on her.

18. ... the commitment is worth it. (Para. 19)

   Meaning: ... your dedication to friendship (as shown in your helping them out) is not in vain, and you will find great reward from it.

╒══════════════════════════════════════╕
Text-related Information
╘══════════════════════════════════════╛

1. **New England**: The northeastern part of the United States, including the states of, by space, north to south, and east to west: Maine, New Hampshire, Vermont, Massachusetts, Rhode Island, and Connecticut.

2. **Summer school**: study programs offered during the summer to those who wish to obtain their degrees more quickly, make up credits for courses failed, or supplement their education.

3. **Alexandre Dumas**: (1802~1870), known as "Dumas *père*," French writer of swashbuckling historical romances, such as *The Count of Monte Cristo* and *The Three Musketeers* (both 1844). His son Alexandre (1824~1895), known as "Dumas *fils*," was a dramatist whose works include *La Dame aux Camélias* (1852).

4. **Robert Louis Stevenson**: (1850~1894), British novelist, essayist, poet, most notable works including *Treasure Island* (1883), *The Strange Case of Dr. Jekyll and Mr. Hyde* (1886), and *Kidnapped* (1886).

Text B   Friends, Good Friends—and Such Good Friends

╒══════════════════════════════════════╕
Close Study of the Text
╘══════════════════════════════════════╛

1. In the first two paragraphs, the coordinator "and" appears between each pair of conjoints, which is more than grammatically required. Such construction like *A and B and C and D* is called *Polysyndeton*. It is used for stylistically marked effects, such as to emphasize a dramatic sequence of events or an open-ended list of events. For example:

   The wind roared, and the lightning flashed, and the sky suddenly turned as dark as night.

   In the first paragraph, polysyndeton is used to emphasize the increasing number of things that the author used to think women friends would do for each other, while in the second paragraph, it emphasizes an open-ended list of what women friends share in common.

2. In the first three paragraphs "Women are friends...when" and "I once would have said" appear two and three times respectively. This type of repetitive pattern of structures and words is called *Parallelism*, which is used to emphasize the similarity of the thoughts. Because of these regularly patterned structures, parallelism brings with it a sense of

rhythm, and also of beauty to the language.

3. ...and bare to each other the secrets of their souls... and tell harsh truths... (Para. 1)

   Meaning: ...reveal to one another their deepest feelings that they would not let anyone else know... and tell unwelcome truths.

4. ...have the same affection for Ingmar Bergman, plus train rides... (Para. 2)

   Meaning: ...have a common love for Ingmar Bergman as well as train rides...

   plus: (*infml*) as well as

   e. g.: We've got to fit five people plus all their luggage into the car.

5. ...I once would have said that a friend is a friend all the way, but now I believe that's a narrow point of view. (Para. 3)

   Meaning: ...I used to believe that a friend is always totally a friend in all ways, but now I think that opinion is rather limited.

   all the way: completely; without reservation

   e. g.: He was all the way back to normal.

   　　　The door opened all the way.

   point of view: opinion; attitude

6. ...of the soul sisters... that of the most nonchalant and casual playmates. (Para. 3)

   soul sister: a woman with whom one has a deep lasting friendship and understanding

   nonchalant: casual, not feeling or showing great interest or enthusiasm

7. ...if our paths weren't crossing all the time, we'd have no particular reason to be friends... (Para. 5)

   Meaning: ...if we didn't always see or encounter each other in the course of other activities, we would not have become friends. *Or* we have become friends only because we always run into each other.

   cross sb. 's path: to meet sb. , usually by chance

   e. g.: I hope I never cross her path again!

8. ...a woman in our car pool... (Para. 5)

   car pool: a number of cars whose drivers agree to perform certain tasks for others in turn, such as driving a group of children to school or a number of others to work

   pool: a common supply of funds, goods or services which are available to a group of people to be used when needed

9. ...Co-op Nursery... (Para. 5)

   co-op = cooperative

   Note: A Co-op Nursery is a nursery owned and run by the families of a neighborhood or area, in which each mother or father takes turns to render unpaid service.

10. ... we maintain a public face and emotional distance. (Para. 7)

    Meaning: ... with these convenience friends, we let them know only those aspects of ourselves that can be shown to all and remain emotionally detached from them.

11. I'll talk about being overweight but not about being depressed... worried sick over money. (Para. 7)

    Meaning: I'll tell these convenience friends that I am fatter than I should be, but not in low spirits; that I am angry but not that I lose my judgment because of my fury; that my husband and I are short of money but not that we feel very much distressed and troubled about it. All in all, with convenience friends we might tell them more or less surface facts about ourselves but not our deeper emotional stress or pain.

    pinched: not having enough of sth.

    sick: severely distressed; disgusted; not healthy emotionally

    e. g. : He's sick about his son's failure in school.

    She left her husband because she was sick of him.

    How can you laugh at that cripple dragging himself along the street? You're really sick! (That's really sick!)

12. And for the most part, that's all they discuss. (Para. 10)

    Meaning: And usually, they only talk about these things.

    for the most part: usually, mostly; on the whole

    e. g. : Japanese TV sets are, for the most part, of excellent quality.

    For the most part, he is honest, but don't ask him about his love life!

13. ... what we're doing is *doing* together, not being together. (Para. 11)

    Meaning: ... we accompany each other in what we do together (i. e. playing tennis), but we do not share other aspects of our life.

14. I don't have the time to keep up with what's new in eyeshadow... (Para. 13)

    Meaning: I don't have the time to follow the latest developments in fashion.

    keep up with: to move or progress at the same rate (as sb. /sth.)

15. ... whether the smock look is in or finished already... (Para. 13)

    Meaning: ... whether the smock style of clothes is still in fashion or already out of style.

    in: fashionable; popular

    finished: over, not existing anymore; ruined

    e. g. : Isn't that TV program finished yet?

The milk is finished. We have to buy more.

The politician was not finished even though he lost the election. He will run for election again some day.

16. ... maybe way back... (Para. 14)

way back: a long time ago

way: (*infml*) (used with a preposition or adverb) far; very

e. g. : She finished the race way ahead of the other runners.

Do you see that man way in the distance?

The shot was way off target.

The price is way above what we can afford.

17. ... but we're still an intimate part of each other's past. (Para. 15)

Meaning: ... but we still constitute a close and private part of each other's younger days.

18. ... before our voice got unBrooklyned... (Para. 15)

Meaning: ... before we lost the way of speaking common to Brooklyn...

19. And who, by her presence, puts us in touch with an earlier part of our self, a part of our self it's important never to lose. (Para. 15)

Meaning: With her being there, we are reminded of what we used to be and that past is something that we should never completely forget.

20. ... having a sister without sibling rivalry. (Para. 16)

Meaning: ... having a sister without the competition frequently found among sisters.

21. We know the texture of each other's lives. (Para. 16)

Meaning: We know the characteristic quality of each other's lives.

22. The sexual, flirty part of our friendship is very small, but some—just enough to make it fun and different. (Para. 21)

Meaning: Men-women friendships always contain some small sexual element of playful courting, and that is what makes it enjoyable and sets it apart from friendships with those of the same sex.

23. ... I've made friends with men, in the sense of a friendship that's *mine*, not just part of two couples. (Para. 22)

Meaning: ... I have formed friendships with men, who are to be understood as "my male friends," rather than my husband's friends or my women friends' husbands.

24. ... achieving with them the ease and the trust I've found with women friends has value indeed.

Meaning: ...I feel as comfortable, relaxed and trusted with my men friends as I do when I am with my women friends, and this feeling is really something valuable.

25. Under the dryer... putting on mascara and rouge... (Para. 22)

Meaning: While drying my hair and applying make-up to my face...

26. Peter, I finally decided, could handle the shock of me minus mascara under the dryer. (Para. 22)

Meaning: I finally came to the conclusion that Peter would not be astonished to see me wet-haired, without make-up.

minus: (*infml*) without, lacking; deprived of

e. g. : He came back from the war minus a leg.

Note: The example illustrates the previous statement that she feels equally at ease in the presence of her male friends as with her women friends, because drying one's hair and putting on make-up are considered things that should be carried out in private or in the presence of female friends. It is viewed as inappropriate to do these things before males whom one hopes to impress.

27. ...is calibrated with care. (Para. 23)

Meaning: ...is carefully adjusted.

Text-related Information

1. **Ingmar Bergman:** (1918 ~), Swedish filmmaker, director whose critically acclaimed films, such as *The Silence* (1963) and *Fanny and Alexander* (1983), are characterized by slow pace, laconic dialogue, and heavy use of symbolism to explore the psychological states of the characters.

2. **Albert Camus:** (1913 ~ 1960), French novelist, playwright, essayist and philosopher whose works, such as *The Stranger* (1942) and *The Plague* (1947), concern the absurdity of the human condition. He won the 1957 Nobel Prize for Literature.

3. **Newark:** a port city in northeastern New Jersey.

4. **Lawrence Welk:** (1903 ~ 1992) conductor and entertainer, one of America's favorite bandleaders. He and his band made their debut on national television in 1955 with a program of dance music that would be produced for the next 26 years. He developed a style of music called "Champagne music."

5. **Brooklyn:** a borough of New York City, at the far western end of Long Island. A

"Brooklyn accent" is the object of many jokes among the resident of Manhattan, the business, shopping and cultural borough of New York City. One feature of Brooklyn pronunciation is the repetition of the "g" sound: sing-ging, ring-ging, bring-ging.

Text C　Friendship

╔══════════════════════════════════╗
Close Study of the Text
╚══════════════════════════════════╝

1. ...I thought the world was caving in... but I still measure all pain by the hurt René caused me. (Para. 1)

   Meaning: ...I thought the world was collapsing... but the pain René caused me has become a standard unit for me to determine how painful other experiences are to me.

   cave in: to collapse; fall inwards

   e. g. : All opposition to the scheme has caved in.

2. ...very earthed, and the table was very important. (Para. 2)

   Meaning: ...very attached to/influenced by farming, and the food served at the table was very important to us.

   earthed: This is a strong, unexpected usage as the word does not exist in this sense ("being attached to/influenced by"). The expression "down to earth" is frequently employed, and means "realistic and practical."

   e. g. : We adopted a down to earth approach to the problem.

   I enjoy talking to her. She's down to earth.

   Note: 1. Examples of being "earthed" are given in the following paragraph where a number of examples of food collected from the wild appear:

   "... produce that grew in the wild... mushrooming... frog hunting... cèpes"

   "Produce" refers to vegetables: "farm produce," the "produce section" in a supermarket.

   2. Frog legs (or, frog's legs) are considered a delicacy in France.

   3. Cep or cèpe is a species of edible mushroom (*Boleteus edulis*) widely distributed in French woodlands, and widely esteemed in French cooking.

3. The adventures that children go through in the making of friendship... (Para. 4)

   in the making of: in the course of being made, formed, developed

4. ...these things create a fantastic fabric to the friendship. (Para. 4)

   Meaning: These adventures give a wonderful structure to the friendship.

5. I waited quietly for the news to sink in... (Para. 9)

Meaning: I did not cry but waited quietly so as to get a full understanding of the news all by myself.

sink in: (of words, etc.) to be fully understood

e. g. : The scale of the tragedy gradually sank in.

6. ... I couldn't see life without my friend... (Para. 10)

Meaning: I could not imagine what my life would be like without René.

7. ... it was my dramatic side to see only the negative side, self-pity in a way. (Para. 13)

Meaning: ... the dramatic aspect of my character did not see things from a constructive or helpful point of view, and that revealed, to some extent, that I felt pity and sorrow for myself.

8. There is not a single bitter note, there are no power games. (Para. 14)

Meaning: There is no feelings of envy, hatred or disappointment in our friendship, no control of one over the other.

9. There is nothing secret, there is nothing which detracts from the purity of it. (Para. 14)

Meaning: We do not hide anything from each other, and our friendship is so pure that nothing can make it seem less valuable.

detract from sth. : to make sth. seem less valuable or less important

Unit 5　Personality of a Leader

Suggestions for Teaching

1. *Inferential reading*: To understand what a writer means requires understanding more than what that writer puts on paper. Writers seldom state everything openly or put every idea on paper. Their texts would be excessively long—and boring—if they did. They are obliged to assume that readers possess appropriate background knowledge and that they as writers have given the readers enough new information to trigger the response the writers hope for.

   Inferencing is a general strategy of guessing, on the basis of literal meaning, what meaning is needed but is not known. Thoughtful teachers have come to recognize that the ability to infer seems paramount in comprehending texts in which difficulties arise.

   An inference may be an explanation, a conclusion formed about the previous part (*backward inference*) or a prediction made about the following part (*forward inference*). The latter process largely depends upon the former one, for every sound prediction can only be made on the basis of full understanding of available information.

   Here is a passage for which two reasonable inferential conclusions follow:

   In 1865 Jules Verne wrote a book entitled From the Earth to the Moon. *In it three men and some animals took off from Florida for the moon in a spaceship. Over 100 years later men did blast off from Cape Kennedy in Florida and landed on the moon. The heroes in Verne's book made a journey that few people believed would ever be taken. In addition, one of Verne's best-known books,* Twenty Thousand Leagues Under the Sea, *tells about adventures in a submarine.*

   Inferential conclusions:

   1) Jules Verne predicted scientific accomplishments long before others considered them possible.

   2) Once a view of future development is put forward, scientists may attempt to realize it.

2. How can teachers help students become better at inferencing? Clearly, a student's ability to understand the literal meaning serves as the basis for inferencing, and, just as clearly, the enhancement of that ability itself needs a certain amount of training. However,

141

teachers should not wait until every student understands nearly all the literal meanings of most materials (that is both impossible and unrealistic—inferencing and comprehension go hand in hand). Teachers should start training students in inferences along with discussion of materials. Teachers can provide training, practice, and encouragement in every text analysis. In **Text A**, the following conclusions might be made:

Conclusion 1: Americans are not as polite as they once were, so they have to look for a figure in the past as an example of courtesy.

Conclusion 2: Washington began to learn rules of civility in his early days, and it was by chance that the author found this deed of Washington.

Conclusion 3: Generally, today's Americans do not consider the rules of civility as important as they once were.

Conclusion 4: They are common and useful suggestions for everyday life.

Conclusion 5: Washington made efforts to practice the rules personally.

Conclusion 6: If followed, the common suggestions for everyday courtesy may matter a great deal, as we see in the case of Washington.

3. **Dashes** can be used to mark the separation of included units when the units are in a middle position in the text, in which case two dashes must be used or in a final position, in which one dash suffices.

The other man—David Johnson—refused to make a statement.

I have not yet obtained a statement from the other woman—Ann Taylor.

The **comma** is the least obtrusive correlative punctuation mark and for that reason is generally preferred unless:

1) there is a disruption of the syntactic structure of the clause:

"I hope that you," His voice broke.

2) or a danger of confusion with other neighboring commas:

In 1949 Chairman Mao, born in Hunan, from the rostrum of Tian'anmen Square, in Beijing, announced the founding of the People's Republic of China.

3) or a failure to mark adequately a rather lengthy inclusion:

At that time, the students, goodness knows for what reason, reversed their earlier, more moderate decision, and a big demonstration was planned.

In the cases above, **dashes** or **parentheses** would be employed:

1) *"I hope that you—" his voice broke.*

2) *In 1949 Chairman Mao (born in Hanan) announced the founding of the People's*

142

Republic of China from the rostrum of Tian'anmen Square (in Beijing).

3) *At that time, the students—goodness knows for what reason—reversed their earlier, more moderate decision, and a big demonstration was planned.*

or

At that time, the students—goodness knows for what reason—reversed their earlier (and more moderate decision), and a big demonstration was planned.

Dashes tend to give a somewhat more dramatic and informal impression, suggesting an impromptu aside, whereas **parentheses** are planned inclusions. Underneath the choice between dashes and parentheses, lies the psychological purpose of highlighting the importance of information (dashes) or de-emphasizing the importance (parentheses).

Communism—as defined by Marx—aimed at freeing workers from capitalist control.

Communism (as defined by Marx) aimed at freeing workers from capitalist control.

The difference between the two examples above is heard when read aloud: the voice is louder and more emphatic for the first; softer, faster, and less emphatic for the second.

4. In addition to reducing clauses, the writer will use punctuation as a tool to produce clear and forceful writing. For our purposes, the most important of these are: *parentheses* ( ), *dashes*—, *colons*: (*BritE*: two dots), and *semicolons*; (*BritE*: dot comma).

Parentheses appear in pairs: one *parenthesis* alone appears only in grammatical examples. In reading aloud one would say "open parenthesis" for (and "close parenthesis" for). What is enclosed between these parentheses is termed *a parenthetical remark*: when speaking, one would say, "Let me remark parenthetically that...". **Parentheses** are employed to present equivalent information, secondary information, and dates, or to remind the reader of something:

A soccer field measures 120 yards by 75 yards (110 meters by 70 meters).

The government of the People's Republic of China (proclaimed in October, 1949) envisioned a better future for all Chinese.

Adam Smith (1723~1790) achieved fame with the publication of his book The Wealth of Nations (*1776*).

Each of the U. S. government branches (executive, legislative, and judicial) became involved in the dispute.

On rare occasions, an author might choose to include a parenthetical remark within a parenthetical remark; if so, one would use **brackets** [ ]:

The Wealth of Nations (*published in 1776 by Adam Smith [1723 ~ 1790]*) *established economics as an area of study.*

Although a common occurrence in academic writing up to roughly 1920, brackets within parentheses (as in the example above) rarely appear today.

Dashes appear also in pairs within a sentence; in reading aloud one would say "dash" and "dash." They serve primarily the psychological purpose of highlighting the importance of information that, between parentheses, would be de-emphasized:

Communism—as defined by Marx—aimed at freeing workers from capitalist control.

A set of **dashes** also figure when the writer wants to comment on information:

This goal—with which the citizenry heartily agreed—was rapidly achieved.

A single dash is sometimes used before the end of the sentence:

This goal was rapidly achieved—the citizenry was delighted !

Or, on occasion, towards the end of the sentence when one is listing:

A professional tennis match requires at least four participants—two players, a referee, and a ball retriever.

However, the **single dash** used in these two ways is not common in academic writing; in both cases, the **colon** is preferred.

For **Colons** and **Semicolons**, see suggestions for Teaching, 5. in Unit 1.

Note that an English sentence or completed thought ends with a period ".". Within a given sentence, other information is separated by using a comma ",". In Chinese, a thought is separated from other thoughts by a comma, and the entire group of thoughts ends with a small, open circle.

Text A   What Happened to Civility?

Close Study of the Text

1. Businesses put callers on hold, forcing us to listen to annoying music. (Para. 1)

   Meaning: When you telephone a company, if they cannot immediately connect you with the person you want, they ask you to wait (on hold), and play music for you.

   put...on hold: to put into a state of interruption or suspension

2. People push in and out of elevators like hockey players facing off over a puck. (Para. 1)

   Meaning: To get into the elevators, people do not let those off first, but push their way in, while the others push their way out, just like hockey player confronting rivals for the first hit of the puck.

   face off: to confront, as in a contest; (Ice Hockey) to begin a game or period with a face-off (the act of putting the puck into play by dropping it between two players on opposing teams)

3. Biographers gloss over Washington's list of rules as a boyhood exercise... (Para. 4)

   Meaning: Biographers explain this as a penmanship exercise that Washington performed in his childhood or early adolescence, rather than focusing on the importance to Washington of these rules.

   gloss over: to give a deceptively good appearance to; mask; cover up

   e. g. : The Japanese history textbooks written by Japanese nationalist historians gloss over Japan's past aggressions against its Asian neighbors and ignore the great sufferings inflicted upon Asians by the Japanese military.

4. ... Washington's is curiously up-to-date. (Para. 5)

   Meaning: ... Washington's list contains information that is still surprisingly useful for the present.

   curiously: oddly, strangely; unusually

5. He had grown to embody their spirit... and ours... (Para. 7)

   Meaning: As he became older, Washington acted on these rules and used his own behavior to exemplify their essence, especially those that contained the most important moral lessons, those of his day learned and we today should learn.

   embody: to give a concrete form to; exemplify or personify

   e. g. : To me he embodies all the best qualities of a teacher.

145

6. Politeness did not come naturally to Washington, whose temper Thomas Jefferson described as "most tremendous." (Para. 8)

   Meaning: It was not an easy matter for Washington to be so polite, because his temper was dreadful according to Thomas Jefferson.

   naturally: easily; instinctively

   e. g. : He's such a good athlete that most sports come naturally to him.

   tremendous: (*infml*) dreadful or awful; terrifying; very big

7. ... he kept it under tight rein. (Para. 8)

   Meaning: ... he had firm control over his temper.

8. But it's also about good judgment, and *deliberating* before you *do*. (Para. 8)

   Meaning: But it also concerns making objective or wise decisions, and thinking carefully before you take action.

   Note: Alliteration occurs in "*deliberating* before you *do*". Alliteration is the occurrence in a phrase or line of speech, etc. of two or more words having the same consonant sound (in this case "d"). This rhetorical device is used for emphasis, to underline the meaning, to produce a sound effect in the given phrase. Rhetorical devices are also known as "flowers." They make the sentence pretty.

   e. g. : A bit of better butter makes a bitter batter better.

   Marriage makes or mars a man.

9. The lesson took. (Para. 9)

   Meaning: That piece of advice had its desired effect.

   lesson: a useful piece of practical wisdom acquired by experience or study

   take: to have the desired effect or intended result

   e. g. : The vaccination took.

   He said your scheme was too fanciful to take.

   Watch the audience to see how my speech takes.

10. ... no harum-scarum, ranting, swearing fellow, but sober, steady and calm... (Para. 9)

    Meaning: ... Washington was never a reckless fellow who spoke violently or theatrically or used profane language; rather he was quiet, rational and composed...

    harum-scarum: (adv. *old-fashioned*, *informal*) (behaving) wildly and thoughtlessly

    e. g. : The children ran harum-scarum around the playground.

    sober: quiet or sedate in demeanor

    steady: settled, regular, unchanging

11. ... Washington laid his shoulder "to the great points, knowing that the little ones would follow. " (Para. 9)

    Meaning: ... Washington worked on the major issues, as he knew the minor problems would fall into place once the more important ones were settled.

12. Washington needed all the courtesy he could muster to hold together a people so diverse... (Para. 10)

    Meaning: Washington needed to use all the good manners he had to get all the different national groups in the United States to act as one nation...

    a people: a nation, a race

    e. g. : The Americans are a hard-working people.

    All the peoples of Asia suffered during the war.

13. Slavery split the country north and south, while the Appalachian Mountains split it east and west. (Para. 10)

    Meaning: At the same time as the country was divided into east and west by the geographical barrier of the Appalachian Mountains, it was split between the north and the south by the practice of owning slaves.

14. Politicians accused each other of treason and other infamies at the drop of a hat. (Para. 10) '

    Meaning: Politicians accused each other of betrayal of the country or other wicked acts at the slightest provocation.

    at the drop of a hat: suddenly and almost without explanation, usually an element of unreasonableness

    e. g. : She expects me to rush over and help her at the drop of a hat.

    He is so angry that he's willing to cancel the order at the drop of a hat.

    She loves playing the piano and will do so at the drop of a hat.

15. Americans were passionate about politics because the stakes were so high. (Para. 10)

    Meaning: Americans had great enthusiasm about politics because their personal interests were closely linked with the political future of the country and it would be too disappointing should the newly-founded republic fail to work.

16. Fortunately for him and for us, he had a model of personal behavior to fall back on. (Para. 11)

    Meaning: It is fortunate for him and for us that he could rely on a pattern of personal behavior as his guide.

    fall back on: to rely on; (be able to) go to sb. for support or use sth. when in difficulty

    e. g. : She is completely without support—at least I have my parents to fall back on.

Take notes during class, and you will have something to fall back on before the exam.

Note: "Curiously" (see note 4), "personally" (see note 5) and "fortunately" are all what are grammatically named *disjuncts*. Compared with the sentence elements, they are syntactically more detached and in some respects "super-ordinate" in that they seem to have a scope that extends over the sentence as a whole.

Disjuncts can be divided into two groups:

(i) style disjuncts that convey speaker's comment as to a) manner (*e. g.*: truthfully, bluntly) and b) respect (*e. g.*: personally)

(ii) content disjuncts that make an observation as to a) degree of truth of content (*e. g.*: really, certainly), and b) value judgment of content (*e. g.*: wisely, understandably).

"Personally" belongs to the first category, while "curiously", and "fortunately" belong to the second. Sometimes students tend to mistake such adverbials for those that modify only the verbs or adjectives in a sentence:

He was *seriously* injured. (severely, badly)

Seriously, are you going to give up your job? (Answer me in a serious way.)

Generally, adverbs as style disjuncts can often be expressed by a clause in which the same adverb becomes an adjunct, with a verb of speaking (*say* or *tell*) and the subject of which is "I". Thus, *frankly* in:

Frankly, I am tired.

Is equivalent to:

I tell you frankly or *I say frankly.*

As for content disjuncts, many of them correspond either to

1) "It is + adjective form of the adverb + *that* clause/ of sb. to do sth. "

2) or to "sb. + be + adjective form of the adverb + infinitive phrase"

3) or "sb. + verb form of the adverb + *that* clause"

For

1) *Regrettably*, James declines our offer. (I *regret* that James declines our offer. / It is *regrettable* that James declines our offer.)

2) *Rightly*, John returned the money. (John was *right* to return the money)

3) *Evidently*, he doesn't object. (It is *evident* that he doesn't object.)

17. The sentiments he copied into his exercise book, practiced for decades, gave him the

framework. (Para. 11)

Meaning： The rules that he copied into his exercise book and acted upon accordingly for decades provided him with a set of principles for his judgment and decisions as President.

sentiments： [pl] (*fml* or *rhet*) points of view; opinions; feelings

e. g. : What are your sentiments on the matter?

framework： set of principles or ideas used as a basis for one's judgment or decision

18. Respecting his fellow Americans was a stepping stone to respecting their rights. (Para. 11)

stepping stone： the means or stage of progress towards achieving or attaining sth.

19. Washington's courtesy didn't fail him even on his deathbed when he assured his doctors they had done their best. (Para. 12)

Meaning： Washington was still courteous even when he was dying; he told his doctors earnestly that they had done every thing they could possibly do.

20. "When a man does all he can, though it succeeds not well, blame not him that did it."
(Para. 12)

Meaning： Do not blame the person who does all he can about something even if it does not turn out well.

Text-related Information

1. **George Washington：** (1732～1799) Commander-in-Chief of the Continental Army during the American Revolution and first President of the U. S. (1789～1797).

2. **Thomas Jefferson：** (1743～1826) third President of the U. S. (1801～1809) and author of *the Declaration of Independence*.

3. **Quaker：** a member of the Society of Friends, a Christian denomination founded by George Fox in 1650.

Text B　What Makes a Leader?

Close Study of the Text

1. In easy times we are ambivalent—the leader, after all, makes demands, challenges the

status quo, shakes things up. (Para. 1)

Meaning: When times are good we have mixed feelings about a leader—on the one hand we want to have one, but on the other, the leader obliges us to do things we may not want to do, questions the state of affairs as it is, reforms and reorganizes things.

2. Great leaders are almost always great simplifiers, who cut through argument, debate and doubt to offer a solution... (Para. 3)

Meaning: Great leaders almost always excel in simplifying the ideas they want to convey; they make a path through argument, debate and doubt to present a way out.

3. ...they must have bigger-than-life, commanding features. (Para. 4)

Meaning: ...they must have impressive features.

bigger-than-life (larger-than-life): exaggerated in size, so as to seem more impressive

e. g.: Many film stars seem to be larger-than-life to the mass of everyday citizens.

commanding: impressive; seeming to have authority

4. A trademark also comes in handy. (Para. 4)

Meaning: It is also useful if the leader has a distinctive characteristic.

come in handy: to be useful some time or other

e. g.: Don't throw that cardboard box away. It may come in handy.

5. We want them to be like us but better, special, more so. (Para. 5)

Meaning: We want them to be like us average citizens, but they should be better than us, have something special or distinctive about them, and they should be so (better and special) to a greater extent than we are.

6. Even television, which comes in for a lot of knocks as an image-builder that magnifies form over substance, doesn't altogether obscure the qualities of leadership we recognize, or their absence. (Para. 6)

Meaning: Television receives much criticism because it makes a leader's appearance seem more important than his or her abilities actually are: it creates a better picture of them. Even so, it doesn't completely hide the qualities of leadership we identify in a leader, or the lack of these qualities in a leader.

come in for: to be the object of sth.; attract sth.; receive sth.

e. g.: The government's economic policies have come in for much criticism in the newspapers.

knock: (*infml*) an adverse criticism; a financial or emotional blow

e. g.: He likes praise but can't stand knocks.

The Wall Street stock market suffered some hard knocks recently.

The school of hard knocks made him the murderer he is.

7. He should be able... to give a good, hearty, belly laugh, instead of the sickly grin that passes for good humor in Nixon or Carter. (Para. 8)

Meaning: He should be able to give a loud, cheerful, unrestrained, thorough laugh, rather than the weak, unhappy, broad smile that is accepted as a sign of good temper in Nixon or Carter.

good: complete; thorough

e. g. : give sb. a good beating

Take a good look at this book.

8. Ronald Reagan's training as an actor showed to good effect in the debate with Carter... (Para. 8)

Meaning: Reagan's training as an actor produced a good result in the debate with Carter...

to good effect: producing a good result or impression

e. g. : The room shows off her painting to good effect.

9. The leader follows, though a step ahead. (Para. 9)

Meaning: The leader follows people's wishes and desires, though he or she is slightly in advance and leads them to accomplish that goal.

10. A leader rides the waves, moves with the tides, understands the deepest yearnings of his people. (Para. 10)

Meaning: A leader makes use of widespread attitudes, conforms to accepted opinions, understands the most intense desires and longings of his people.

ride the waves: to go along with a widespread attitude or tendency

e. g. : Having found a way to ride the wave of tax payer revolt, he was re-elected governor of Illinois.

11. ... he must dignify our desires... give us a sense of glory about ourselves. (Para. 11)

Meaning: ... he must make our desires seem worthy and impressive, convince us that we are great history-makers, and make us feel proud and noble.

12. A leader must stir our blood, not appeal to our reason... (para 11)

Meaning: A leader must rouse us to excitement, not emphasize rational thinking.

stir one's/the blood: to rouse sb. to excitement or enthusiasm

13. ... the leader himself should have fire, a spark of divine madness. (Para. 12)

Meaning: ... the leader himself should have great passion, a trace of godlike enthusiasm.

14. ...for the leader is like a mirror, reflecting back to us our own sense of purpose...
(Para. 13)

Meaning: ...in the leader we see what we feel we want to achieve...

15. ...he is, in the final analysis, the symbol of the best in us, shaped by our own spirit and will. (Para. 14)

Meaning: ...he, in sum, embodies our best qualities, and is influenced by our courage and determination.

16. He is... merely the sum of us. (Para. 14)

Meaning: He is only us added together.

Text-related Information

1. **Winston Churchill** (1874~1965): British Prime Minister (1940~1945, 1951~1955).

2. **Franklin Delano Roosevelt** (FDR) (1882~1945): 32nd President of the U. S. (1933~1945).

3. **V(ladimir) I(lyich) Lenin** (1870~1924): Russian revolutionary leader, Soviet Premier (1918~1924).

4. **Lyndon Baines Johnson** (1908~1973): 36th President of the U. S. (1963~1969).

5. **Ikeda Hayato** (1899~1965): Japanese Prime Minister (1960~1964).

6. **Abraham Lincoln** (1809~1865): 16th President of the U. S. (1861~1865).

7. **John Fitzgerald Kennedy** (1917~1963): 35th President of the U. S. (1961~1963).

8. **Gerald R. Ford** (1913~): 38th President of the U. S. (1974~1977).

9. **Adlai Stevenson** (1900~1965): the unsuccessful Democratic nominee for President in 1952 and 1956.

10. **Nelson Rockefeller** (1908~1979): vice-president of the U. S. (1974~1977), son of John D. Rockefeller Jr., grandson of John D. Rockefeller, who were both U. S. oil magnates and philanthropists.

11. **Richard Nixon** (1913~1994): 37th President of the U. S. (1969~1974), resigned from office as a result of the Watergate Scandal.

12. **Hubert Horatio Humphrey** (1911~1978): vice-president of the U. S. (1965~1969).

13. **Harry S. Truman** (1884~1972): 33rd President of the U. S. (1945~1953).

14. **James (Jimmy) Carter** (1924~): 39th President of the U. S. (1977~1981.

15. **Ronald Reagan** (1911~): 40th President of the U. S. (1981~1989).

16. **Confucius:** (551? B. C. ~478? B. C.) Chinese philosopher and teacher.

Text C   The Qualities of Leadership

Close Study of the Text

1. For one thing, you must show... (Para. 2)

   for one thing: (used to introduce a reason) the reason that first comes to mind; sometimes followed by "for another"

   e. g. : We'd better give up the idea of taking a long trip for the coming holiday. For one thing, there isn't enough time; for another, we don't have enough money.

2. In practical terms, this means... (Para. 2)

   terms: ways of expressing oneself

   in practical terms = when we consider the reality of things

   e. g. : Students often forget that, in practical terms, teachers are human beings: they become tired of the same errors, angry at ceaseless talking in the classroom, and bored with carelessly done assignments.

3. You can develop this all-important quality by... (Para. 5)

   all-important: very important, most important

4. ... you are likely to come up with new ideas... to contribute at the next meeting. (Para. 5)

   Meaning: ... it is probable that you will think of new ideas... to share with others at the next meeting.

   come up with: to find or produce (a solution or an answer)

   e. g. : During the exam, I couldn't come up with a single original idea.

Unit 6　Love and Marriage

Suggestions for Teaching

1. Teachers frequently give students pre-considered questions to enhance students' readiness to read: questions certainly provide direction for the students' focus. However, another way to enhance readiness—and one that better reflects "real-life" reading where there are no questions—is to show students how to anticipate the outcome. In this way, students provide their own motivation, which should prove more satisfying and productive in the long run than guidance that is offered by someone else.

To anticipate the heart of the story and the outcome, students may use the title, the information received from skimming or simply the beginning of the story. They can speculate about these matters, but they should always indicate what has led them to predict a given path. They should also check their predictions by identifying the portions of the story that confirm or cancel them. Students can also be encouraged to think ahead and the teacher, while reading to them, may stop and ask what will happen next or how the story will end.

It is also possible for students to anticipate what is likely to follow when they are reading informational material.

In the "lizard" passage, for example, the author has provided clues that prepare the reader for what is to come. Below the words that indicate what information may be anticipated are shown in *italics*; the purposes suggested are noted in parentheses.

Yet even if lizards didn't have such a long and impressive history (the preceding paragraph probably deals with the history of the lizards), *they'd still be a fascinating form of animal life.* (In what way would they be fascinating?) There are *over three thousand different species* of lizards. (How are the species different?) They are tiny, large, fat, skinny, speckled, checkered, striped, spotted, smooth, warty, blotchy, spiny, shiny, iridescent, bright, drab, or able to change color!

Some lizards are legless. Some have a *third or parietal "eye,"* (What is the eye for?) which may aid the lizard in controlling its body temperature. Some Indonesian lizards have *"wings"* (Can they fly?) with which they can glide for distances up to eighty feet. The basilisk lizard can run across the surface of the water. And most gecko species have *toe pads* (For what purpose?) that allow them to walk up a wall or upside down on a ceiling.

Additional paragraphs may deal with the lizard's utility in the environment, their usefulness to man, and so on. The eventual conclusion will probably deal with a re-statement of the great variety of lizards, or a summary of their history, their variety and their utility.

Passages such as this can be selected from various sources and used to teach students what kind of words will help them to anticipate information. The teacher could indicate what questions might be raised by the first few clues and then ask the students to suggest questions for the others. Later, the students could seek out clues on their own and discuss what question they would raise about the content and what information they might expect to follow.

2. **Text C** is an informational or expository essay (it "exposes" or presents information) whose title, "Anti-nuclear Reaction," is chosen to catch the reader's attention. A "nuclear reaction" suggests to the reader that the article will deal with life-threatening explosions at atomic energy power plants. The prefix "anti," however, suggests that the article will argue against this: a somewhat expected view. The first sentence, however, indicates that the article will deal with the "nuclear family," and the reader appreciates the joke played. The author's view that what is commonly considered a decline in moral values does not in fact represent social disintegration, but rather a return to older traditions. The concept of a nuclear family, the author argues, came into being recently, and its weakening was to be expected. His is a comparatively complex article. Teachers should urge students to grasp the main standpoint of the author and ignore all the conceptually minor details such as facts and dates. This approach will prove to be the best way for a general reader to reach over-all comprehension. This approach will be discussed in the next unit.

Text A　Appointment with Love

Close Study of the Text

1. ... whose written words had been with him and sustained him unfailingly. (Para. 1)

   Meaning: ... whose written words had accompanied him, and kept him cheerful and alive at all times.

2. ...just beyond the ring of people besieging the clerks... (Para. 2)

   Meaning: ...just outside the circle of people who were crowding around the ticket sellers...

   Note: The primary sense of "besiege" is "to surround (a place) with armed forces in order to make it surrender." The scene of the clerks being surrounded closely by people reminds the lieutenant of his war experience when his plane was surrounded by a group of Japanese planes.

3. ...when his plane had been caught in the midst of a pack of Zeros. (Para. 3)

   a pack of sb./sth.: (*often derog.*) a number of people or things (used esp. in the expressions *a pack of fools; a pack of thieves; a pack of lies*)

   Zero: a model of Japanese war planes in WWII.

4. Yea, though I walk through the valley of the shadow of death, I shall fear no evil, for Thou art with me. (Para. 4)

   Meaning: Although I am under the threat of death, I shall not be afraid of evil, for the Lord (God) is with me.

5. His face grew sharp. (Para. 5)

   Meaning: As the meeting time drew increasingly near, he grew alert, searching among the crowd for the woman he was waiting for.

6. ...Lieutenant Blandford started. (Para. 6)

   Meaning: ...he made a sudden movement, thinking she might be the woman he was waiting for.

7. ...the book the Lord Himself must have put into his hands out of the hundreds of Army library books sent to the Florida training camp. (Para. 7)

   Note: The lieutenant thought that it was the Lord's purpose that he should choose, out of the hundreds of Army library books, that particular book, which later brought him to correspond with the woman.

8. *Of Human Bondage*, it was; and throughout the book were notes in a woman's writing. (Para. 7)

   Note: This is an inverted sentence, with fronting and inversion occurring in the first clause and the second clause respectively. Placing into a lead position an element which usually comes later is known as *thematic fronting*. The fronted element is called the *marked theme*. The difference between fronting and inversion lies in the order of the subject and the verb. If the normal order of SV (the subject followed by the verb) is kept in the sentence with a marked theme, we call it *fronting*, whereas if the verb precedes the subject, we say *inversion* has occurred.

Fronting and inversion can be used to:

a) move a key idea into a more emphatic position so as to attract attention.

b) balance a sentence when its subject has a long modifier (and also to ensure the end-weight principle).

c) link two sentences more closely.

The title of the book *Of Human Bondage* is placed in the lead position to establish a close relation with the previous sentence, identifying "that book;" the adverbial "throughout the book" as the marked theme functions so as to show emphasis.

9. He had always hated that writing-in-habit... (Para. 7)

writing-in-habit: (compound word) "the habit of writing in (a book)"

write in: to include in or add to a text by writing

e. g.: The teacher wrote in corrections between the sentences.

10. ... she had faithfully replied, and more than replied. (Para. 8)

Meaning: ... she had answered his letters conscientiously, and actually she had not only replied but had written in such a way as to encourage continuation.

Note: "More than" can mean "not only/not simply," or "greatly/extremely;" this expression is often followed by nouns, verbs, adjectives and adverbs.

e. g.: She was more than plump. (Para. 16, Text A) (She was not slightly heavy but rather overweight.)

This more than satisfied me. (I was very much/greatly satisfied.)

11. I'd always be haunted by the feeling that you had been taking a chance on just that, and that kind of love would disgust me. (Para. 9)

Meaning: I would always think that you had written to me because you were risking the possibility that I might be beautiful, and that kind of skin-deep love would make me sick.

12. ... he pulled hard on a cigarette. (Para. 10)

Meaning: ... he drew the cigarette smoke deep into his lungs.

13. Then Lieutenant Blandford's heart leaped higher than his plane had ever done. (Para. 11)

Note: Hyperbole is employed in this sentence to exaggerate Lieutenant Blandford's great excitement at seeing the young woman.

Hyperbole is a kind of overstatement, a conscious exaggeration for the sake of emphasis, not to be understood literally. It appears most commonly today in advertising for cars ("The fastest car on the road."), books ("The best book ever written."), movies ("A heart-breaking love story."), and so on. In literature or daily speech its use is more subtle:

e. g. : I love Ophelia: forty thousand brothers

could not, with all their quantity of love

make up my sum. (Shakespeare, *Hamlet*)

He ran down the avenue, making a noise like ten horses at a gallop.

14. ...as he moved, a small, provocative smile curved her lips. (Para. 13)

Meaning: ...as he moved, the young woman smiled slightly and in a sexually seductive way.

Note: The young woman intended to test the lieutenant; as soon as she saw him moving towards her, obviously attracted by her beauty and elegance, she tested him a little more.

15. "Going my way, soldier?" she murmured. (Para. 14)

Meaning: "Are you going in the same directions as I am? If so, we can walk together."

Note: This phrase was commonly used during wartime by prostitutes (professional whores, street-walkers, or, humorously, sidewalk hostesses) to indicate their willingness to have sex for money. Other expressions for the time were "Hello, sailor," "Hi, big boy," and so on. Hollis uses this expression perhaps to determine if Blandford is out for a "good time" only, and would miss their arranged meeting for casual sex. It is doubtful however that she would continue with the game. She is merely testing him, as with his behavior with the 40-ish year old woman.

16. Blandford felt as though he were being split in two... and there she stood. (Para. 18)

Note: In this sentence, we find the rhetorical device of simile, a comparison of two essentially unlike things, often introduced by *like* or *as*: "How like the winter hath my absence been" or "So are you to my thoughts as food to life" (Shakespeare). "*As though he were being split in two*" is a simile. "*There she stood*," on the other hand, shows fronting. These devices help show graphically Blandford's dilemma: on the one hand he was deeply attracted to the lovely young woman, yet on the other he wanted so much to talk with the older, unattractive-looking woman, who (as identified by a red rose on her lapel) was the woman he had been in correspondence with.

17. Her pale, plump face was gentle and sensible; he could see that now. Her gray eyes had a warm, kindly twinkle. (Para. 18)

Note: After checking his disappointment and regaining his judgment, Blandford was able to see what he failed to perceive at first glance —the kind, gentle sensible side of the woman standing before him.

18. I've got two boys with Uncle Sam myself, so I didn't mind to oblige you. (Para. 22)

Meaning: I have two sons in the service, so I didn't object to doing you a small favor.

Note: Uncle Sam is a personification of the U. S. government or the country itself. He is usually represented as a tall, lean man with white chin whiskers, wearing a blue tailcoat, red-and-striped trousers, and a top hat with a band of stars. This image was used in the Second World War in posters for military recruiting, with the caption "UNCLE SAM WANTS YOU. " A number of countries have adopted personifications to be used in times of war: Marianne for France, John Bull for England, and so on. In peacetime, countries revert to older, invented Latin goddesses: Columbia for the U. S. , Britannia for Great Britain, Hibernia for Ireland, and so on.

Text-related Information

1. **King David** (Para. 4): According to the *Old Testament*, he was the second king of Israel, (reigned c1010 ～ c970BC), successor to King Saul. When one of his sons Absalom rebelled, he fled Jerusalem. Later with his friend Hushai's help, King David survived the rebellion and Absalom died.

2. **The 23rd Psalm** (Para. 4): one of the psalms or songs in *Psalms*, a book of *the Bible* composed of 150 songs, hymns and prayers. The 23rd Psalm is still traditionally recited over the grave of the person to be buried.

Text B   Could You Have Loved as Much?

Close Study of the Text

1. ... and her heart still skipped a beat when he walked into the room. (Para. 1)

Meaning: ... she still felt excitement when he walked into the room.

2. The lonesome months dragged on. (Para. 3)

   Meaning: During these months she was lonely and felt that time passed by very slowly.

3. He had married Aiko, a Japanese maid-of-all-work assigned to his quarters. (Para. 5)

   maid-of-all-work: a maid or servant who does all of the various chores in a household, as opposed to, say, cleaning women today, who will say "I don't do floors or windows". The expression may have been coined after "Jack-of-all-trades," a man who is able to do any or all of the following: replace broken windows, stop water leaks from pipes, fix electrical appliances (TV sets, radios, blenders), build bookshelves, and so on. It is also applied to any male or female who does a variety of different tasks: caring for children, working in an office, teaching.

   e. g. : She/he's a (regular) Jack-of-all-trades.

4. ... if I were making up this story, the rejected wife would fight that quick paper-divorce. (Para. 6)

   Meaning: ... if I were inventing this story, I would have the rejected wife hire a lawyer to protest this quick foreign divorce that is not legal in many states of the U. S..

5. She would want vengeance for her own shattered life. (Para. 6)

   Meaning: She would want to take revenge on them because they had destroyed her life.

6. Sadder were the times when letters came from Aiko. (Para. 12)

   Note: Inversion occurs to lay emphasis on the word "sadder," and to balance the sentence, following the "end-weight principle."

7. ...Edith read the loneliness... (Para. 12)

   Meaning: ... Edith read between the lines and saw Aiko's loneliness.

8. ... the immigration quota had a waiting list many years long. (Para. 13)

   Meaning: ... each year only a limited number of foreigners are allowed to enter America; as a result the number of those people who had been waiting for that chance for several years was very large.

Text C   Anti-nuclear Reaction

Close Study of the Text

1. ... the ratio of divorces to marriages... shot up by more than half... (Para. 1)

   shoot up: to grow rapidly or suddenly

2. Could it be that it was really a fleeting phenomenon... the spread of mass culture? (Para. 2)

Meaning: Is it possible that the concept of the ideal nuclear family was only a phenomenon that passed swiftly? Did it become most popular and widespread in the 1950s, soon after such phenomena as the affluence and prosperity after WWII, a sharp increase in the birthrate and the spread of mass culture?

3. If so, the gloom begins to look less well-founded. (Para. 2)

Meaning: If that is true, the feeling of depression does not seem to have a good basis.

well-founded: based on good reasons

4. Maybe today's western family in all of its many jumbled forms—one-parent-headed, second-time-around-headed... (Para. 2)

Note: "Second-time-around-headed" is a compound adjective. (see Text A, Unit 4 (*Teacher's Book*))

second time around: in general this expression means that you have done something before without much success and that the second time you have done it the results were better (I passed the entrance exam the second time around). "Second-time-around-headed" means that at least one of the parents has been divorced and re-married, probably bringing in children from the first marriage or marriages to form a new family.

5. ... the average duration of marriage began to inch up. (Para. 4)

inch up: to move by small degrees

6. Americans, who have supplied our century with so much of its imagery of the ideal marriage, also had late marriage. (Para. 6)

Meaning: Although Americans have provided the 20th century with many a lot of concepts of what the ideal marriage should be like, they themselves married lately.

7. The 19th-century American male did not rush to be married... (Para. 6)

Meaning: They delayed getting married for some time...

8. That figure dipped gently to a low of 22.5 years in 1959, as the new prosperity, suburbanisation and the celebration of the nuclear family took effect. (Para. 6)

Meaning: The figure decreased gradually to the lowest point ever of 22.5 years in 1959, because post-war affluence, the move to the areas around the cities and the wide publicity given to the concept of the nuclear family began to produce these results.

9. As for staying married, European visitors to 19th-century America were astonished at the ease of divorce. (Para. 6)

Meaning: Regarding marriage duration, European visitors were greatly surprised to find how easy it was to get a divorce in 19th-century America.

10. Rates of extra-marital birth began to take off in the latter half of the 18th century... (Para. 7)

take off: to rise very quickly

11. ... most people for most of the 20th century did not labor under this burden. (Para. 10)

Meaning: ... most people for most of the past 1,000 years did not suffer because of this hard-to-bear obligation of romantic marriage.

labor under sth.: (*fml*) suffer because of (a disadvantage or difficulty)

e. g.: The clinic labored under the disadvantage of not having enough space.

The new government removed the injustices under which the population had labored.

12. In colonial America, settlers seem to have married earlier, and often in opposition to their parents, because they could secure frontier land. (Para. 11)

Meaning: When America was still under British rule, settlers seem to have married earlier, and often ignored their parents' wishes, because they could get frontier land from the government after marriage.

in defiance of: ignoring sth. or in spite of sth.

13. ... the idea of a nuclear family continues to have a powerful hold on the late-20th century imagination. (Para. 15)

Meaning: ... the concept of the nuclear family continues to exert a powerful influence in the late 20th century on people's mental images about the family.

Text-related Information

1. **Nuclear family** (Para. 2): a social unit composed of father, mother and children, as compared to "extended family," which refers to a kinship group consisting of a married couple, their children, and various close relatives.

2. **Baby boom** (Para. 2): a period of sharp increase in the birthrate, such as that in the U. S. following World War II as a result of a rash of weddings for the 4 million men discharged by the army.

3. **Mass culture** (Para. 2): among the benefits that WWII soldiers received from the government was the possibility of a fully-paid university education. A vast number of soldiers took advantage of this, with the result that a BA degree (Bachelor of Arts), once rare, became common. This "mass" of soldiers ("large number") naturally sent their

children to school. At the same time (late 1940's, 1950's), television sets were produced in ever-greater and cheaper quantities, and the programs shown were increasingly designed to please a "mass" audience ("all of those in a group"). "Mass culture" refers therefore to "the things that would interest a large group of people." Note that "the masses" refers to the body of common people or people of low socio-economic status: the term appears in politics and history.

4. **Pre-industrial times** (Para. 4): the entire period before the Industrial Revolution (the complex of social and economic changes resulting from the mechanization of industry that began in England about 1760).

5. **Suburbanization** (Para. 6): the move to the areas around the cities. These areas are called "suburbs" or "outskirts," and the process is known as "suburbanization." After WWII an increasing number of Americans started building their houses or purchasing them on the outskirts of cities, and among them 95% were white, affluent and young. The cities remained the home of the poor, the old and the minorities.

6. **Pre-revolutionary** (Para. 8): before the French Revolution (the revolution in France that began in 1789, overthrew the Bourbon monarchy, and ended with Napoleon's seizure of power in 1799).

7. **Reformation** (Para. 12): the 16th-century movement to reform the perceived religious, financial and sexual abuses of the Roman Catholic Church. The Reformation resulted in the establishment of the Protestant Churches, and has been credited with the rise of capitalism, the pioneering spirit and colonizing missionary activity.

Section Three   Technology and Economy

Unit 7   Technology

Suggestions for Teaching

1. When readers think in a questioning way about and with the printed page, they may be said to be reading critically. As with other aspects of reading for meaning, the teacher must involve students in objective-oriented activities that are designed to foster students' habits of evaluative reading and to refine the quality of their responses.

   Among the activities that students should apply for critical reading are the following: 1) noting the points of view, 2) recognizing the author's purpose, 3) distinguishing between fact and opinion and 4) evaluating the author's final judgment. 1) and 2) will be discussed in this unit and 3) and 4) in the next.

   In the following passage about crows, two points of view are presented: These are identified by (a) and (b). A discussion follows.

   "*If people wore feathers and wings, very few of them would be clever enough to be crows.* (a)" So someone once said.

   That person *was right*. The black-feathered and *quick-witted* crows *are unique in the bird world for their amazing intelligence.* (a) *True*, *sometimes this intelligence leads them into stealing and mischief-making.* (b) *But* as one farmer said, "If it is not your corn that has been stolen, *you cannot help* but admire their skill and daring. (a)"

   One scientist at Johns Hopkins University figures that there are 320,000 crows each year at one winter roost near Baltimore. Another roost near Arlington National Cemetery has held 130,000 crows.

   Obviously, the author supports (a). His tendency can be detected from the *italics in bold* above, as well as from the *true... but* statement. In regard to (b), the author accepts the fact but believes it can be very well ignored. In his final judgment, the author admires crows for their intelligence (despite their faults), and it is to express his liking for these special birds that the author has written the passage. Therefore, in the author's

164

opinion, (for the question in the Reading Skill of *Student's Book*) b. We should admire crows because they are so intelligent, and c. If you are not personally involved with crows, you will like them better.

While the first two paragraphs present views about crows, the third paragraph merely provides information about them.

2. To help students recognize conflicting points of view, have them examine actual or teacher-prepared letters-to-the-editor on a specific topic and lead them to discuss how writers' view differ. Have them later write letters from different points of view: a proposal for a student smoking room from (1) a student who smokes, (2) one who does not, (3) a parent, (4) a physician, (5) a school board member. Ask the students to discuss "how might the point of view of a fire chief differ? of a football coach? of a lobbyist for the tobacco growers? of an owner of a local store? "

Later students may be encouraged to listen to conflicting viewpoints on television or radio and note (1) the backgrounds of the speakers, (2) the "public" and "hidden" purpose they may have, (3) their professions and occupations. Such texts as newspaper articles, printed advertisements, or political appeals may be studied from the same angle: "What is the author's point of view? The author's purpose? Do you think there is a hidden purpose? Could the author be biased? How might the author's background influence the point of view?"

3. Both **Texts A** and **B** are examples of argumentation, and you may ask the students to present a review of the structure of argumentative articles (see Book I, Unit 7). **Text C** is an expository article, and again a review of the article structure can be assigned.

In **Text A**, two opposing points of view are presented towards TV: the positive opinion of the first critics as represented by psychologist Joel Gold, predicting that TV would better American life, and the negative view as posed by the author that TV has vastly disrupted family life, in the sense of shared activities, and has to a great extent replaced the family as the unit that molds in society. The author strongly attempts to dissuade Americans from watching too much TV in order to embrace a more satisfying emotional life. In one sense her opinion is biased, as she considers that all families are "happy families. "

At the same time, we find a good model of popular science articles in **Text B**. In this type of article, the style of language tends to be less formal and the use of colloquial

English can be identified (*I*, *you*, *can't*, *don't* and the many ellipses) to balance the scientific terms and give an impression of simplicity to the readers. Note that the scientific terms are to be mastered by the students. In **Text B**, again, two different opinions are presented towards a new discovery, namely sequencing the human genome. Some express doubt as to its benefit, fearing that to know our genetic code means we will know our irrevocable fates. The author's view is opposed to this, focusing instead on the dual role of genes and environment or upbringing. The author's purpose is to free others from the first fear.

The author of **Text C** is reporting events, analyzing them and offering suggestions. He believes that, hard as governments around the world try to curb the spread of software piracy, eliminating piracy under the current copyright system may ultimately prove impossible. He expresses his own view through his agreement with Michael Godwin that the creators of intellectual property have to find new ways to be compensated for their work. In the future, he suggests, the real value of a piece of software may lie not in the program itself but rather in the secondary services that come with it.

Text A   The Dangers of Television

Close Study of the Text

1. Who could have guessed that a quarter of a century later Mother would be in the kitchen watching a daytime drama, Dad would be in the living room watching a ball game, and the children would be watching cartoons in their bedroom? (Para. 1)

   Meaning: Nobody could have guessed that 25 years later family members would rather go their separate ways watching their favorite programs alone than sit together and share one TV.

   Note: This is a rhetorical question, which differs from an ordinary question in that it does not need an answer. As previously mentioned, a positive rhetorical question is like a strong negative statement, while a negative rhetorical question is like a strong positive statement.

   For example:

   Don't you know that this is a highly classified document? (You surely know that this is a highly classified document.)

2. The time devoted to games, songs, and hobbies—all shared activities—in the years before

TV is now dominated by "the tube. " (Para. 3)

Meaning: Before TV was invented and became widespread in family life, family members spent time together playing games, singing songs, and doing things they enjoyed for pleasure. Now, however, TV has become the most important thing in family time.

the tube: (*infml*) television; also, "the boob tube," stupid or uninteresting television shows

3. Without such communication, family life disintegrates. (Para. 3)

Meaning: If family members do not talk to each other, family life will break up.

4. The ski slopes are nearly empty on Super Bowl Sunday; football on TV takes precedence. (Para. 4)

Meaning: On the Sunday when an American championship football match is televised live, few people go out skiing, as watching football games on TV is the first order of business in their life.

5. Addiction of some sort inevitable follows. (Para. 4)

Meaning: It is unavoidable that children will form the habit of watching TV and will hardly be able to stop doing so.

6. Isn't there a better family life than this dismal, mechanized arrangement? (Para. 5)

Meaning: Family life that has television as its center is cheerless and mechanical; there must be something better than this.

Note: another rhetorical question, expressing the author's concern about the future prospect of family life if the current situation continues.

7. ... if the family does not accumulate shared experiences, it is not likely to survive. (Para. 5)

Meaning: ... if the family does not gradually build up a series of experiences that the members share together, it is very likely to break up.

8. ... if parents and children alike do not change their priorities, television will continue to exert its influence on American family life... thus supplanting the place of the family in society. (Para. 5)

Meaning: ... if parents and children still place television above everything else in their lives, then TV will continue to play its many roles: taking care of the baby while the parents are away, comforting children's anger and anxiety, teaching them, setting them examples for imitation and providing them with social customs and standards of behavior, hence shouldering the social functions of the family.

Text B   It's Not "All in the Genes"

Close Study of the Text

1. ... many people get nervous at the prospects of that scientific milestone. (Para. 2)

   Meaning: ... many people become worried about what that significant scientific event, namely sequencing the human genome, might lead to.

2. Will it mean that our behavior, thoughts and emotions are merely the sum of our genes, and scientists can use a genetic roadmap to calculate just what that sum is? (Para. 2)

   Meaning: Will it mean that how we behave, what we think and feel are simply decided by adding up our genes, and that scientists will use the genome sequences to tell what we are going to be like?

3. Will knowing our genetic code mean we will know our irrevocable fates? (Para. 2)

   Meaning: Will knowing our genetic code mean we will know what will happen to us in the future, a future that cannot be changed?

4. At the crux of the anxiety is the notion of the Primacy of Genes. (Para. 3)

   Meaning: What makes people so anxious is the belief that genes are the fundamental components of living creatures and that as they come first in importance, they determine everything else.

5. Everything is preordained from conception. (Para. 3)

   Meaning: All things are decided beforehand from the time of pregnancy.

6. ... nurture reinforces or retards nature (Para. 4)

   Meaning: ... environmental factors facilitate or slow down the development of inborn elements.

7. There is genetic vulnerability, but not inevitability. (Para. 4)

   Meaning: One may have genes that are susceptible to something awful, but that does not mean one is sure to have it.

8. ... the buck starts and stops there. (Para. 5)

   Meaning: ... genes act on themselves and take full responsibility for their actions.

   Note: This sentence is adapted from "The buck stops here." This was a motto on President Truman's desk, meaning "this is where the ultimate responsibility lies; don't shift responsibility to someone or somewhere else." This expression in turn came from "passing the buck," in which "the buck" was a false or counterfeit dollar bill. Obviously, one did not want to lose money so one "passed the buck" on to the next person.

9. In some instances, chemical messengers from other parts of the cell. In other cases, messengers from other cells in the body (this is the way many hormones work). (Para. 7)

    Note： These are two elliptical sentences (where only part of the sentence is written or spoken) to answer the question "What regulates those switches?" An elliptical sentence may be defined as a legitimate abbreviation of a complete sentence. The omitted elements are readily understood either from the context (textual ellipsis) or from the situation (situational ellipsis).

    i) textual ellipsis：ellipsis of the words that are somewhere in the context

    　　For example：

    　　—What on earth are you doing? —(I am) Singing.

    　　Whether (he is) right or wrong, he is your father after all.

    　　"Do you want to see that movie?"—(I do) Not really (want to see that movie).

    ii) situational ellipsis：ellipsis of subject and auxiliary/modal.

    　　For example：

    　　Oh well, (it) can't be helped.

    　　(Are you) Coming?

    　　(Does) Anybody need a lift?

10. Or a mother rat licking and grooming her infant will initiate a series of events that eventually turns on genes related to growth in that child. (Para. 7)

    initiate： to cause to begin; put into operation

11. That goes for real life, too: genes are essential but not the whole story. (Para. 8)

    Meaning： That applies to real life as well: genes are fundamental components of our lives, but there are other factors that also matter.

Text-related Information

1. **James Watson：** U. S. biologist (1928～).
2. **Francis Crick：** English biophysicist (1916～).
3. **Winston Churchill** (1874～1965)：British Prime Minister (1940～1945) (1951～1955).
4. **Gandhi** (*Mahtma*) (1869 ～ 1948)：Hindu religious leader, nationalist, and social reformer.

5. **Albert Einstein** (1879～1955): German-born American theoretical physicist whose special and general theories of relativity revolutionized modern thought on the nature of space and time and formed a theoretical base for the exploitation of atomic energy. He won a 1921 Nobel Prize for his explanation of the photoelectric effect.

6. **Molecular biology**: the branch of biology that deals with the nature of biological phenomena at the molecular level through the study of DNA and RNA, proteins, and other macromolecules involved in genetic information and cell function.

7. **Genetics**: the scientific study of the ways in which characteristics are passed from parents (or in plants from parent stock) to their offspring.

Text C   Nabbing the Pirates of Cyberspace

Close Study of the Text

1. Nabbing the pirates of cyberspace. (title)

   Meaning: Catching those who conduct piracy through electronic communication.

   nab: (*infml*) to catch sb. doing wrong; seize

   cyberspace: the realm of electronic communication

2. And it is seen by some Italians as an ill-disguised attempt to suppress free speech on a troublesome new medium. (Para. 3)

   Meaning: Some Italians think that this campaign, which assumed the appearance of an anti-piracy effort, barely hid its real intention, which was to prevent free speech by left-wingers on the Internet as a new medium that causes governments many worries.

   ill: unsatisfactorily; poorly

   Similar example: ill-bred, ill-conceived, ill-considered, etc.

3. The underlying difficulty... comes from trying to guard new electronic "property" using laws that were made with printing press technology in mind. (Para. 4)

   Meaning: The fundamental difficulty lies in the fact that people are trying to protect the recent electronic products by using laws that were made for older products.

4. The drafters of copyright never anticipated a day when everyone could violate the laws. (Para. 9)

   Meaning: The persons who worked out the draft of the copyright laws did not realize then nowadays the laws could be so easily broken by anybody.

Text-related Information

1. **Bulletin board** (Para. 1): BBS (Bulletin Board System), a computerized facility, accessible by modem, for collecting and relaying messages and software programs.

2. **Gizmo** (Para. 7): (*infml*) a gadget or device whose name is unknown or forgotten.

   e. g.: "What's this gizmo called?"—"It's a battery-operated warming device for socks and gloves."

   "Where's the gizmo to open this wine bottle?"—"The corkscrew is in the bottom drawer."

Unit 8   Economy

Suggestions for Teaching

1. In this unit, three articles dealing with economics are presented in order to introduce students to what is possibly the most important aspect of China today in regard to their future lives. For those who are interested, there are a number of newspapers and journals that deal with economics, some of these publications written in rather clear and simple terms.

   In this type of economic article, students should be trained to deal with various aspects:

   1) to become familiar with certain economic terms
   2) to learn to read tables, graphs, etc.
   3) to absorb facts quickly
   4) to distinguish opinions from facts
   5) to form their own judgment.

2. It is not always easy to distinguish between facts and opinions particularly when opinions are not identified in any way. Moreover, some statements combine both fact and opinion.

   Then, too, certain facts are more definite than others. For example, it is a fact that Abraham Lincoln was the sixteenth President of the United States: there is hardly any reason to question this statement for the record is clear. But take the "fact" that scientific experiments reveal the speed of light to be 186,000 miles per second. In this instance the record is not quite so clear. Nevertheless, readers tend to accept this fact as readily as the other, even though they cannot confirm it in the same way.

   Students must learn to analyze statements to determine how factual they are:

   The present temperature is 70 °F. This is the high for the day.

   The first sentence contains a verifiable fact. The second is an opinion for the temperature may rise. If the second sentence read *this is the highest temperature recorded for the day*, the sentence then becomes a verifiable fact.

   Today's highest temperature is expected to be 70 °F.

   This is the best restaurant in town.

172

Both of the above are opinions: "best" is usually a personal judgment.

This restaurant is the most expensive one in town.

It is quite possible that this is a fact. One would have to visit the town's restaurants to verify it however.

After distinguishing opinions from facts, students should be encouraged to evaluate opinions on the basis of available information. In the passage below, they can judge how reasonable an opinion is and accept or reject it on suitable grounds (**opinions are boldfaced**):

Tough, resourceful, and sly, crows above all other birds seem to have mastered the problem of survival against heavy odds. One major reason is their amazing communications system.

They seem to have a built-in radar for detecting danger. They also communicate with one another through a relay system. *People cannot understand it, but apparently it is very clear to crows. For example, a crow will make two or more noises at evenly spaced intervals. Far back in the forest, another crow repeats the message with exactly the same note, with the same pitch, at the same intervals. Depending upon the tone, they appear to be passing the message along—"Here's food!" "Lie low...Quiet!" "All clear."*

In addition to this relay system, **crows have a strong sense of caution.** *While on the hunt for food, they appoint a crow to stand guard. High up in a tree, the guard can spot a gun a half-mile away, never mistaking it for a pole or stick. When anyone with a gun comes near, on a signal from the guard, the flock makes a quick, quiet retreat. They fly a speed of perhaps forty-five miles an hour.*

The most general opinion of the writer "**Tough, resourceful, and sly, crows above all other birds seem to have mastered the problem of survival against heavy odds**" is supported by two less general opinions "**one major reason is their amazing communications system. They seem to have a built-in radar for detecting danger. They also communicate with one another through a relay system**", and "**crows have a strong sense of caution.**" Each of the less general opinions is again strengthened by a group of details or facts. Therefore, the writer's opinion "**tough, resourceful, and sly, crows above all other birds seem to have mastered the problem of survival against heavy odds**" can be said reasonably well-supported and made valid.

3. Students should be encouraged to form their own judgment, without which no real comprehension can be achieved. Before forming their own judgment, however, teachers

should ask them to quickly grasp the major points dealt with in the article. Teachers may design other pre-reading questions and should even encourage students to design theirs after a preview skimming.

In **Text A**, the major points are the good and bad aspects of Chinese economy, although some aspects are both good and bad. In a very general way, the **good** aspects are 1) the country enjoys a stable period of sustained high growth coupled with low inflation; 2) China's successful bid to stage the Olympic Games in 2008 may bring in another surge of foreign investment; 3) consumers are gradually becoming more confident. The **bad** aspects are: 1) China is not yet completely out of the deflationary woods and consumers generally remain cautious about purchases; 2) China's GDP growth figures are not matched by a corresponding sense of well-being and security among ordinary citizens caused by the unfairness of allotting system; 3) even a growth of $7\% \sim 8\%$ is not enough to cope with China's fast-rising unemployment; 4) the increase in the value of industrial production slowed month after month between February and July, partly due to slackening external demands; 5) massive spending on housing construction and other infrastructure cannot go on forever without incurring unsustainably high debt; 6) the average cash incomes of rural households are about the same as they were five years ago, while taxes have been soaring. The **good** and **bad** aspects are: China's accession to the World Trade Organization (WTO) may result in throwing more out of work, particularly in the inefficient state sector, etc.. Thus, in effect, the key word seems to be the verb in para. 1, *appear*.

In **Text B**, Malthus was right in believing that the power of population is superior to the power of the soil / land to produce subsistence for man and that the earth's resources are finite. But Malthus was wrong in expecting populations to double every 25 years. In the 200 years since he wrote, the time it takes mankind to double has shrunk from several centuries to 40 years. Besides, he vastly underestimated man's ingenuity in utilising resources more efficiently, and at making new inventions. Furthermore, Malthus did not predicate what was something known now as the *demographic transition*: the way societies alter, as they get richer. First comes a decline in mortality, leading to a short population explosion; then, after an interval of variable length, a steep decline in the birth rate, which slows, halts or may even reverse the rise in numbers.

Note that in **Text B** Malthus' prediction works as a thread, uniting the entire selection.

Text C analyzes the problems in America's economy: 1) the economic outlook remains uncertain since much of that surge was driven by temporary factors, particularly a reduction in the pace at which firms slashed their inventories; 2) the broader outlook for corporate investment is still obscure and profits are small compared with their pre-recession peaks; 3) the prospects of a double-dip recession hinge on further weakness in labour markets. Many make comparisons with the "jobless" recovery of the early 1990s; 4) government spending is running 10% ~ 15% above last year's levels; 5) foreign investors are losing confidence in the American economy.

Text A   Persuading the Reluctant Spenders

Close Study of the Text

1. Officials proclaim that China really has turned the corner after several years of declining growth. (Para. 1)

   Meaning: Officials say that China has actually ended several years of decline in GDP growth.

   turn the corner: to pass a period of difficulties, a critical point in an illness, etc. and begin to improve

   e. g. : We've turned the financial corner.

   He was very ill but he's turned the corner now.

2. ... the country will enjoy an unusually stable period of sustained high growth coupled with low inflation. (Para. 2)

   Meaning: ... China will have an exceptionally stable period characterized by continued high economic growth together with low inflation.

3. China's accession to the World Trade Organization (WTO)... may bring in another surge of foreign investment... (Para. 2)

   surge: a sudden increase or occurrence

4. ... contracted foreign investment soared by nearly 40%... (Para. 2)

   Meaning: ... foreign investment that was formally agreed on went up high...

5. China desperately needs such confidence. (Para. 3)

   Meaning: China is in great need of such consumer confidence.

6. But if there is a "feel good" factor at work, its effects are patchy. (Para. 3)

   Meaning: But if consumer confidence is working, its results are not completely satisfactory.

patchy: not of the same quality throughout; uneven

e. g. : My knowledge of German is patchy.

His piano playing is very patchy.

7. On the positive side, retail sales of consumer goods... (Para. 3)

Meaning: On the good side...

positive: showing confidence and optimism; constructive

e. g. : a positive attitude

positive thinking

positive proposals

Note: "On the good side" is opposed to "on the negative side." Both are alternate ways of saying "on the one hand... on the other."

8. But this is only a moderate spending spree by Chinese standards. (Para. 3)

Meaning: But judging by Chinese standards, such spending levels are not great at all.

9. Nor is China completely out of the deflationary woods. (Para. 3)

Meaning: China has not completely overcome the problem of deflation, either.

out of the woods: (usu. with a negative) free from trouble or difficulties

e. g. : She has regained consciousness but she is not out of the woods yet.

deflation: a reduction in the amount of money in circulation in an economy in order to lower prices or keep them steady; a dropping of prices, the opposite of *inflation*

10. Consumer prices rose by 1. 5% in July compared with 0. 3% in the whole of last year. But prices of clothing, household appliances, transport and communication continued to drop. (Para. 3)

Note: The rise in consumer prices reflects an increase in consumer spending and thus the growing confidence of consumers, which is, of course, healthy for economic growth; while the price decreases in the second sentence indicates that this confidence is not thorough or complete, thus proving the previous statement that "its effects are patchy."

11. At a time of civil-service cuts and closures of state enterprises, these people are not eager to spend with abandon. (Para. 4)

Meaning: At a time when governmental institutions are reducing staff numbers and state enterprises are closing, these people do not have the desire to spend money without thinking.

with abandon: with freedom; without restraint

e. g. : weep with complete abandon

laugh with the abandon of a child

spend money with abandon

12. China's GDP growth figures may look strong, but they are not matched by a corresponding sense of well-being and security among ordinary citizens. (Para. 5)

Meaning: The growth figures may look strong, but ordinary citizens do not feel very happy or secure.

13. A favorite, and reasonable, complaint of urban residents is that an increasingly disproportionate amount of the country's new wealth is lining the pockets of a privileged few. (Para. 5)

Meaning: Urban residents often complain, with reason, that an increasingly large amount of new wealth is going to a few Chinese who enjoy special rights and advantages.

14. ... civil servants might be in for a pay rise, and there would be easier credit and more incentives for exporters. (Para. 6)

Meaning: ... it is possible that civil servants are about to have a pay increase, and that exporters will find it easier to obtain loans from banks and receive better treatment from the government.

15. In reality, China's growth, though definitely positive, may well be lower than the official figure, given the propensity of local authorities to exaggerate. (Para. 7)

Meaning: China's economy is growing for sure, but the actual growth rate is likely to be lower than the official figure if you take into account the tendency of local authorities to exaggerate.

well: (after can, could, may, might) probably, justifiably or reasonably

e. g. : I might well consider it later.

You may well be right.

I can't very well leave now.

It may well be that the train is delayed.

given: taking (sth.) into account

e. g. : Given the government's record on unemployment, their chances of winning the election look poor.

Given that she is not interested in children, I am sure teaching is not the right career for her.

16. But this cannot go on forever without incurring unsustainably high debt. (Para. 8)

Meaning: But such large spending cannot continue for a long period of time without causing a high debt that will be harmful to continuing economic development.

17. The budget deficit is already ballooning. (Para. 8)

    Meaning: The budget deficit is already increasing and swelling greatly.

    balloon: to grow greatly in size

    e. g. : After college, he got a job, married a good cook, and led a settled life. His figure ballooned!

18. ... the government is struggling with the hidden costs of propping up a banking system plagued by bad debts incurred by politically inspired loans to bankrupt state firms. (Para. 8)

    Meaning: ... banks that lent loans to inefficient state enterprises because they received instructions to do so, are now suffering bad debts as these firms go bankrupt, and the government, in turn, must try hard to deal with the hidden costs of supporting such a banking system.

19. What then of rural China as an engine of growth? (Para. 9)

    Meaning: What is the situation of rural China as a driving force of growth?

20. Even a moderate downturn could cause an employment crisis with far-reaching social and political consequences. (Para. 10)

    Meaning: Even a slight slide in growth could lead to an employment crisis that will have a great impact on the social and political life of China.

Text B   Like Herrings in a Barrel

Close Study of the Text

1. Give or take the odd 100m of us, 6 billion. (Para. 1)

   Meaning: Now the world's population is around 6 billion, plus or minus 100 million of us; that is, it ranges from 5. 9 billion to 6. 1 billion.

   give or take sth. : plus or minus a specified amount; more or less

   e. g. : The man is 80 years old, give or take a year.

2. When Malthus wrote, there was no widespread sense that numbers were running out of control. (Para. 2)

   Meaning: At the time when Malthus wrote this essay, most people of his day did not feel that the world's population was becoming too large to be handled.

3. ... a few prophets of doom had begun to give forth. (Para. 4)

Meaning: ...a few pessimists had begun to air their opinions on population.

4. ...either let matters take their course, thus inviting "positive" checks... (Para. 5)

   Meaning: ...either let matters develop as usual, thus bringing about "helpful" external factors to reduce population...

5. ...and it was barely under way by his day... (Para. 7)

   Meaning: ...and it had not started by his day...

   be under way: to be in the process of happening or beginning

   e. g. : Is the concert under way yet?

   We were /got under way at 6 a. m.. It was a long drive.

6. But something else was happening there that would have taken Malthus by surprise. (Para. 9)

   Meaning: Should Malthus be alive, there was something else that would have shocked him.

7. ...they also found that children were no longer an economic asset that could be set to work at an early age, but a liability... (Para. 9)

   Meaning: ...parents also discovered that they could no longer consider children as money-earners or force them to work when they were young; rather children became a burden for parents...

8. Nor were offspring any longer a guarantee against a destitute old age... (Para. 9)

   Meaning: When parents grew old and poor, they could no longer rely on their children to support them...

9. The know-how needed to avoid premature death... not far behind the rich world's. (Para. 12)

   Meaning: The knowledge to keep young children from dying too early was learned worldwide so that even people in many poor countries live nearly as long as those from the rich ones.

10. In China, ... the demographic transition is already almost complete. (Para. 13)

    Meaning: Although far less rich than those European countries, China also comes to the later period of the demographic transition—firstly population exploded to over 1. 2 billion people with a decline in mortality, then a decline in the birth rate results from the family-planning policy.

Text-related Information

1. **Benjamin Franklin:** U. S. statesman, philosopher, inventor, one of the founding fathers

of the U. S. A. .

2. **The Mediterranean**: The Inland sea enclosed by Europe, Africa, and Asia. It measures as much as 2,300 miles (3,700 km) east-west, and occupies an area of about 970,000 sq. mi (2,512,000 sq. km).

3. **Black Death**: an outbreak of bubonic plague that spread over Europe and Asia in the 14ᵗʰ century and killed an estimated quarter of the population.

4. **Thirty Years War**: a series of wars (1618~1648) that began as a conflict between German Protestants and Catholics and developed into a struggle for power among the Catholic and Protestant European nations.

5. **New World**: the part of the globe west of the Atlantic, including North and South America, their islands, and the surrounding waters, as opposed to the Old World, Europe and Asia.

6. **Tuscany**: a region of northwest Italy between the northern Apennines and the Ligurian and Tyrrhenian seas. Inhabited in ancient times by the Etruscans, it fell to Rome in the mid-fourth century B. C. . Long a cultural center, Tuscany was a grand duchy under the Medicis (1569~1860) and subsequently became united with the kingdom of Sardinia.

Text C   Why No Longer So Alluring

Close Study of the Text

1. Thanks to the productivity miracle, output grew fast enough to push unemployment to historic lows without fuelling inflation. (Para. 1)

   Meaning: Because of the surprisingly high productivity, output grew so fast that the unemployment rate was driven to historical lows, while inflation was not made worse.

   fuel: to make sth. increase or become more intense

   e. g.: The economic boom was fuelled by easy credit.

   His anger was fueled by jealousy.

   Her success was fueled by determination.

2. ... investors could not get enough of this magical state of affairs. (Para. 1)

   Meaning: ... investors worldwide were more than happy and willing to see the American economy keeping up such an unusually lucky, strong momentum.

   Note: "This magical state of affairs" refers to "charmed economy (Para. 12);" "magical" and "charmed" are used to describe the economy that the author thinks developed in an unexpected, strange and wonderful way, as if helped by some supernatural power.

have/get enough (of sth.): to be unable or unwilling to tolerate sth. /sb. any more

e. g. : After three years without promotion he decided he'd had enough and resigned.

I left early because I had enough of the speaker.

Note: In the negative, the meaning of this phrase is reversed: to be able or willing to tolerate

e. g. : I'm surprised you haven't had enough of him yet—I found him very boring.

I can't get enough of this book. I've read it six times already!

3. Despite the bursting of the stock market bubble... (Para. 2)

Meaning: Although what seemed to be a wonderful situation in the stock market came to an end...

the bubble has burst: a situation or idea which seemed wonderful has ended or has stopped seeming wonderful

e. g. : It was only a matter of time before her bubble burst and she left him.

4. ... consumers remain resilient... (Para. 2)

Meaning: ... consumers are quickly recovering from the recession and remain active in their purchases.

5. Higher profits should bode well for future investments. (Para. 4)

bode well/ill (for sb. /sth.): to be a good/bad sign

e. g. : The poor trading figures do not bode well for the company's future.

His late nights at the disco bode ill for the final exams!

6. ... by most measures America's firms still have plenty of spare capacity. (para . 4)

Meaning: ... judging by most standards, America's firms are still able to produce in great quantities.

spare: not in use but kept for use if needed

e. g. : a spare tire

a spare bedroom

7. That leaves the burden where it has long been—on the American consumer. (Para. 5)

Meaning: As outside investment cannot do much to improve the overall economy in the near future, such responsibility has to be shouldered by American consumers, just as it has been for a long time.

8. There is little sign that Americans have, up till now, lost their appetite forever more high-priced purchases. (Para. 5)

Meaning: So far, nothing indicates that Americans have lost their desire to buy more expensive items.

9. For the economy to fall back into recession, consumption would have to collapse dramatically. (Para. 6)

Meaning: Only if consumption fell suddenly and noticeably would the economy decline again.

10. ...weekly pay envelops have held up surprisingly well... (Para. 7)

Meaning: ...it is surprising to see that those who are working have not suffered a loss in the amount they receive.

hold up: to stay in a reasonably good state

e. g. : Children's wear is one area that is holding up well during the recession.

Sales held up well.

We hope the weather will hold up.

Although she's 75, her health is still holding up.

11. Ruined expectations also play a role. (Para. 11)

Meaning: Another reason for investors' fear is that people who had high expectations about the economy are disappointed at its neither-good-nor-bad performance.

12. ... Wall Street assumed that fast growth and fat profits were round the corner. (Para. 11)

(a) round the corner: very near

e. g. : My new place is just round the corner.

13. ... economic weaknesses... loom large. (Para. 12)

Meaning: ... investors now find the economic disadvantages that they had long ignored threatening.

loom large: appear threatening or important

e. g. : The terrible problem of armed crimes now looms large in our society.

The prospect of war loomed large in everyone's mind.

14. America's enormous current-account deficit... has risen sharply on the radar screens. (Para. 12)

Meaning: It is considered by those who watch the market that America's enormous current-account imbalance is continuing to rise (to surpass the pre-set goal of 5% of GDP).

Note: "Radar" is used to discover by using radio signals, the position or speed of objects such as aircraft or ships when they cannot be seen. Here the "radar screen" refers metaphorically to "economic monitors. "

15. For many Wall Street economists, a sudden dollar collapse is the biggest threat to the

recovery, aside from a terrorist attack or another oil shock. (Para. 12)

Meaning: Many Wall Street economists believe that if the American dollar depreciates suddenly, it will do as much harm to the current economic recovery as a terrorist attack or another rise in oil price would.

16. It is a cruel irony that if foreigners give up on America too quickly, they will ensure that the charmed economy disappears. (Para. 12)

Meaning: If foreigners lose hope in America and stop their investments soon, then this will guarantee that the wonderfully successful American economy will disappear. This is in direct contrast to what they want to happen.

give up on (sb. /sth.): to lose hope in sb. /sth. , no longer believe sb. or sth. is going to be successful

e. g. : When she caught him in his last lie, she gave up on him.
I've given up on this novel. It's too dull.

charmed: lucky, as if protected or helped by magic (used mainly in English); pleasant or beautiful to extent of being separate from the real word

e. g. : lead/have a charmed life
the charmed atmosphere of Oxford in the 20th century

Text-related Information

1. This article first appeared in *The Economist* on June 1st, 2002.
2. **"Profits and losses"** (Para. 6) refers here to balance sheets, written statements of the amount of money and property a company has, including amounts of money that it owes and is owed. "A good/bad balance sheet" refers to the general good or bad financial state of the company.
3. **Morgan Stanley:** one of the world's largest diversified financial services firms, whose business ranges from securities and investment management to credit services.
4. **J. P. Morgan:** an American investment bank founded by John Pierpont Morgan (1837~1913) whose money came from his reorganization and control of major railroads, and his consolidation of the U. S. Steel Corporation.
5. **Goldman Sachs:** a global investment banking, securities and investment management firm.
6. **Enron:** an American energy giant, was plagued by accounting scandals and went bankrupt.

Key to Exercises

Unit 1

Text A

Pre-reading Focuses

2. ☑ exaggerated (Some students may think it satirical. Let them hold their opinion.)

Post-reading Focuses

I. Reading Comprehension

(1)~(5) c b d a b   (6)~(10) c d a a b

II. Micro-writing Skills Practice

1. (1) Tourism   (2) announcement   (3) poisonous   (4) flooded   (5) stimulate
   (6) lawsuit   (7) leisure   (8) unconventional   (9) accusation   (10) haunted

2. (1) up   (2) on, as   (3) of   (4) away   (5) up
   (6) about   (7) over   (8) on   (9) at   (10) into

3. (1) tourist   (2) conductor   (3) musician   (4) murderer   (5) psychologist
   (6) optician   (7) pragmatist   (8) hiker   (9) supervisor   (10) racist

4. (1) the only one that is close to a panacea
   (2) the one he had been waiting for all these years
   (3) a house many times larger than the little cottage
   (4) a farmhouse (that) he thought was empty
   (5) a group of ants that did not have anything special about them
   (6) the kind of school which was believed to send few students to college
   (7) the crisis that had crippled so many Southeast Asian economies
   (8) the right that is the dream of so many of the world's cities

(9) Chinese peasants who seek employment in the cities

(10) the only one in China that is still inaccessible by (any) road

5. (1) characterized   (2) collectivism   (3) nations   (4) individuality

   (5) English   (6) when   (7) characteristics   (8) speech

III. Functional Training

1. (1) strange   (2) queer/odd   (3) odd   (4) peculiar

2. See *Teacher's Book*, 5 (referring to the 5ᵗʰ point in the **Suggestions for Teaching** in the same unit).

3. —They don't care.

   —They never budge.

   —They never move.

   —They don't read them.

   —They don't mind.

   —They don't even know it.

These statements generally express the same idea: Americans are too haughty to care about the opinions of other nations. The different diction in these statements on the one hand supplies variations, and on the other pushes the paragraph into a climax in the last expression: they don't even know it.

Text B

Pre-reading Focuses

1. (1) ☑ ironic

     ☑ exaggerated

(2) The writer hates the British custom of drinking tea with milk, regarding it as one of those established national practices that characterize British society. He believes that others, just like him, dislike this beverage, but dare not oppose it openly altogether, for fear that they will not be considered part of civilized society.

Post-reading Focuses

I. Reading Comprehension

(1)~(4) b a c b   (5)~(8) c c a b

II. Micro-writing Skills Practice

1. (1) eminence   (2) high-sounding   (3) putting their heads together

   (4) unorthodox   (5) feel like   (6) spoiled

   (7) exotic   (8) barbarism   (9) bore fruit

   (10) eternity

2. (1) that strong young American swimmer

   (2) a small shiny black leather handbag

   (3) both major Danish political parties

   (4) our numerous splendid African tourist attractions

   (5) these crumbling gray Gothic church towers

3. *Sample*

   The question of the correct way to speak and write English continued to exercise a great influence in British life throughout the twentieth century. Many English users in the 1990s adhered to the model of standard English advocated / formulated / decided upon / used in the nineteenth century, believing it to be the real or true English language. Those believing this remain anxious about what they consider to be falling standards in spoken and written English.

III. Functional Training

1. *Sample*

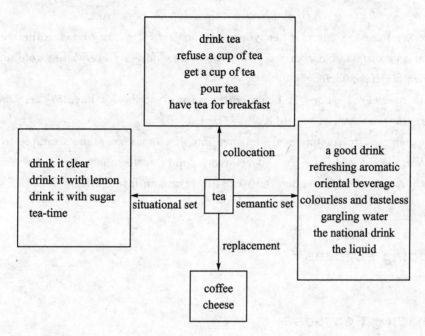

2. —They suggested that if you do not drink it clear, or with lemon and sugar, *but* pour a few drops of cold milk into it and no sugar at all, the desired object is achieved.

—There are some occasions when you must not refuse a cup of tea, *otherwise* you are judged an exotic and barbarous bird without any hope of ever being able to take your place in civilized society.

—When you are disturbed in your sweetest morning sleep, you must not say: "Madame (or Mabel) I think you are a cruel, spiteful and malignant person who deserves to be shot." *On the contrary*, you have to declare with your best early morning smile, "Thank you so much. I do adore a cup of early morning tea, especially early in the morning."

You use *but* to introduce something which contrasts with what you have just said.

You use *otherwise* after stating a situation or fact, in order to say what the result or consequence would be if this situation or fact was not the case.

You can use *on the contrary* when you are disagreeing emphatically with something that has just been said or implied, or are making a strong negative reply.

3. —*The most eminent* British scientists put their heads together, and *made complicated biological experiments* to find a way of spoiling it.

187

—*To the eternal glory of British science* their *labour* bore fruit.

—There are some occasions when you must not refuse a cup of tea, otherwise you are judged an exotic and barbarous bird *without any hope of ever being able to take your place in civilized society.*

—I drink *innumerable* cups of black coffee during the day. I have *the most unorthodox and exotic* teas even at tea-time.

—The other day, for instance—I just mention this as a *terrifying* example to show you *how low some people can sink*—I wanted a cup of coffee and a piece of cheese for tea.

The author uses highly exaggerated words to create an ironic effect.

Text C

Pre-reading Focuses

1. ☑ modest

Post-reading Focuses

I. Reading Comprehension

(1)~(4) F T F T   (5)~(8) T F T F

II. Micro-writing Skills Practice

(1) Intelligence   (2) competitive   (3) Dogmatism   (4) haughty   (5) Modesty

III. Functional Training

—Generally, Canadians can be described as intelligent, hardworking, friendly, open, reasonable, and do not feel that their opinion is the only one possible.

—Moreover, they are modest.

—Whatever they had or produced must be inferior to the cultural level, the skill or the standards of colonial powers.

—Some Canadians don't think much of themselves.

—Modesty makes it easier for one to get on well with others.

—Canadians don't have the haughtiness which characterizes those from a superpower.

—Canadians are conditioned from infancy to think of themselves as citizens of a country unsure of itself, having a confusing past and a hazardous future.

—Canadians have learned to take things as they are.

—They are well aware of the fact that there is a limit to human effort.

—Therefore, one of their favorite sayings is, "It can't be helped."

Unit 2

Text A

Pre-reading Focuses

1. (3) See *Teacher's Book*, 2.

2. (1) By introducing two kinds of sports, tennis and bowling, the author describes clearly the different handling of American and Japanese styles of conversation through the comparison with the sports. Then the two styles of conversation are formed in contrast as the two sports are.

Post-reading Focuses

I. Reading Comprehension

(1)~(4) d c a b   (5)~(8) c d b a

II. Micro-writing Skills Practice

1. (1) back and forth   (2) challenging   (3) no wonder   (4) startling
   (5) falling apart   (6) object   (7) came to a halt (8) called on
   (9) registered   (10) even if   (11) refer to   (12) dependent on
   (13) previous   (14) knock down   (15) switched to   (16) Even though
   (17) responded   (18) join in   (19) take turns   (20) in line

2. (1) a. Whoever leads a life full of love and happiness
       b. Whoever wants to have greater power
       c. Whoever pollutes the environment
       d. Whoever is with him
       e. Whoever comes first

(2) a. (Just) as some people are born artists, so are some born sportsmen.

b. (Just) as the lion is the king of beasts, so is the eagle the king of birds.

c. As a man lives, so does he die.

d. (Just) as two Americans proved in 1903 that man could fly through the air, so did three Americans again prove in July, 1969, that man could fly into limitless space, land on the moon, and then safely return to our planet Earth.

e. As you sow, so shall you reap.

f. As you have made your bed, so must you lie on it.

g. Just as they must put aside their prejudices, so must we be prepared to accept their good faith.

3. (1) woman   (2) Chinese   (3) his   (4) Chinese

(5) surprise   (6) misunderstanding   (7) question   (8) would

(9) if   (10) child   (11) should

III. Functional Training

3. **simple sentences with the word *different*:**

—Japanese-style conversations develop quite differently from American-style conversations.

—We were unconsciously playing entirely different conversational ballgames.

—Tennis, after all, is different from bowling.

paired sentences:

—I realized that just as I kept trying to hold American-style conversations even when I was speaking Japanese, so were my English students trying to hold Japanese-style conversations even when they were speaking English.

—An American-style conversation between two people is like a game of tennis. A Japanese-style conversation, however, is not at all like tennis or volleyball, it's like bowling.

Text B

Pre-reading Focuses

1. (1) (1) indecent   (2) proper   (3) nonverbal

(2) (4) four main distances in American social and business relations

    (5) 45   (6) 45～80   (7) 1. 30 meters to 3 meters   (8) 1. 30～2

(3) (9) avoided   (10) unpleasant   (11) apology

(4) (12) advisable

    (13) a truly bilingual person switches his body language at the same time he switches
       languages

2. (1)～(3) a a a   (4)～(6) a c b

Post-reading Focuses

I. Reading Comprehension
(1)～(4) c c d d   (5)～(7) a d a

II. Micro-writing Skills Practice

1.
infeasible	imbalance	independent	disobedience	inaccurate
uncertain	uncommon	inappropriate	inadvisable	disgrace
disapproval	unreliable	incredible	non-fiction	disorder
irresolute	incompetent	impartial	nonconformity	unavoidable
dissatisfaction	inadequate	immature	illiterate	

2. I.   Introduction

    A. The problems when speaking with foreigners

    B. The answer to the problems (thesis statement)

  II. Distance

    A. Arab

    B. American

    C. English-speakers

 III. Physical contact

    A. A study of different peoples

    B. English-speakers

    C. Chinese

IV. Eye contact

   A. American

   B. Puerto Rica

V. Conclusion

III. Functional Training

In this text, Mr. Deng illustrates different body languages in different cultures so that the reader may avoid improper gestures or body movements when dealing with foreigners. The author avoids imperative sentences as much as possible so that the tone sounds polite and patient, and the essay informative and educative.

Text C

Pre-reading Focuses

(2) By illustration or example.

Post-reading Focuses

I. Reading Comprehension

(1) F   In response to a compliment on his Chinese, an Englishman would **not** express his agreement.

(2) F   Chinese tend to refuse a compliment because they **do not want to be considered arrogant.**

(3) F   **When you think the compliment is not really true,** you could refuse it.

(4) T

(5) F   When you do not want to accept or refuse a compliment directly, you could always respond by **making a related comment.**

(6) T

(7) F   Partial refusal or partial acceptance of a compliment is another common strategy to handle compliments.

   Or: **You could honestly refuse a compliment** when you find a compliment is totally untrue.

(8) T

II. Micro-writing Skills Practice

(1) (e)   (2) (e)   (3) (c)   (4) (d)   (5) (b)

(6) (a)　　　　(7) (e)　　　　(8) (e)

Unit 3

Text A

Pre-reading Focuses

3. (1)～(5) b a a c b　　　(6)～(9) a b a b

Post-reading Focuses

I. Reading Comprehension

(1)～(4) a b c d　　　(5)～(8) a c a b

II. Micro-writing Skills Practice

1. (1) comes down to　(2) overwhelmed　(3) brooks　(4) work out
   (5) drawn up　(6) face up to　(7) speaking up　(8) go beyond
   (9) on average　(10) clean up　(11) counts　(12) consistent
   (13) accounting for　(14) has incurred　(15) befall　(16) readily
   (17) put away　(18) buckles down

2. (1) his face grave
   (2) Our work done
   (3) Everything taken into consideration
   (4) The last bus having gone
   (5) Head down
   (6) her hands in her pockets, and a smile on her face
   (7) Circumstances having changed
   (8) she alone remaining at home
   (9) Weather permitting
   (10) all expenses to be paid by his company

3. (1) either　(2) top-students/super-achievers　(3) interruption
   (4) concentrate　(5) organized　(6) scheduled

(7) absorb (8) Finally (9) approaches

III. Functional Training

1. —super-achievers
   —A students
   —the kids at the top of the class
   —top students
   —the best students

2. **students' activities connected with study：**
   —a member of the mathematics society
   —exhibited at the science fair
   students' activities connected with hobbies：
   —klutzes at sports
   —is on the tennis team
   —sings in the choral ensemble
   —played varsity soccer and junior-varsity basketball
   —did student commentaries on a local television station
   —played rugby and was in the band and orchestra
   students' study achievements：
   —get high grades
   —maintained a 4.0 grade-point average (GPA), meaning A's in every subject achieved a GPA of 4.4—straight A's in his regular classes, plus bonus points for A's in two college-level honors courses
   students' posts in student body：
   —serves on the student council
   —student-body president
   —was chosen for the National Honor Society and National Association of Student Councils

Text B

Pre-reading Focuses

1. (1) It was 1976, and the ugly shadow of racism was still a fact of life.
   (2) Pride in a good name keeps families and neighborhoods straight, and a sense of shame is the reverse side of that coin.

Post-reading Focuses

I. Reading Comprehension
(1)~(4) b a c b   (5)~(8) c b c a

II. Micro-writing Skills Practice

1. (1) propelled   (2) patronage   (3) vulgarize   (4) initiated
   (5) dampened   (6) abused   (7) restoration   (8) upholders
   (9) pervading   (10) charitable   (11) transgression   (12) profane

2. *Sample*

   One summer day my father sent me to buy wire and fencing and we had to ask for credit. Since our family was honest, the storeowner agreed to give me the credit. So I discovered that a good name could bestow a capital of good will of immense value. The good name my father and mother had earned brought our whole family the respect of our neighbors. A good name, and the responsibility that came with it, forced us children to be better than we otherwise might be.

   While we take pride in a good name, which keeps families and neighborhoods straight, we should also store a sense of shame, the reverse side of that coin. Once the social ties and mutual obligations of the family disintegrate, communities fall apart. Many of today's kids have failed because their sense of shame has failed. They were born into families with poor reputations, not caring about keeping a good name.

III. Functional Training

I. One summer day...

II. That day I discovered that a good name could bestow a capital of good will of immense value.

III. I thought about the power of a good name when I heard Gen. Colin Powell say that we need to restore a sense of shame in our neighborhoods.

IV. Today, when I'm back home...

Text C

Pre-reading Focuses

1. (1) When we need to make decisions when the full information does not exist, our best guess will often be the best we can do.

   (2) illustration/example

2. (1) the Pacific Ocean

   (2) six nautical miles deep

   (3) Enrico Fermi

   (4) does not contain all the information you need to solve it precisely

   (5) how much heat do other colors between black and white absorb

   (6) Stan Mason

   (7) the shape of a mushroom cloud

Post-reading Focuses

I. Reading Comprehension

(1)~(5) b a b c a

II. Micro-writing Skills Practice

(1) Gently as her words were spoken, there was no doubt that she was displeased. (h)

(2) I have told this story just as it happened. (d)

(3) The night has turned cold, as is usual around here. (i)

(4) I have to go now, as my sister is waiting for me. (f)

(5) He is a doctor, as was his wife before she had children. (g)

(6) As time went on, their hopes began to wane. (a)

(7) The question is so obvious as to need no reply. (j)

(8) As a child, he lived in Japan. (b)

(9) Such people as knew Tom admired him. (c)

(10) The policy is as cynical as it is dangerous. (e)

III. Functional Training

—**Suppose, for example,** you've been asked to write a marketing plan for a new telephone device that will send your name, company, address and telephone number to a visual display or printer on another person's phone.

—**The question about** phone stores **was an example of** what scientists call a Fermi problem, named after Nobel Prize-winning physicist Enrico Fermi, who used problems such as this to teach his students how to think for themselves.

—**Here's another puzzle.**

—**One of my favorite** "guesstimators" is Weston, Conn., inventor Stan Mason, who developed microwave cookware specially designed to position food in the best spot for cooking.

Unit 4

Text A

Pre-reading Focuses

1. (1) Expository article.

Post-reading Focuses

I. Reading Comprehension

(1)~(4) a a b c   (5)~(8) d a c d

II. Micro-writing Skills Practice

1. (1) treated   (2) awesome   (3) commitments   (4) underestimate
   (5) moan   (6) faultless   (7) endear   (8) vent
   (9) demanding   (10) frailties   (11) seeming   (12) perplexed
   (13) overflowing   (14) feigned   (15) matter   (16) risky
   (17) enrichment   (18) trivial   (19) drifted   (20) impulsive

2. (1) keep score   (2) stand by   (3) blurt it out   (4) opened up
   (5) shrugged off   (6) get hung up on (7) forget about   (8) the hard way

(9) aren't yourself   (10) do a favor for

3. (1) (d)   (2) (a)   (3) (f)   (4) (b)   (5) (c)   (6) (g)   (7) (e)

4. (1) a struggle involving life and death

  (2) a divide-and-rule policy

  (3) a not-so-strong football team

  (4) the too-eager-not-to-lose old champion

  (5) a never-to-be-forgotten night

  (6) an individual with run-of-the-mill opinions

  (7) Ours is a Papa-knows-best family.

  (8) What he follows is the-end-justifies-the-means philosophy.

  (9) There was an air on his face which said "I told you so!".

5. (1) only if he works hard

  (2) Only if I complete my homework

  (3) If only somebody had told us

  (4) only if a teacher has given permission

  (5) there is some hope only if proper medicine is obtained

  (6) I'll only come if you promise me that you won't invite Henry.

  (7) If only I had invited her to dance!

  (8) If only I were a millionaire!

6. (1) Friends   (2) difference   (3) lit   (4) childhood   (5) when

  (6) liked   (7) cared   (8) doesn't   (9) questions

III. Functional Training

1. (1) **Make friends a priority.**

  Many of us say, "I'd like to have more friends. I just don't have time." Yet we all have time for those things we truly want to do. To make room for friends, you simply need to be more creative.

  Note the little things.

  Standing by friends during difficult times is important. But the seemingly trivial acts of caring are what keep friendships going: the birthday call, the note scrawled in a greeting card to ask, "How's your back?"

Risk being yourself. Some people resist telling friends their deepest feelings. They're afraid to vent their fears, disappointments and negative emotions. But there comes a time in all friendships when you must open up.

Don't keep score.

Too often people get hung up on the duties of friendship: who was the last one to phone or write? When you forget about getting as much as you give, you'll make more friends.

(2) Each part is organized in the following general way: the common attitudes that people hold—a better view of friendship—an example to illustrate the author's point—the author's conclusion.

2. —**Steven Duck, author of *Friends*, *For Life*, asked people to** recall the most important conversations they'd had during a day. He found the talks that matter most tend to last only two or three minutes. "It's not the long meaning-of-life conversations that remind old friends you care," says Duck, "but the brief comments like 'Good luck on the job interview.'"

Duck notes that, especially in the early stages of friendship, it's endearing to admit your faults.

—Because she practices the art of friendship **as French novelist Alexander Dumas defined it:** "Forgetting what one gives, and remembering what one receives."

—**In the end, you realize that Robert Louis Stevenson was right when he said,** "A friend is a present you give yourself."

Text B

Pre-reading Focuses

1. ☑ The intensity of friendships depends on various factors.

Post-reading Focuses

I. Reading Comprehension

(1)~(4) d c b d   (5)~(8) a b d c

II. Micro-writing Skills Practice

1. (1) keep up with   (2) pinched   (3) rival   (4) endurance
    (5) for the most part   (6) intimate   (7) beyond a doubt   (8) cross his path
    (9) nonchalance   (10) way back

2. (1) (b)   (2) (e)   (3) (c)   (4) (g)   (5) (a)   (6) (d)   (7) (h)   (8) (f)

3. (1) harsh (Para. 1)—soft, gentle
    (2) mutual (Para. 8)—one-sided/individual
    (3) crucial (Para. 17)—unimportant
    (4). intimacy (Para. 29)—aloofness
    (5) tolerate (Para. 31)—eliminate/criticize

4. (1)~(5) a d b b c   (6)~ (10) a b a b c

5. *Sample*

     A friend is a person whom one knows, likes, and trusts. We have best friends, close friends, and just friends. There are many types of friendships. There are friendships based on activities, social groups, and work—a category that is becoming increasingly important. There are crossroad friends that we connect with during transitional times in life, and there are the friends that come at 3:00 A.M. when you need them.

III. Functional Training

1. —good Friends, such Good Friends, a friend all the way, convenience friends, special-interest friends, a shopping friend, historical friend, a friend who knew us when, crossroad friends, women friends, medium friends, pretty good friends, very good friends indeed, our very best friends, the best of friends, 12-year-old girl friends

2. **convenience friends**: These are the women with whom, if our paths weren't crossing all the time, we'd have no particular reason to be friends.
    special-interest friends: The value of these friendships lies in some interest jointly shared.
    historical friends: We all have a friend who knew us before we grew up to become the mature individual / person we are today.
    crossroad friends: Crossroad friends are important for what was—for the friendship we

shared at a crucial, now past, time of life.

men who are friends: Those friends of the opposite sex we can share ideas with.

3. (1) illustration   (2) enumeration   (3) classification   (4) compare/contrast

Text C

Pre-reading Focuses

—sheer disbelief, numbness, the most incredible pain I have ever experienced, the worst loss I have ever had in my life

Post-reading Focuses

I. Reading Comprehension

(1)~(4) F T T F   (5)~(8) F T F F

II. Micro-writing Skills Practice

(1) cave in   (2) table   (3) in the making   (4) teased
(5) adventurous   (6) sink in   (7) abounds   (8) purified
(9) detracted   (10) impact   (11) credibility   (12) traumatic

III. Functional Training

See *Teacher's Book*, 2.

Unit 5

Text A

Pre-reading Focuses

2. See *Teacher's Book*, 2.

Post-reading Focuses

I. Reading Comprehension

(1)~(4) c d a d   (5)~(8) a c d b

II. Micro-writing Skills Practice

1. (1) cut across   (2) facing off   (3) embodiment   (4) assurance
   (5) counselor   (6) infamous   (7) entrusted   (8) take
   (9) at the drop of a hat (10) fall back on   (11) muster   (12) presided over
   (13) deliberation   (14) inspiration

2. (1) although   (2) during the time that   (3) whereas   (4) as long as
   (5) although   (6) whereas   (7) whereas   (8) as long as she/he is
   (9) at the same time as

3. (1) Confidentially, I am resigning next year.
   (2) Frankly, there is nothing more I can do about it.
   (3) Fortunately for the latecomer, the train was late too.
   (4) Honestly, I don't know what you're talking about.
   (5) Personally, I find the music too arid.
   (6) Curiously, they never asked for charity even though they were virtually penniless.

4. (1) President   (2) But   (3) not   (4) deliver   (5) matter
   (6) recited   (7) over   (8) earth   (9) speech

III. Functional Training

1. —"Put not another bit into your Mouth 'til the former be swallowed."
   —"Cleanse not your teeth with the Table Cloth."
   —"Spit not in the Fire."
   —"Sleep not when others Speak."
   —"In the Presence of Others Sing not to yourself with a Humming Noise."
   —"Think before you Speak."
   —"When a man does all he can though it succeeds not well blame not him that did it."
   —Setting a good example influences people more than precepts.
   They are all (except the last two) imperative.
   The negative sentence is formed by "a verb + not".

2. —Mom *would have liked* Rule 97 ("Put not another bit into your Mouth 'til the former

be Swallowed") and Rule 100 ("Cleanse not your teeth with the Table Cloth").

—Boy Scout leaders *can use* Rule 9: "Spit not in the Fire."

—Rule 6 *is good for* the corporate boardroom: "Sleep not when others Speak."

—Personally, I *like* Rule 4: "In the Presence of Others Sing not to yourself with a Humming Noise."

—Rule 73 *counsels* "Think before you Speak."

—Did he *recall* Rule 44: "When a man does all he can, though it succeeds not well, blame not him that did it"?

—It's all a matter of Washington's Rule 48, which *observes* that setting a good example influences people more than precepts.

Text B

Pre-reading Focuses

1. (2) A great leader is the symbol of the best in us, shaped by our own spirit and will.

Post-reading Focuses

I. Reading Comprehension
(1)~(4) F F T T   (5)~(8) F T F T

II. Micro-writing Skills Practice
subject + must/should/have/be to:
—The leader <u>must appear</u> on the scene at a moment when people are looking for leadership.
—When he comes, <u>he must offer</u> a simple, eloquent message.
—<u>A leader should have an unforgettable</u> identity, and permanently fixed in people's minds.
—<u>A leader must know how to</u> use power (that's what leadership is about), but he also has to have a way of showing that he does.
—<u>He has to be able to</u> project firmness.
—<u>A leader must have</u> the grace of a good dancer, and there is a great deal of wisdom to this.
—<u>A leader should know how to</u> appear relaxed and confident.
—<u>His walk should be</u> firm and purposeful.
—<u>He should be able to</u> give a good, hearty, belly laugh.
—<u>His purpose must</u> match the national mood.
—<u>His task is to</u> focus the people's energies and desires, to define them in simple terms, to

inspire, to make what people already want seem attainable, important, within their grasp.

—He must dignify our desires, convince us that we are taking part in the making of great history.

—A leader must stir our blood, not appeal to our reason. . .

—A great leader must have a certain irrational quality, a stubborn refusal to face facts, infectious optimism, the ability to convince us that all is not lost even when we're afraid it is.

—While the advisors of a great leader should be as cold as ice, the leader himself should have fire, a spark of divine madness.

subject + be/verb:

—Great leaders are almost always great simplifiers, who cut through argument, debate and doubt to offer a solution everybody can understand and remember.

—The leader is like a mirror, reflecting back to us our own sense of purpose, putting into words our own dreams and hopes, transforming our needs and fears into coherent policies and programs.

—A leader rides the waves, moves with the tides, understands the deepest yearnings of his people.

we+verb:

—We have an image of what a leader ought to be.

—We even recognize the physical signs: leaders may not necessarily be tall, but they must have bigger-than-life, commanding features.

—We expect our leaders to stand out a little, not to be like ordinary men.

—We want them to be like us but better, special, more so.

other forms:

—It also helps for a leader to be able to do something most of us can't.

III. Functional Training

1. **in favor:**

   —LBJ's nose and ear lobes

   —Ike's broad grin

   —Lincoln's stovepipe hat

   —JFK's rocker

   —FDR—overcame polio

   —Mao—swam the Yangtze River at the age of 72.

—Lincoln, FDR, Truman, Ike and JFK—give a good, hearty, belly laugh

—Ronald Reagan—his easy manner and apparent affability managed to convey the impression that in fact he was the President and Carter the challenger.

—Winston Churchill—managed, by sheer rhetoric, to turn the British defeat and the evacuation of Dunkirk in 1940 into a major victory.

—FDR's words turned the sinking of the American fleet at Pearl Harbor into a national rallying cry instead of a humiliating national scandal

out of favor:

—Adlai Stevenson—too cerebral

—Nelson Rockefeller—too rich

—Nixon's insecurity—the sickly grin that passes for good humor

—Humphrey's fatal infatuation with his own voice.

—Ford—physical clumsiness

—Carter—rapid eye movements

2. See *Teacher's Book*, 4.

Text C

Post-reading Focuses

I. Reading Comprehension

(1)~(4) a d a b   (5)~(8) d d c b

II. Micro-wring Skills Practice

1. (1) acquainted   (2) contributive   (3) respectful   (4) respectable

   (5) afflicts   (6) hesitant   (7) modesty   (8) willing

2. (1) Once I make up my mind to do something, I do it immediately.

   (2) Once you show fear, he will attack you.

   (3) You cannot get out, once you are in.

   (4) Once children are involved, divorces are particularly unpleasant.

   (5) We can leave once you're ready.

   (6) Once a wrong is done, it cannot be undone.

III. Functional Training

1. —president of your class, school, or student council
   —fellow students
   —school activities
   —joining clubs, attending dances and other social functions, and going out for athletics
   —schoolmates
   —circle of friends and contacts
   —sell ten tickets to a dance
   —make your organization successful
   —members of a club
   —sit passively through a meeting
   —club matters
   —the time comes for election of class or student body officers
   —a possible candidate
   —to declare yourself a candidate

2. (1) *Because* introduces a direct reason. It is usually placed after the main clause unless it is stressed, as is the case here.

   (2) *For* is used in semi-formal and formal writing to replace *because*. Unlike *because* it can only appear after the main clause and must be accompanied by a subject/verb.

   (3) *As* introduces an explanation or a reason which may place a certain emphasis on the time sequence involved; this is the case here. In other cases, *as* may be used for a reason that is not as obvious or important as the reason introduced by *because* and which is already widely known (*As she is hard-working, she is very successful*). An *as*-clause is usually put at the beginning.

   (4) *Since* is the semi-formal and formal replacement for *as*.

3. —... you must first demonstrate that you have the <u>potentials of leadership</u>.
   —<u>For one thing</u>, you must show that you are interested in your school and in your fellow students.
   —If you consciously strive to overcome shyness by going out to meet people, you will find yourself <u>at the same time</u> developing <u>another quality</u> of <u>leadership</u>—understanding.
   —<u>Another quality</u> of <u>leadership</u> which you can develop is willingness to do a bit extra.
   —<u>A fourth quality</u> of <u>leadership</u> is imagination—the ability to see a way through problems

and to develop new ideas.

Unit 6

Text A

Post-reading Focuses

I. Reading Comprehension

(1)～(4) b d c d   (5)～(8) c b b d

II. Micro-writing Skills Practice

1. (1) started   (2) obliging   (3) get hold of   (4) unfailing
   (5) What of it   (6) sustained   (7) renewal   (8) besieged
   (9) a pack of   (10) confession   (11) faithful   (12) held out
   (13) sensible   (14) provoked   (15) saw into   (16) disgusting
   (17) take a chance on (18) pulling on

2. (1) Neither fame nor gain does he seek.
   (2) Until you conquer your fear of being an outsider, an outsider you will remain.
   (3) After weeks of drought came the rains.
   (4) Fool he may be; but thief he is not.
   (5) The door burst open and in rushed the angry crowd.
   (6) Never had he believed that a woman could see into a man's heart so tenderly, so understandingly.
   (7) The committee has asked him to resign. That he will not do.
   (8) The road we have long been traveling in pest control is deceptively easy, but at its end lies disaster.

3. (1) job   (2) ever   (3) while   (4) shoes
   (5) no   (6) would   (7) driving

III. Functional Training

1. **the girl**

—wearing a red flower in her suit lapel, but it was a crimson sweet pea, not the little red rose they had agreed upon

—too young, about 18

Hollis Meynell

—A young woman.

—Her figure was long and slim; her blond hair lay back in curls from her delicate ears.

—Her eyes were blue as flowers, her lips and chin had a gentle firmness.

—In her pale green suit, she was like springtime come alive.

—A small, provocative smile curved her lips.

the-middle-age woman

—a woman well past 40

—her graying hair tucked under a worn hat

—more than plump

—her thick-ankled feet were thrust into low-heeled shoes

—wore a red rose in the rumpled lapel of her brown coat

2. **The importance of Hollis for Blandford in the 13 months:**

—... he would see the woman who had filled such a special place in his life for the past 13 months, the woman he had never seen, yet whose written words had been with him and sustained him unfailingly.

—And he had remembered; he had heard her imagined voice, and it had renewed his strength and skill.

—For 13 months, she had faithfully replied, and more than replied. When his letters did not arrive she wrote anyway, and now he believed he loved her, and she loved him.

—... yet so deep was his longing for the woman whose spirit had truly companioned and upheld his own; and there she stood.

Blandford's eagerness and nervousness in the six minutes:

—His heart was pounding with a beat that shocked him because he could not control it.

—Now he was going to hear her real voice. Four minutes to six. His face grew...

—One minute to six—he pulled hard on a cigarette.

—Then Lieutenant Blandford's heart leaped higher than his plane had ever done.

3. **the waiting line:**

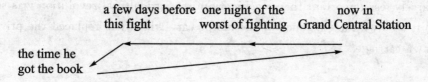

six minutes to six　　four minutes to six　　one minute to six

the recall line:

a few days before　one night of the　　　　now in
this fight　　　　worst of fighting　Grand Central Station

the time he
got the book

Text B

Pre-reading Focuses

1. (1) The author.

　　　The function centers around the following possibilities:

　—to re-define the meaning of "story" ("an untrue narrative") so that the reader understands that it is a narrative of factual events;

　—to show the difference between what happens in non-real "stories" and what happens in "real-life stories;"

　—to alert the reader to the fact that what will follow is not what one would expect.

(2) The 13th paragraph.

(3) —A newspaper columnist, involved with human and political problems, helpful.

Post-reading Focuses

I. Reading Comprehension

(1)~(4) T F T F　　(5)~(7) F F T

II. Micro-wring Skills Practice

1. Inversion often serves the function of so arranging clause order that the most important part of the message falls at the end. This avoids a weak ending for the sentence. At the same time, inversion may serve to link the first part of the inverted sentence with what has preceded while simultaneously leading into the following sentence through the second part of the inverted sentence.

(1) A year ago, two crashes occurred at the corner, and more recently has come the news of a third.

(2) Of drugs or medicines she had almost none.

(3) Only in Africa is population growth still rampant.

(4) Scarcely less important than machinery in the agricultural revolution was science.

'(5) To it we owe the existence of the motor car, which has replaced the private horse-drawn carriage.

2. *Sample*

Letters have to be better-organized and more precise than ordinary conversation because letters don't give you the opportunity to go back and complete or clarify your remarks. But if you think of writing letters as way of communicating with someone—rather than as a piece of paper—your writing will be more natural, clearer and more convincing. Follow the four c's: be clear, concise, courteous and correct.

III. Functional Training

1. —He'd write that

—. . . his letters were coming less and less often.

—a postage stamp

—came a letter

—a mail-order divorce

—she wrote Karl, asking him to keep her in touch with his life.

—he wrote back

—the terrible letter

—his last letters

—letters came from Aiko

—Edith Taylor wrote me, asking if I could help.

2. **in conditional sentences to introduce the circumstances in which an event might happen:**

—*If* his job as government-warehouse worker took him out of town, he would write Edith each night and send small gifts from every place he visited.

—Now, *if* I were making up this story, the rejected wife would fight that quick paper-divorce.

—What *if* she should hate this woman who had taken Karl away from her?

—She wrote that, *if* Aiko was willing, she would take Maria and Helen and bring them up in Waltham.

in indirect questions where the answer is either yes or no:

—(Tell me) *If* Maria or Helen cry or not.

—It was then that Edith Taylor wrote me, asking *if* I could help.

to introduce a subordinate clause in which you admit a fact which you regard as less important than the statement in the main clause:

—Edith knew that, *if* she had been afraid, Aiko was near panic.

3. —The story begins early in 1950 in the Taylors' small apartment in Waltham, Massachusetts.

—In February 1950, Karl was sent to Okinawa for a few months to work in a new government warehouse.

—The lonesome months dragged on.

—Then, after weeks of silence, came a letter.

—Edith now built her life around this thought.

—And then the terrible letter.

—Then Edith knew that her last gift to Karl could be peace of mind.

—For many months after Karl's death, Aiko would not let the children go.

—In November 1956, she sent them to her "Dear Aunt Edith."

—Petitions were started, and, in August 1957, Aiko Taylor was permitted to enter the country.

—As the plane came in at New York's International Airport, Edith had a moment of fear.

Text C

Pre-reading Focuses

1. See *Teacher's Book*, 2.

Post-reading Focuses

I. Reading Comprehension

(1)~(4) d a b d   (5)~(8) c a b d

II. Functional Training

—**The past 25 years** have seen a new and unusual burst of worrying in western society about the collapse of the family.

—**Between 1970 and 1998**, the ratio of divorces to marriages in the United States shot up by more than half; the rate of out-of-marriage births more than tripled, to about one in three.

—Maybe today's western family in all of its many jumbled forms—one-parent-headed, second-time-around-headed, grandparent-headed, peopled with half-siblings or step-siblings, or combinations thereof—is simply returning to the complex, diverse state in which in fact it spent most of the previous 1,000 years.

—Measured merely by their duration, marriages **in the mid-20th century** were more stable than at almost any other time in history.

—**In the mid-1950s** American, a couple could expect their marriage to last, on average, **a full 31 years**.

—As living standards, household and public sanitation and health improved, **in the later 18th century**, people lived longer and the average duration of marriages began to inch up.

—**Between 1600 and 1850**, outside towns, the average bridegroom at his first marriage was aged 27 or 28, the bride at hers 25 or 26, though rich girls tended to marry quite a lot younger.

—Rates of extra-marital birth began to take off **in the latter half of the 18th century**, rising **by 1850** to 6.5% in Britain, over 7% in France, and 9% in Sweden.

—**For the first two-thirds of the 20th century**, however, rates dropped to only about 4% in England and Wales.

—**Not until the 1960s~1970s** did the figures accelerate, to a third of all births in England and America **by the 1990s.**

—Either way, **by the late 17th century** in England the idea that two people could choose to marry for love became increasingly widely held.

Unit 7

Text A

Pre-reading Focuses

1. See *Teacher's Book*, 3.

Post-reading Focuses

I. Reading Comprehension

(1)~(4) F F F T   (5)~(8) T F F T

II. Micro-writing Skills Practice

1. (1) ultimate   (2) dominant   (3) disintegration   (4) dismal
   (5) consequent   (6) Elimination   (7) enormous   (8) devotion
   (9) takes precedence (10) invariable   (11) exerts...influence on (12) unpredictable
   (13) supplanted

2. (1) Aren't they wonderful dresses?
   (2) Do you call that a poem?
   (3) If winter comes, can spring be far behind?
   (4) Can't we learn from the tragic experiences of others?
   (5) Aren't there other alternatives to the chemical control of insects?
   (6) Don't you know that this is a highly classified document?

3. I.   Introduction
      A. TV would better American life in past experts' views.
      B. TV has changed American life in a bad way. (thesis statement)
   II. TV exerts bad effects on American family life.
      A. TV often limits family outings.
      B. TV destroys family time together at home.
      C. TV dominates family life.
   III. Conclusion
      A. TV arranges family life in a dismal, mechanized way.

213

B. TV will supplant the place of the family in society.

III. Functional Training

1.

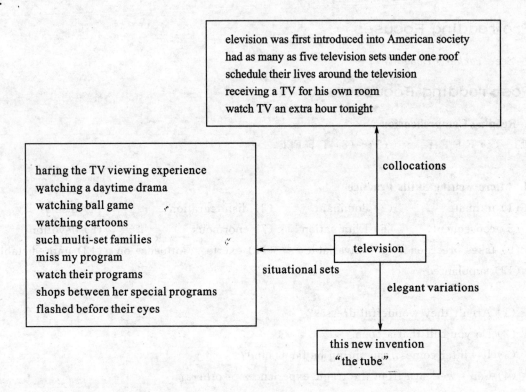

```
┌─────────────────────────────────────────────────┐
│ elevision was first introduced into American society │
│ had as many as five television sets under one roof │
│ schedule their lives around the television        │
│ receiving a TV for his own room                   │
│ watch TV an extra hour tonight                    │
└─────────────────────────────────────────────────┘
```

collocations

```
┌─────────────────────────────────────┐
│ haring the TV viewing experience     │
│ watching a daytime drama             │
│ watching ball game                   │
│ watching cartoons                    │
│ such multi-set families              │
│ miss my program                      │
│ watch their programs                 │
│ shops between her special programs   │
│ flashed before their eyes            │
└─────────────────────────────────────┘
```

┌────────────┐
│ television │
└────────────┘

situational sets

elegant variations

```
┌──────────────────────┐
│ this new invention    │
│ "the tube"            │
└──────────────────────┘
```

2. —*Television has certainly changed American life, but not the way the first critics predicted.*

—*Perhaps more important than the lack of family outings is the destruction of family time together at home.*

—*Isn't there a better family life than this dismal, mechanized arrangement?*

These sentences both introduce the new paragraphs and conclude the previous paragraph at the same time.

3. They all show the effect of certain behavior and they are widely used in argumentation.

Text B

Pre-reading Focuses

1. See *Teacher's Book*, 3.

2. (1) It is no surprise that virtually every list that appeared of the most influential people of the 20th century included James Watson and Francis Crick, right up there alongside Churchill, Gandhi and Einstein.

   (2) It will no doubt be a revolution, but there are some fundamental questions about how we will think about ourselves.

   (3) For example, research indicates that "having the gene for schizophrenia" means there is a 50 percent risk you'll develop the disease occurs only when you have a combination of schizophrenia-prone genes and schizophrenia-inducing experiences.

   (4) Or a mother rat licking and grooming her infant will initiate a cascade series of events that eventually turns on genes related to growth in that child.

Post-reading Focuses

I. Reading Comprehension

(1)～(4) d b b a   (5)～(8) b c a c

II. Micro-writing Skills Practice

(1) overwork   (2) precautions   (3) poetic   (4) publicity   (5) irrational

(6) envious   (7) disengage   (8) validate

III. Functional Training

1. Words with the same root can be mastered together.

   gene—genetic—genetics—genome—carcinogens:

   root—gen: race, offspring, to give birth

   molecular: root—mole: small mass

   biology: root—bio: life   log: word/study

   schizophrenic—schizophrenia—schizophrenia-prone—schizophrenia-inducing

   root—schizo: split   phren: mind

   pathologically: root—patho: disease, suffering

2. See *Teacher's Book*, 3, under **Text B**.

3. —*Yet hardly any genes actually work this way. Instead, genes and environment interact; nurture reinforces or retards nature.*

   —*However, that view is far from accurate too. Within the staggeringly long sequences of DNA, it turns out that only a tiny percentage of letters actually form the words that constitute genes and serve as code for proteins. More than 95 percent of DNA, instead, is "non-coding."*

   The author uses a transitional connective to start his points.

4. The rhetorical questions are probably the questions that would actually appeal to the general interest of most readers. They quickly catch the readers' attention and serve to raise the opposing viewpoint for the whole article at the very beginning.

Text C

Pre-reading Focuses

See *Teacher's Book*, 3.

Post-reading Focuses

I. Reading Comprehension

(1)~(4) F T F F   (5)~(8) T T F F

II. Functional Training

—computer bulletin board, software, modems, floppy disks, computer programs, electronic networks, internet, hard drives, frequent upgrades

Unit 8

Text A

Pre-reading Focuses

1. See *Teacher's Book*, 3.

Post-reading Focuses

I. Reading Comprehension

(1)~(4) c d b a   (5)~(8) a c a d

II. Micro-writing Skills Practice

1. (1) disproportion   (2) prop up   (3) scaled   (4) far-reaching

   (5) boost   (6) lining their own pockets   (7) patchy   (8) abandon

   (9) turned the corner   (10) slack   (11) plagued   (12) scraping

   (13) acceded   (14) inspiration   (15) out of the woods

   (16) may well

2. (1) Given their inexperience

   (2) Given enough manpower and financial support

   (3) Given his advanced years/ Given that he was advanced in years

   (4) Given peace and quiet

   (5) Given patience

   (6) Given that this was his first offence

III. Functional Training

1. —consumers, domestic demand, retail sales, consumer goods, a moderate spending spree, the deflationary woods, price, the sell-off of state-owned housing, buy homes and spend money on furnishing and decorating, purchases, big or small, spend with abandon

2. —Officials proclaim that China really has turned the corner after several years of declining growth.

—Growth is widely predicted to reach 7.5%～8% this year.

—That may be down a fraction from last year's 8%, but it would still be remarkably healthy for a country suffering from a sharp contraction in its export growth as a result of the global slowdown.

—... the country will enjoy an unusually stable period of sustained high growth coupled with low inflation.

—Officials say China's successful bid to stage the Olympic Games in 2008 will stimulate industries ranging from tourism to construction, adding as much as 0.3 percentage points to China's annual GDP growth.

—As export growth slows (exports are likely to grow by a mere 5%～8% this year, down from nearly 28% last year), domestic demand is becoming all the more crucial.

—... retail sales of consumer goods rose by 10.3% in the first six months of this year, slightly higher than the 9.7% growth of last year.

—Even growth of 7%～8% is not enough to cope with China's fast-rising unemployment.

—In reality, China's growth, though definitely positive, may well be lower than the official figure, given the propensity of local authorities to exaggerate.

—Moreover, despite GDP growth in the first six months of 7.9%, the increase in the value of industrial production slowed month after month between February and July, from 19% to just over 8% compared with the same months a year ago.

—Chinese officials realize that maintaining high levels of growth over the long term will depend on the rural market.

—In the villages, retail sales in the first half of this year rose 7.4%, compared with 11.6% in the cities.

Text B

Pre-reading Focuses

1. See *Teacher's Book*, 3.

Post-reading Focuses

I. Reading Comprehension

(1)～(4) c b a a   (5)～(7) c b d

II. Micro-writing Skills Practice

（1）他获得的选票比对手多出三倍。

（2）自 1976 年以来，电视机的销售量增加了 14 倍。

（3）在过去一百年左右的时间里，欧洲人口只增长了 80％，达到 7 亿 3 千万；而同期亚洲人口则翻了近两番，总数超过 36 亿。

（4）世界人口在 1,000 年内激增了 19 倍。

（5）The firm's profits are rising four times faster than those of other companies. / The firm's profits are rising four times as fast as other companies'.

（6）The latest survey revealed a threefold increase in breast cancer worldwide.

（7）In 1980 the output value of our city's light industry multiplied 6 times (sixfold) over 1967.

（8）He boldly ventured that the world's population was likely to double every 25 years.

III. Functional Training

—At the time the world's population was close to 1 billion, having risen slowly and erratically from maybe 300m at the start of the millennium.

—The human race would double from its then total of around 650m in about 600 years' time, and ventured boldly：

—Unless checked, most populations were likely to double every 25 years, increasing at a geometric rate (1,2,4,8,16 and so on).

—The population doubled or trebled.

—The population spurted, as Malthus had predicted.

—Between 1800 and 1900 Europe's population doubled, to over 400m, whereas that of Asia, further behind in the demographic transition, increased by less than 50％, to about 950m.

—Thanks to Europe's newfound restraint, in the past 100 years or so its population has risen only 80％, to 730m, and most countries' birth rate is now so low that numbers are static or falling.

—In contrast, Asia's population over the same time has nearly quadrupled, to more than 3. 6 billion.

—North America's too has grown almost as fast, but largely thanks to immigration. Africa's has multiplied 5½ times, and Latin America's nearly sevenfold.

Text C

Pre-reading Focuses

1. See *Teacher's Book*, 3.

Post-reading Focuses

I. Reading Comprehension

(1)~(4) F T F T   (5)~(8) T F T T

II. Functional Training

—In many ways, today's economic recovery is equally attractive.

—The economy surged in the first three months of 2002; productivity growth remains extraordinarily strong; consumers remain flexible; corporate profits, as measured in the national income accounts, are showing signs of life, and inflation is nowhere to be seen.

—Certainly first-quarter GDP growth—5.6% at an annual rate, according to revised figures released on May 24th by the Commerce Department—was unexpectedly strong.

—Though financial markets are not bright, consumers' profits and losses are still buoyed by a booming housing market. Sales of existing houses rose sharply in April, and the price of the typical American house is up 7% from a year ago.

—Americans' incomes are still rising, although more modestly than they were earlier this year.

—Taken together, this evidence leads most economists on Wall Street to conclude that the most likely thing to happen is continued growth, although at a more moderate pace than in the first quarter.

附　录

以学科互动的观点定位阅读与写作课程

梁晓晖

　　阅读与写作训练为何能够也必须结合？阅读与写作课程应该怎样进行内容定位、难度定位及培养方向定位，从而建立一个科学有效的课程模式以适应人才培养的需求？本文即从它与各门课程的关系入手从理论上阐述阅读与写作课程（本文暂以它为大学一年级课程来进行探讨，各学校可依据自己学校的学生水平而定）的定位问题。

一、以横向联系定位

　　阅读课既可理解为精读课，也可理解为泛读课。在传统课程的模式中，一年级同期开设的精读、泛读、写作课程之间存在着牢固的横向联系，它们之间的关系决定了阅读与写作这门新型课程的基本框架。笔者认为针对我国现阶段的人才需求，阅读课可以更偏重泛读课的方针。这一点可以从传统的精读课与泛读课的比较中看出。

1. 泛读与精读的对立统一

　　首先，泛读与精读的发展阶段不同。长期以来有两种现象非常值得思考。第一，经常有人提到这位精读教师教课什么风格，那位精读教师教课什么风格，而众多优秀的精读教师确实各有所长，其授课也以自己独特的魅力受到学生的欢迎。相反，大家对泛读教师的授课褒奖甚少，一旦提及，也只是谈到"这位老师上泛读课有一套方法。"这些反应其实都说明了一个事实，即精读课在长期实践中已形成了一套相当固定的授课模式，而教师们都在这个模式下尽力发挥各自所长以有所突破。而泛读恰恰相反。泛读课还缺乏一个广为接受的授课模式，没有一个标准，各位教师的授课风格也就无从谈起——大家在五花八门的泛读授课实践中正在摸索一个科学而有效的体系。

　　另一种现象更需加以注意。泛读教师们一向没有相对固定的教材，各个学校的英语老师给学生加印材料最多的可能当数泛读教师。一些依据个人喜好、方便选取的材料几乎占据了课堂教学的主流。而这些材料很难保证经过精心取舍、专家论证，从而缺乏统一的取材思路，也就很难确保一个明晰的教学思想。所以精读与泛读在教学模式及教材选定上处在一高一低两个不同的发展阶段，而泛读教学也急需一个规范体系来指导。

　　其次，泛读与精读的模拟对象相反。随着语言学与心理学相结合的产物心理语言学的发展,外语教育工作者不仅加深了对语言学本身的研究,也更加关注学习者本身的心理因素。这对各门课程教学的影响都很重要。认知心理学认为,青春期以后的外语学习者(大学生)与习得母语的儿童相比是有差异的。儿童进入青春期后,控制分析和智力功能的大脑左侧开始起主导作用,强于控制情感功能的大脑右侧。由于大脑的这种变化,成年人倾向于更多依赖分析能力和注意外语学习。这与儿童那种无意识和自发地习得母语形成对照。同时,儿童接触语言的机会远远多于成人。只要儿童不处于睡眠状态便是在学习语言,他听父母谈话,与小朋友交流,读随处可见的儿童书籍,都是在学习语言。儿童是在语言的海洋里泡大的,而外语学习者是在课堂上有限地接触外语。实际上精读课就是把学生当做成人来教授的。它针对学生已进入青春期、开始注重分析能力的特点,以语法翻译法为核心方法进行教授。也正是因为学生确已形成成人思维,无论精读课的教学方法怎样变革,以注重语言分析为主的语法翻译法将长期占据主导地位。

另一方面,教师们都鼓励学生课下进行大量阅读,这就是让学生尽量模仿儿童习得母语,心情放松地大量接触外语。也就是说这种广泛阅读模拟的对象是幼儿。事实上我们一直所称的泛读课并不是真正意义上的泛读——只有课下那种大量阅读才称得上是泛读——泛读课课上并不进行泛读,而是应该指导课下大量阅读,泛读课是帮助业已成年的大学生在精读授课的基础之上转而适应模拟幼儿习得语言。泛读课应教授学生方法去克服在课下泛读中所遇到的各种困难,进入较为轻松地阅读状态。

再次,泛读与精读的授课重点相反。同样是针对文章的词、句、文分析,泛读与精读强调的重心是相反的。在精读课上,词汇学习主要依赖于词汇的语义关系,从词汇的上义词、下义词、同义词、反义词、同源词的角度深刻理解词汇。下面是北京大学主编的精读教材《大学英语》教师用书的两个条目,是典型的精读词汇讲解模式。

—very few pesetas(1. 17)

Compare：

1)（very）few：not many（negative）

2) a few：a small number（positive）

3)（very）little：not much（negative）

4) a little：a small amount（positive）

"（Very）few" and "a few" are used with countable nouns, while "（very）little" and "a little" are used with uncountable nouns. Note that "only a few" and "only a little" are negative, expressing the idea of too small a number or amount.

...

—Arab—member of a race inhabiting Arabia and North Africa

A number of words related to "Arab"：

1) Arabia：*n.* peninsula in southwestern Asia, between the Red Sea and the Persian

Gulf, homeland of the Arabs

2）Arabian：*adj.* of Arabia or the Arabs

　　　　　n. another words for an Arab

3）Arabic：*adj.* of Arabia, the Arabs, or their language

　　　　　n. language of the Arabs

…

当然，词汇的使用语境、应用搭配也不容忽视，这会更有益于词汇在语义关系中的把握。

与精读课相比，泛读课则更强调词汇的语境关系，从某一词汇形成情景词汇串的词汇关系入手来把握词汇，以便复用。在下面一段课文中，按照泛读课的要求学生应掌握单身及婚姻生活词汇串（画线词汇）：Ask a <u>bachelor</u> why he <u>resists marriage</u> even though he finds <u>dating</u> to be less and less satisfying. If he's honest, he will tell you that he is afraid of <u>making a commitment</u>. For commitment is in fact quite painful. The single life is filled with fun, adventure, excitement. <u>Marriage</u> has such moments, but they are not its most distinguishing features.

Similarly, <u>couples</u> who choose not to <u>have children</u> are deciding in favor of painless fun over painful happiness. They can dine out whenever they want, travel wherever they want and sleep as late as they want. Couples with <u>infant children</u> are lucky to get a whole night's sleep or a three—day vacation. I don't know any <u>parent</u> who would choose the word "fun" to describe <u>raising children</u>.

But couples who decide not to have children never experience the pleasure of hugging them or tucking them into bed at night. They never know the joys of <u>watching a child grow up</u> or of <u>playing with a grandchild</u>.

对于句型，两种课型也有不同的侧重点。精读更注重对句型结构本身的掌握，而泛读则强调句型所反映的功能。例如：Nothing in my life has meant as much to me as Von Sauer's praise。精读需操练句型"Nothing（or no＋noun）… more"。如：Nothing is more valuable than health. 从句型角度讲这是一个比较级。再如：I have never read a novel better than this.。而泛读课则需提醒学生此句型在功能上反映的是最高级，而与普通型最高级"… best…"相比它更具强调作用。

同样，两种课型对文章的分析也各有重心。精读课主要分析个体文章的结构特点，以深入理解此文内容。而泛读课则要从多个各体文章结构推演到整类文章结构规律，以指导课下大量泛读。例如，记叙父母之爱的故事大多有一种结构模式，讲述人与人交往的故事也有一种结构模式，而他们一起又都符合记叙文的整体结构模式。

纵然泛读与精读存在着种种区别——相对的而非绝对的——但它们却具备至关重要的相同点：终极目的。它们都服务于学生的课下泛读。因为学生课下的大量阅读是他们将来走上工作岗位后阅读英语的真正方式。

总之,与平行设立的精读课相比,泛读课更强调培养学生从语境组合中记忆生词,从功能角度掌握句型,从篇章结构规律出发阅读理解文章。

阅读与写作课的阅读部分一方面应参照吸收精读课的方法,同时更要遵循泛读课的原则,从而有效提高学生课下大量阅读的能力。

2. 阅读与写作相辅相成

阅读与写作之间的相互促进关系决定了二者应在授课时融为一体。

首先,写作能够调动阅读的心理准备。阅读前先布置一篇内容相关的写作任务会使学生产生关于信息储备、思想表达、文章组织等多方面的困惑,这时候再让学生阅读文章学生会有一种求知若渴的感觉,会对原文中的信息内容、表达方式、文章结构极为敏感,从而阅读速度及理解力也大大上升。同时,学生利用阅读中所汲取的词、文知识再反过来修改他们在阅读前所完成的作文会大大提高他们的写作水平。所以从泛读转型来的阅读课应与写作课相结合,从而互相促进。

阅读与写作课最重要的结合点在于结构归纳法,对于同一类型的文章进行文章结构归纳,会大大促进学生在阅读中遇到同类文章的预测本领、猜测技能及理解能力,结构归纳法对学生阅读能力的提高远胜于其他单项技能——如猜词能力、预测下文能力、以意群为单位阅读的习惯——的作用,可以说它是其他技能训练的基础。而这种结构归纳法对写作课也是至关重要的。学生在初期不知道怎样下笔写作文,除了在英语语言掌握运用能力上的欠缺,很重要的一点是不知道英文文章的行文脉络,于是很多中文写作水平很高的学生也是一到英文写作就头疼。文章结构仿佛盛咖啡的壶,学生的具体思想及表达思想的语句都是咖啡,没有容器再好的咖啡也煮不出来。而有了能够容纳表达思想的那些语句的结构容器,再反过来提高学生的语言能力要容易得多。因此,以结构归纳法为统领可以把阅读与写作完美地结合在一起。

二、以纵向联系定位

阅读与写作作为一年级的课程还与高年级的相关课程存在衔接问题,在这个纵向关系上为阅读与写作定位,可以使学生在未来的学习中有一个良好的英语语言基础及丰富的知识储备,可以使它更好地为高年级相关课程服务。

1. 与高年级写作课相配合

在二年级进行系统的作文理论传授及按部就班的写作技能训练之前,应在一年级让学生有一定的写作实践,从而在二年级有的放矢。

首先要对一年级学生及早进行文章结构意识的培养,否则学生写出来的东西顺序零乱,很难进一步提高语言的地道性。如果学生总是延用中式式构建文章的思路或干脆没有任何文章结构思路可言,便谈不上英语语言的合理使用。正如一个穿着长裤马褂或赤身裸体的人是很难融入西方主流社会的。可以说,越早培养文章结构意识,学生会越容易下笔,语言也越容易提高。下面是一篇在讲授对比结构后学生限时完成的作文,抛开个别处语言应用的不当(括号中为改正部分),作文结构对称而明晰,从而思想表达甚是清楚。例文:

I left Shanghai to enter a university in Beijing this year. Soon, I found the difference between the roads in Beijing and those in Shanghai. Roads in Beijing are mostly wide, straight and orderly. They run parallel or cross perpendicular. Thus,(去掉) you(首字母大写)find it just like a chessboard. People(Thus people,但此句最好用被动句) can easily find their way on this chessboard. Roads in Shanghai, however, are on the contrary (not straight). All of them (They) are tortuous except a few main roads. They're not straight. So(去掉) the(首字母大写)roads are just like a complicated spider net. People from other cities may always lose their way in this spidery net, as well as Shanghainese themselves.

在一年级写作训练初期,还应训练学生对衔接和连贯的认识。连贯即文章意义上的流畅与贯通,它体现句与句之间意义相互关联,既不无理重叠,也不无理跳跃。而衔接是作者为协助理解、表达连贯而使用的各种手段。学生如在这方面没有很好的训练,即使到了三、四年级,写出的东西还会前言不搭后语,很难清晰地展现主题思想。

另外,还应训练学生在功能思想的统领下掌握词句。以功能为核心记忆的词汇容易复用,而所掌握的句子更是能够正确使用。下面是一个毕业生论文的开头。例句:"It is a truth universally acknowledged, that a single man in possession of a good fortune, must be in want of a wife." This marvelous ironic sentence came out at the very beginning of *Pride and Prejudice*, which also define the theme of the novel as courtship and marriage. 句子虽无任何语法错误,但因忽略了主要动词 define 应该在主句中表达,结果把次要动词 came out 当作了句子主句的谓语,结果本末倒置。应改为:This ironic beginning of *Pride and Prejudice* indicates the theme of the novel ——courtship and marriage.

总之,如果拿重塑花瓶这个艺术过程来比喻学生学习英语写作,那么一年级是教师把花瓶打碎了让学生按原有的形状拼出来,只有这样学生才会充分意识并深刻记忆花瓶的细节构造。而二年级是让学生照着花瓶自己塑造,是模仿的高级阶段。到了三、四年级学生才能学习自己创造性地重塑花瓶——在被参照花瓶的基础上,加上自己创造性的思维。如果去掉一年级的写作训练这个环节,那么在二年级学生照着样本花瓶自己塑造时,就不能仔细观察并清晰记忆花瓶的细节,自己塑造出来的作品就会出现问题甚至面目全非。

2. 为二年级文化课铺路

在二年级开设文化课的目的在于帮助学生提高逻辑思维和分析能力,扩大知识面,掌握更多的文化背景知识,特别侧重英、美等主要英语国家比较深入的背景知识。而一年级的阅读与写作课在学生阅读习惯的养成、文化知识的积累及文化思维方式的形成上都为二年级文化课铺平了道路。

首先,二年级的文化知识需要在教师课上文化体系教学的指导下在课下大量阅读相关英、美文化书籍。而这种课下大量阅读的良好习惯来自于一年级的阅读指导。良好的阅读习惯不是朝夕之功，也不是单靠教师的严格要求逼出来的。它的养成靠的是一切与阅读有关的兴趣的激发、心理素质的培养、各种技能的训练，而这正是以写作带动阅读这门课程所要达到的效果。

其次，一年级的阅读与写作课程在授课中指导学生非系统地大量涉猎各种文化知识，这种积累会大大促进学生进入二年级后系统学习文化课的兴趣，而这种由点及线的学习也使系统授课相对容易。

再次，学生刚刚进入大学课堂就具备一定文化思维方式对以后的英文阅读是至关重要的。在《实话实说》的一期节目中，主持人崔永元与来访的剑桥大学校长谈到了剑桥招生都要进行面试的问题。这时崔永元拿出一个精美的紫砂壶送给剑桥大学校长并幽默地说道："我想知道是不是所有人都要参加面试。"在场观众哄堂大笑。同声传译后校长先生犹豫良久才明白崔的意思。这句话实际蕴含着一个极其中国味儿的"关系"问题。中国观众因为没有文化障碍所以能立即明白，而这位来访的英国人尽管机智过人，也一时语塞。相同的情况中国学生在接触英文过程中会随时遇到，而学生必备的从文化角度进行阐释语言的能力是不可或缺的。

3. 为高年级文学课打基础

学生进入三、四年级后课下任务量会陡然增加。而文学课所布置的原文小说的阅读任务大多数学生很难完成。如果在一年级的阅读课上教师有目的地安排指导学生阅读高年级要学习的小说的简写本并简单介绍相关知识，学生会在此基础上从二年级开始就进行这些名著的原文阅读，这会为高年级的文学课打下很好的基础。

同时，一年级的阅读与高年级的文学课实际上形成了阅读的低高层次。阅读过程分为不同层次，各个层次有机联系，互不分割。但随着英语水平的提高，阅读者会更好地完成更高层次的阅读。第一个层次是对字面意思的反应，这是一种理解性阅读。但完成这一层次还不够，还应达到第二个层次即对字间意思的探知，也就是推测性阅读。作为一个成熟的读者，不应该只接受信息，还应该同时在脑中反映信息，这就要形成对字外意思的评价，这就是第三个层次的批判性阅读。

如果成功地达到了以上三个层次，读者经过训练会根据所阅读材料的不同文体分析其语言的风格、与自己经历的统一点等等，这就形成了最高层的欣赏性阅读。它与前几个层次息息相关：因为只有真正掌握了字面意思，明白了字间意思，形成了自己的评判观点，读者才能真正有可能进行欣赏性阅读。一年级的阅读课更针对于前三个层次的培训，三、四年级的文学课主要培养学生欣赏性阅读的能力。但由于阅读层次的不可分割性，学生都在自觉不自觉地、或好或坏地同时进行四个层次的阅读，所以一年级时也应对欣赏性阅读稍加引导。有能力欣赏所读材料才是学生坚持课下大量阅读的长久动力。

总之，一年级的阅读与写作课程在横向上与传统的精读课和泛读课相对照，在纵向上与高年级课程相呼应，是培养学生应用语言技能的一门重要课程。

英语阅读能力培养机制探究

梁晓晖

进入大学教育阶段,在听、说、读、写四项英语学习的基本技能中,阅读能力的提高是最紧迫的任务。因为,第一,阅读能力是听、说、写等技能提高的基础。第二,阅读是学生最薄弱的环节。中国学生由于长期受到应试教育的影响,过于局限于课本知识,缺乏进行快速大量阅读的能力。表现在英语上就更为突出。这一点严重阻碍了学生各方面技能的进一步提高。导致学生没有养成良好的阅读习惯,自学能力较差。第三,绝大部分英语毕业生面临的最主要任务就是阅读整理大量英文资料,以了解国外经济技术的发展或与国外进行贸易文化交流。在21世纪知识经济飞速发展、信息产业迅猛腾飞的时代,人们的日阅读量成倍增加。

那么,阅读能力的提高为什么会影响其他英语技能,而大学阶段英语课程的设置能否完全解决学生阅读能力不足的问题呢?本文将结合习得语言及学习语言的理论分别进行探讨。

一、阅读能力对其他技能的影响

阅读能力以特定的方式影响着听、说和写等技能的提高。

首先,阅读能力是听力的放大。这包括三个方面的内容。第一,听力词汇量小于阅读词汇量,并与阅读词汇量成比例增长。在学习英语的过程中,一般来讲,中国学生首先掌握的是阅读词汇,通过听力练习,阅读词汇会转化为听力词汇。阅读词汇量越大,听力练习做得越多,听力词汇量也就越大。第二,阅读为听力提供了谋篇知识。在阅读材料中文章大体分为信息类和叙事类。信息类文章基本都是三段论结构,即引言导入主旨句—文章主体各段共同论述或解释主旨句—结论在主旨句基础上进行预测或提出建议。这与听力材料中的信息结构是相对应的。阅读中的叙事类文章在开头引入特定时间背景下的人物,继而人物为某一目标的实现而经历若干事件,并通过高潮事件解决问题。这又与听力中的新闻五要素即时间、地点、人物、事件、起因相对应。通过阅读积累篇章知识会为听力提供最为实际的心理准备,是提高听力水平的重要环节。第三,听力所需的克服障碍的经验是在阅读中练就的。一个人处理问题时表现出的有条不紊和镇定自若的程度可用歧义容忍度来表示。容忍度高者往往能够接受与他的信仰和知识结构不同的观点和意见,接受互相矛盾的内容,能够在模棱两可的情况下把问题整理出头绪。容忍度低者往往无法忍耐模糊不清的事物,回避不明确的东西,拒绝与他们想法不一致的观点。研究表明,学习者的歧义容忍度是影响其外语提高速度的重要因素。歧义容忍度高的人会在阅读中接受不明因素的干扰,确定主旨大意。阅读是有形材料,听力是无形材料,有形材料要比无形材料易于把握,所以学生只有通过阅读材料训练自己的歧义容忍度,才能去应付更为触不可及的听力材料。无论是阅读材料还是听力材料,学生都会遇到不懂的词句。如果学生在阅读中习惯于利用上下文猜测未知词句的意思,具备把握主题大意而忽视若干细节的心理素质,就会在听力练习中应用相应的技巧应对个别没有听懂的词句。更为关键的是,即使个别没听懂的地方无法猜出,学生也能继续往下听,不至于被个别不懂的地方所羁绊。

其次,读是说的源泉。许多中国学生因口语水平难以提高而一筹莫展。学生感觉无论是在课堂讨论中还是在英语沙龙的自由会话中都无话可说。这不仅是词汇量的问题,也不只是口语练习少的缘故,关键是他们只要用英语进行交流就找不到合适的句子表达自己的意思。知识储备不足是根本原因。学生要提高口语水平,就要有足够的英语输入。多听当然非常重要。但一方面听力练习毕竟有限,另一方面学生对听力材料的把握也很有限,难以吸取有用知识。这样,增大阅读量就显得非常重要。学生要通过阅读报刊书籍了解英语世界的有趣事件、英语国家的文化观点,当然也包括所需的英语表达,才可能用英语进行交流,不至于在讨论中冷场。

最后,在四种英语基本技能中,学生普遍认为写作能力是最难提高的。他们写作文时,不知如何开头、展开、结尾,结果写出的作文前言不搭后语,语法错误更是不可避免。许多老师批改作文时以纠正语法错误为中心,还有的老师把全班学生的语法错误打印出来供大家借鉴。这如同阅读中的自下而上的训练方法,即从细节入手把握文章的方法。这样做确实可以解决学生写作中的许多细节问题。但是这样做的同时还应更多加入作文结构的训练,也就是说写作辅导中也应加入自上而下的训练方法,即从宏观角度把握文章的方法。我们知道,中文有中文的作文准则,英文有英文的行文规范。学生的语法错误一部分是源于学生的语法知识基础欠缺,更源于学生在作文结构知识上的匮乏。学生在东一句西一句地写作文凑字数时,最容易言不达意,以致犯语法错误。如果从低年级起让学生广泛阅读结构典型的英文文章,从模仿入手开始写作,学生就不会为无据可寻而抓耳挠腮了。下面是一位大一学生的两篇习作。

习作一:

My Father

My father is not only my father but also my instructor. In my opinion, he is the greatest man in the world.（主旨句不恰当）

Four years ago, when I was informed that I failed to entrance (**enter**) the senior middle school(**,**) I was so sad that sleepless（病句）, I was worring(**worrying**) not only my future but also the attitude that my father would showed（后半句 **awkward**,且动词时态错误）. "Will they(**he**)feel sorry for me?" I thought. To my surprise, my father treat(**ed**) me as before and even better. One night, he asked me if I would have a walk with him, I said sure. While we were walking, neither of us had a word. Finally, he broke the silence, "You shouldn't have (**be**) so upset. " He said, pointing to the sky. "You're the best one, just like the star. (**With**) More confident(**ce**) and more courage, you'll be successful finally. You'll give off lights like the star. In a word, you'll never let me down, never!"

I was deeply moved,（缺少连词）my father's love is the greatest love.

习作二：

Spring

It all Happens so quickly：The days turning longer, the pasture going green(**er**) in the garden and girls becoming more and more beautiful.

Then one day you notice that swallows are singing happily on the top of the tree and fragrance is diffusing the air. And you're aware that your winter clothes feel all wrong—The color too dull, the shoes too hot to wear. Yogurt have (**has**) to be put into refrigerators and gray is no longer the only color in the world.

Officially spring comes in March. It begins with putting away thick clothes and getting out with your lovely T-shirt. It begins with the melting of snow, raindrops pelting down and the ground getting soften(**ed**). It begins with waking up when you find you're bathing in the golden sunlight.

The beginning of spring is lovely, just like a poetess' description："Spring is not only the breeding season but the beginning of a flood of life. It is just like a song, a poetic song."

第一篇写于入学初,整篇文章错误百出(文中的括号里编者提供了修改意见),显然该生的英文基础较差。第二篇写于第二学期初,经过短短三个月从阅读到写作的模仿训练,第二篇作文不仅结构工整,而且语法错误极少。这是只依靠语法纠正即自下而上的训练方法难以取得的效果。

总之,在英语学习中,阅读能力的培养是重中之重。但通过什么途径才能有效培养学生的阅读能力呢? 这需要了解一下习得理论。

二. 习得理论对外语学习途径的影响

20 世纪 70 年代中期,应用语言学家克拉申(Krashen, S.)把"习得"与"学习"两个概念进行了明确的区分。语言习得一般指 0 至 4 岁儿童学习母语,这是一个生理发育的过程,是长期大量无意识地接触语言的结果,不是社会学习和有意教学的结果。而外语学习是指人们,尤其是成人,在正规的课堂和学校环境里有意识地学习语言。成人学习外语相对儿童习得母语来讲最大的区别在于,成人更关注语言规则的学习。在克拉申看来,第二语言也能习得。学习者要尽量和儿童习得母语一样,不把学习的注意力集中于语言的形式,而是潜意识地学习。

大学生的年龄已经超过了习得语言的最佳阶段,他们的思维活动接近于成人。他们的头脑中已经形成了关于母语的全部规则,他们要通过学习外语与其母语的区别来掌握外语。于是,正规教授外语规则的课程是不可缺少的。

然而,不容忽视的是,大学生依然处于成长发育阶段,他们接受新鲜事物的能力远高于成人。所以,教师要积极为学生创造条件,形成习得外语的氛围。也就是要求学生要大量地接触英语,多听多读,增大英语输入,在大量接触中去摸索英语的规则和词句的用法。而对于中国学生来讲,增大英语输入最为实际的途径就是大量阅读英文资料。同时,针对中国学生将来面对的工作要求及社会需求,大量阅读英语材料,在阅读中更关注材料的大意而不去深究细节及规则,就显得更为重要了。

那么,这种阅读大量英语材料的实践与训练可否单纯依靠课上来提供呢? 我们的培养机制能否完全解决学生的阅读问题呢?

三、课程设置对阅读能力的影响

在大学课程中,与阅读关系最为紧密的当为精读课和泛读课了。那么这两种课程是怎样培养阅读能力的呢?

首先,精读课历来在我国被视为主打课程。依照传统,精读课重视语言作为规则的性质,强调学习中要记忆词汇和语法规则,并通过大量翻译、课后练习来强化这些记忆。精读课中也会涉及词汇和语法规则所处的篇章知识、文化背景,但这些宏观介绍是服务于微观字、词知识的传授的。这是一种自下而上把握文章的方法。这与习得理论中的"学习"外语相对应。

对于快速理解大量材料而言,学生更需要的是自上而下的阅读能力,即先去把握文章总体大意,如有必要,再以主要意思为基础理解文章中微观词句的意思。如果只是整理资料、寻找有用信息,自上而下的阅读就足够了。只有在对有用信息再进行分析的时候才有必要进行自下而上的阅读,即从研究微观词句的角度入手去分析文章。当然,自上而下阅读习惯的形成必须要有一定自下而上阅读的经验为基础,是自下而上阅读训练提高后的结果。

由此比较可以看出,精读课的教授准则并不真正针对阅读能力的提高。它的必要性在于,当学习者已经超越了学习语言的最佳时期,已经掌握了母语的全套规则后,在学习外语时,他们需要洞悉外语区别于母语的规则。而精读课就提供了这种规则。精读课的时效性在于它为阅读能力的提高提供了必备的字、词、句知识。也就是说,精读课是教授成年人学习语言的,不是针对学生学习阅读的。

泛读课顾名思义是针对阅读的。它主要传授大量谋篇知识,以及在此基础上领悟难词难句的知识。与以自下而上把握文章为原则的精读课相比,泛读课提供了自上而下阅读文章的基本训练。但泛读课上有限的训练(一周几篇文章)并不可能解决阅读的全部问题,它只是为阅读者提供了阅读的基本技能,而技能只有经过应用后才能变为能力。

根据习得理论以及大学课程设置实际,要培养阅读能力,只有通过课下大量的阅读实践,即要努力去习得外语。精读课为这种实践提供了字、词知识基础,泛读课为这种实践提供了方法与技能。

然而,即使是进入大学英语教育后,学生也深受课本与课程的局限,以为课程本身已经基本提供了足够的英语训练,忽视了自己课下进行大量阅读的必要性。这是学生阅读能力难以提高的根源。基于阅读能力在整个英语学习中的重要地位,缺乏课下大量阅读也是学生综合英语水平难以提高的症结所在。

北京外国语大学副校长、博士生导师何其莘教授曾经提到:"用英文思维是许多英语学习者都希望达到的一种境界,因为这是用英语流畅地表达思想的基础。对于一个生活在非英语环境中的中国学生来说,要做到部分或全部用英文来思考确有很大难度,但也不是可望而不可及的。从自己学习英语的经历中,我体会到坚持大量阅读是实现这一目标最有效的途径之一。"许多英语教育家像何教授一样,充分强调了坚持大量阅读的必要性。

要提高阅读能力不能单纯依赖课堂讲解,必须通过课下大量阅读,可以说,课下大量阅读是英语水平提高的根本途径。

四、阅读实践中的具体问题

学生要做到有效地大量阅读,首先就是选材恰当。许多学生在一年级阅读初期由于选择了难度过大的书籍而倍感受挫,以致"一朝被蛇咬,十年怕井绳"。有些英语专业毕业生在写毕业论文的时候才后悔自己竟未曾从头至尾完整地读过一本英文小说。一般来讲,学生应在入学后的前两三个学期充分阅读简明读物,要至少达到 8 本以上才可开始阅读简单的未经删改的原文书籍。

同时,学生要在阅读每一本书时为自己定下一个明确的阅读目标。有了阅读目标,学生阅读就有主动性,而不必依赖老师来强加任务。如小说类读物可定为寻找主要人物所经历的三大事件;文化类读物可定为分析中国文化与英、美文化在某一问题上的区别。带着目的阅读,学生才能更多关注所读材料的主要意思,而忽略一些不懂的细节。总之,要在自上而下阅读的统领下提高自己的歧义容忍度。随着阅读量的增多,学生对细节的理解水平会不自觉地提高。

学生经常反映不知如何把握查字典的频率。总的来讲,在故事类文章中,描写人物关系的语句中反复出现的生词以及描写故事进展的过程中反复出现的生词要查字典。而对于大量的景物描写的部分中出现的生词可以忽略。对于信息类文章,如果生词出现在段落的开头或结尾可以查阅,而段中的生词要尽量忽略。

总之,学生只有通过大量的阅读实践才能真正把握解决问题的方法,提高阅读能力,应对信息时代的要求。

附录三

学生习作一览

　　下面三篇是大一学生模仿下册第一单元 Text A 的习作,供大家参考。经过一个学期阅读与写作课的训练,学生们在写作上都有了长足进步,写作水平都有了明显的提高。我想这套教材最大的优势在于对学生读写技能的双项培养。值得一提的是在这一次的写作任务中,全班有三分之二的同学的作文都达到了下面三篇例文的水平,而第一篇恰恰是出自班里的老师和同学们公认的基础几乎最差的学生。最后一篇是来自基础较好的一位同学,这一篇不只是内容与结构,连句型都在模仿 Text A。

　　当然例文反映出学生在思想深度上还有待提高,观点正确与否我们也不敢苟同(因此我们删去了第一篇例文第三段中两个地名,用××代替)。而这恰恰是学生要在阅读中逐渐解决的问题。但作为大一的学生,能够全班同学都能写出大致这样水平的习作,逻辑清晰,文字流畅,有自己的想法,甚至还有 Text B 中的幽默,这是值得肯定的。还有一个很有意思的现象细心的读者应该能够发现:学生已经开始注意语言的变化了——他们在有意识地应用上册第三单元讲到的 elegant variation!

例文一:

The Queer Chinese

　　The Chinese are queer people:they love to sleep. They sleep on soft beds,on crowded buses,even in important conferences. In cinemas,if they think they won't get anything interesting from the film,their first plan would be to close their eyes and then to sleep.

　　The Chinese are queer people:they love to drink. In history,many wise men enjoyed drinking,and many wonderful things came from drinking. Drinking and sleeping were just the two things Ji Kang did everyday. And most of Li Bai's poems were written when he was tipsy.

　　The Chinese are queer people:they love to fight. In ×× province,if you quarrel with anyone,even a little child,or an old woman,there will be a crowd of furious people gathering around you in no time. And if you boldly give a fist to a man in ××,you will see lots of hoes flinging towards you. If anyone wants to fight with a Chinese at the moment,I have to tell him:"Poor fellow,you have gotten the poorest idea."

例文二：

The Queer Chinese Etiquette

The Chinese etiquette is really a queer thing.

Whenever you meet a friend on the road, the first regards would be: "Have you had your meal?" It does not mean he wanted to invite you to eat together, but simply "Hello!"

When you are invited to someone's home, the host will ask you: "Would you like something to eat?" Just answer "No, thank you. Don't bother." Never reply like this: "I would like some chocolates."

When you are about to leave, your host will request: "Stay a little longer, please." Then you must say: "Thank you very much, but I really have to go. Next time, OK?" Of course, both your host and you will never need to worry about the "next time".

At last, you will hear: "Walk slowly!" Don't really walk as slowly as a snail, it just means "Walk carefully!"

Therefore, you must always be aware of all the etiquette in China, and never be so frank and direct, otherwise you will be a big joke.

例文三：

The Chinese Are Queer

The Chinese are queer: they are so friendly. They can preserve their relationships with others very well even when they can't get any benefits from those friends. And they can easily forgive their former enemies if these guys admit their faults from the bottom of their hearts.

The Chinese are queer: they are so obstinate. They successfully defeated the Japanese invaders last century; they bravely fought with the Allied Forces of the Eight Powers for the safety of their motherland and their family. They couldn't keep silent when some friends denied their historical faults.

The Chinese seem queer. In fact, they aren't queer at all. They just act with their conscience: be friendly to their friends no matter how weak they are; be cruel to their enemies no matter how strong they might be.

例文四：

Paradoxical Character of Japanese

To many people around the world Japanese are a mystery. Anthropologists analyze them while finding no definite words to explain them. Scholars do research on them while failing to reach a clear conclusion. Tourists travel around their country while getting confused when they find this nation surprisingly different from the description in textbooks or reports. And in my opinion, the reason why Japanese are so mysterious is that their character is paradoxical.

Japanese are both cooperative and competitive. Unlike Americans' preference to individualism, Japanese appeal for cooperation. They depend upon each other, help each other, and learn from each other with a strong sense of community. No privilege is allowed in a team. No wonder a popular saying goes that a group of Japanese ants can knock down an American elephant. However, when a rival relationship is established between Japanese and others, they can be extraordinary competitors, or even enemies. With a keen smell of danger, they set themselves against any form of existence that may pose potential threat to them. As a solid whole, they strive for united wisdom in economy, culture and military capacity, to verify its great competency in global competition, despite the fact that they are, more often than not, accused of being aggressive.

Japanese are self-abased while proud of themselves. As Japan is an island country lacking in natural resources, they are extremely anxious about their future, fearing that one day they will be conquered and eliminated by greater powers in the world. And this anxiety goes even stronger when they find some of their neighbors are gradually taking off in some aspects. However, instead of constant complaints, they choose to take action. They've been applying advanced western civilizations to their own national construction since Meiji Restoration, which finally lists the nation high in the world in integrated powers. And that explains why they are complacent on the other hand. The great success in national rejuvenation brings a sense of unprecedented superiority to them. They become confident and even overconfident. They once exaggerated their potential capability and turned it into the unpractical aspiration of insulting the less developed countries and dominating the world. But they finally paid out for their abnormal massacres in World War II.

As the American anthropologist Benedict says, Japanese were born with double faces. They are contradictory, naturally and historically. Even if you've been quite acquainted with your Japanese friends, it's not a simple matter to truly understand them. There still can be moments when you are not so sure about the people you are dealing with. So remember, their character is paradoxical.